Praise for Blackbird Blues

"A musical coming of age story lies at the heart of *Blackbird Blues'* meditation on race, religion, and gender in midwestern America. At a time of personal crisis in the early 1960s, teenaged singer Mary Kaye struggles to free herself from the orbit of an arch conservative Catholic family. Caught between the pull of a convent's regimented life and her discovery of the expressive freedom of jazz, her muse leads her across racial lines in Chicago's nightclubs, embroiling her in a web of intimate relationships. The story's surprising twists and turns build steadily to its deeply-affecting climax—like a masterful jazz performance itself. As *Blackbird Blues* is true to the sounds of jazz, it is true to the sacrifices of love, family, and community made by individuals who find one another in the jazz world." — Paul Berliner, author of *Thinking in Jazz: The Infinite Art of Improvisation*

"This is an absorbing novel that proves on page after page that what we do affects others. Jean Carney deftly recreates the summer of 1963 as lived by a talented, devout young white woman who chafes at her limited options and becomes increasingly aware of racial injustice. With graceful language and engaging and complicated characters, *Blackbird Blues* gives us a portrait of a time and place that makes us examine our own era. Carney writes with elegance and authority, whether she takes us inside a convent, a Chicago jazz club, an illegal abortion clinic, or a young woman's heart. Like *The Bell Jar,* but more communal and publicly aware." — S.L. Wisenberg

"Jean Carney has written a masterful novel. She has the rare capacity to combine almost surgically precise prose with warm and compassionate understanding of human misery and spunk. *Blackbird Blues* made me see, taste, smell, and touch the world in which Mary Kaye, Maureen, and Lucius lived, with all their fears, desires, regrets, and contradictions, as if they were my own. Reading *Blackbird Blues* is a powerful experience. It left me with a greater sense of hope and a more sympathetic attention to despair. It will stay with me for a long time." — Stefania Tutino, author of *Uncertainty in Post-Reformation Catholicism: A History of Probabilism*

"*Blackbird Blues* portrays an early-60s world on the cusp of radical change—racial, social, sexual—with deep insight into the cross-currents of the era. It intertwines the travails of Mary Kaye, a young woman questioning the depth of her religious commitment, with those of Sister Michaeline, her free-spirited ideal and mentor, the prizefighter-turned-musician Lucius, his imprisoned son Benny, the members of Mary Kaye's large and chaotic family, and other memorable figures. The novel's graceful plot and spare style evoke the existential complexities of these haunting characters and the times in which they lived with poignancy and power." — Zachary S. Schiffman, author of *The Birth of the Past*

blackbird blues

Jean K. Carney

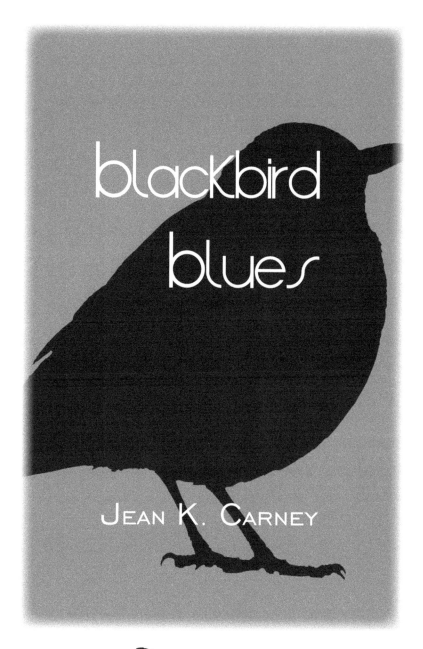

blackbird blues

JEAN K. CARNEY

BInk · *Bink Books*
Bedazzled Ink Publishing Company • Fairfield, California

9978-1-949290-22-6 paperback

Cover Design
by

Bink Books
a division of
Bedazzled Ink Publishing Company
Fairfield, California
http://www.bedazzledink.com

To Constantin Fasolt
My Beloved Husband, whose Boundless
Love and Generosity
Make Everything Possible

Note

In depicting social and political events in the 1940s and 1960s, I have tried to represent them as I understand them historically. However, the characters in this novel are all products of my imagination. Any resemblance to people living or dead is coincidental.

1

AT FIRST SHE didn't see the bodies. She was lost in the beat of the music coming up from the church basement where the Friday night sock hop rocked. She scrubbed the sanctuary floor in time with Buddy Holly's "That'll Be the Day." She sang softly, feeling the music in her legs—the guitar twang, the bass pluck, and especially the brush and beat of the drums. Drums were Buddy Holly's weakness too. He'd let them get carried away till they took over a whole record.

Tony would be downstairs. Maybe she didn't have to wait to talk with him until she knew for sure that she was pregnant. She would ask Sister Michaeline. Sister was her voice coach, but she was more than a mentor. Since Mary Kaye had been a kid, Sister had guided her through the bedlam that had been Mary Kaye's childhood.

As dark descended, Mary Kaye couldn't see by the light of the Easter candle, so she walked to the sacristy and turned on the sanctuary lights.

Walking back to the sanctuary, she saw them: two caskets, lying in front of the altar. The polished wood had been almost invisible in the earlier darkness. She frowned. A double funeral was unusual and she hadn't heard that anyone in the parish was failing. She imagined the funeral for whoever lay resting inside: as usual, she and Sister Michaeline would sing the Requiem. Singing took the edge off; that would be the time to tell Sister her worry.

She stepped forward. The two caskets were open and resting on separate biers. A few inches had been left between them so they would not touch.

Then she stopped, alarmed at the familiar sight of the Franciscan habit. She couldn't see faces yet, but around each nun's head circled a braided crown of thorns. She looked above the caskets, above the altar steps, and focused on the golden tabernacle at the center of the altar. She looked back and forth deliberately between the floor and the altar. As a child, she had taught herself to slow things down when she was getting overwhelmed. She had a system. She focused on each detail, one by one. She took a breath and peered inside.

She recognized at once the face of her sixth-grade teacher, Sister Jane Denise. It was spooky to see the nun with her eyes closed. The casket lid covered the lower part of Sister Jane Denise's body, but other elements of her dress were familiar. The nun's hands were folded above her waist, entwined in a black rosary. The big crucifix hung around her neck. The floor-length skirt was mostly hidden, but there was the full-sleeved blouse and the rectangular scapular that hung like a sandwich board in front and behind.

Mary Kaye had always wondered whether the bibs were made of heavily starched fabric or some kind of plastic. She bent over Sister Jane Denise's body and tentatively touched the white bib. She still couldn't tell.

The nun's face was luminous. Her complexion was preternaturally smooth. Thick pancake makeup gave her a tan unlike anything she'd likely ever had in real life. Mary Kaye had the impulse to press a fingertip into Sister Jane Denise's skin, but was afraid the makeup, and the skin underneath, would cave in like frosting on a cake. Sister Jane Denise looked like she had been starched, but she looked like herself.

The other nun did not. Mary Kaye tried to stifle her senses and muffle reality but her usual self-protective system crashed and she had to steady herself on the casket. She heard herself wailing. It could not be Sister Michaeline! Bending down into the casket, she lay her head on Sister's breast, but there was no give. The body was hard, overstuffed. She sobbed, stammering until the words turned to gibberish, "No, no, no. What'll I do without you?"

This lifeless mannequin could not be Sister Michaeline. Sister Michaeline walked like a speedboat, chin tilted up, head bouncing. Sister Michaeline pushed up her sleeves with gusto, twisting the edge into a little knot, like a magician twirling the end of a silk scarf out of a top hat. Sister Michaeline lifted the chorus to a swell as she reached high on tiptoes, wielding the baton, and, bending forward, shrank everything to silence. Mary Kaye sobbed, imagining Sister Michaeline sitting abruptly upright in her coffin: "Hey kiddo. How's tricks?" Sister had never sounded like a woman of 1963, but even after sixteen years in the convent she still had not sounded like the other nuns either.

Mary Kaye hugged herself. Her impulse was to go home and sleep, to manage the shock as she had dealt with other, lesser shocks: by keeping her own counsel, and making her own plan. Yet she was afraid to be alone.

What would Sister Michaeline advise? Mary Kaye felt certain that, even if Sister had known what she and Tony had done, she would say: Straighten your skirt. Ditch the scrub pail and get down to the church basement. Sister would tell Mary Kaye to find Tony and, for Heaven's sake, give him a hug.

Mary Kaye went back to the sacristy and stood in front of the full-length mirror where the priest donned his vestments. The music had shifted and Little Eva was calling from downstairs. Little Eva was at the top of the pop charts. She was Mary Kaye's age and, like her, had begun singing in a church choir. "That's how you get your start," Sister Michaeline had said. Looking into the mirror, Mary Kaye stretched to her full five-feet-eight-inches and shook herself. There was a catch in her throat as she mouthed Little Eva's words to her reflection. "Come on baby, do the loco-motion."

Her ears were aflame. Sister Michaeline always said that was Mary Kaye's tell when she was trying to smother emotion. She wiped the mascara off her cheeks, fluffed out her long curls, and flipped the ends under along her neck and over her shoulder. On the left side, her better side, she tucked the strands behind her ear and straightened the tortoiseshell barrette she had filched from her mother. Mom's hair was dyed blonde. The barrette looked better against Mary Kaye's dark brown locks. She moaned. It was taking all her powers of concentration to distract herself and not collapse in grief.

The sock hop shifted to Roy Orbison, the unmistakable tah-duh, tah-duh, drums and strings together, strings darting off on their own.

"Blue Angel." The song Tony had sung to her in the car. "Sha la la, dooby wah, Blue Angel." He couldn't reach the top notes, so she finished some of the lines. Which meant that after he sang "if you just say you're mine," she'd been the one to finish, "I'll love you till the end of time." That wasn't true now, but it felt OK then—"Blue Angel" was maybe the most beautiful song ever sung. Drums in the background where they belonged, back-up singers up front, human percussion. Roy's voice out there naked, open to everybody, the way she wished she could sing. The way she wished she could be.

She hadn't told Tony she might go to the convent until after they had slept together. She could tell he was hurt. He'd been quiet, then said, "You know your own mind, and I love you for that. But you just plow through. You decide what you're going to do and you do it. Too bad for anybody who tries to stand in your way." That had been almost seven weeks ago.

Maybe it was the way the guitars, the piano, the drums, the voices blended together like an orchestra; maybe it was the thought of Tony tousling her hair. Mary Kaye turned to go to the basement, warmed by the idea of seeing Tony, holding him, telling him what she had seen in the sanctuary. Maybe Sister Michaeline would have been right. Maybe that was not such a bad idea.

2

IN THE BASEMENT "Teen Angel" was playing. The few lucky couples danced at the center of the wood floor, foreheads touching, arms wreathed around each other's necks, torsos leaning inward, feet separated always by a good six inches. The other girls and boys hovered nearby—except Tony, who was talking to Father Moriarty and nodding vigorously. He was hunched, in deference to Father, but still towered over the other kids, his black flat-top like a mountain plateau.

Mary Kaye felt a twinge of affection. She and Tony had been on and off for seven years, since sixth grade. She had known he wasn't smart enough, but he was a good egg. Nobody had ever been more devoted to her than Tony.

She kicked off her loafers into the pile of shoes in the corner and headed for Tony and Father Moriarty. After the breakup she had taped a script next to the phones in the kitchen, the foyer, and her parents' bedroom. The O'Donnells could stick to a story. When Tony had called, they'd told him Mary Kaye was out. Now, though, she needed to talk to him.

Seeing her coming, Tony sidestepped away from the priest. She loved his walk, how he moved with a side-to-side sailor sway, slightly oafish, like Marlon Brando in *On the Waterfront*. She let him speak first.

"What in hell are you doing here?"

"I'm on sacristy duty. The music is so loud. I heard it upstairs."

"You OK? You don't look OK." Tony's eyes narrowed and seemed to turn browner as he took her in.

"You look great, though," she said. "And you sound like yourself. Swearing like a sailor."

The little bump in the middle of Tony's nose twitched as he laughed; he would have said it moved a "tesch." Tony played catch with words from the old country the way other guys threw a baseball. His people had come over from Sicily near the end of the last century—later than Mary Kaye's had come from the Rhineland and County Donegal—and had clung to their ways, not feeling the shame of it.

"What's up?" he asked, slipping his hand to her behind. Mary Kaye swatted it away.

"Listen. Really listen. I've got something to tell you. Sister Jane Denise . . ."

Tony looked into her eyes and bent toward her, cocking his left knee. Mary Kaye's shoulders drooped. She loved it when he leaned into her. "She's dead," she muttered.

He flicked his head a little to the side, the way he had when he'd had an Elvis Presley wave. "What do you mean 'she's dead'?"

"I mean 'she's dead.'" She touched the tip of her pointer finger to her lips. Her hand was shaking. "She and Sister Michaeline are laid out in the chapel upstairs."

"Holy shit. You're not kidding."

"Sister Jane Denise kind of looks like she's sleeping. Sister Michaeline looks dead dead. Not like people are supposed to look when they're gone. She's not at rest. Go see for yourself."

"No siree, Bob," Tony said, shaking his head. "The sight of you is enough of a shock."

They paused as Father Moriarty approached and put a hand on each of their shoulders.

"I guess you're talking about the Sisters," Father said, eyeing Mary Kaye. "We should have thought not to assign you sacristy duty today."

"What's the story, Father?" Tony said.

"Father Schultz doesn't want anybody talking about it until he speaks at all the Masses on Sunday. Sorry. My hands are tied." Father Moriarity took his hands back and gestured to Mary Kaye. "She's in shock, Tony. Make sure she gets home."

"Yes, Father. Good idea, Father." Tony sounded like Perry Como; usually he sounded like Jimmy Dean. Mary Kaye let Tony take her hand. She had missed his smooth touch, softened by the special cream his father brought back from business trips to Sicily.

"We better get a move on." He slid toward the pile of shoes. "Come on. I'll find ours."

"Wait a sec. I want to listen to this. You hear the strings? How do they do that? How do they do that thing where they make the strings float?"

Tony grinned. "You're a sucker for mush." He slipped his hand around Mary Kaye's waist and nestled a fingertip in the curve under her ribs. She let him slide his forearm down the side of her skirt, find her hand, and fold it in his. "Don't let the nuns throw you. At least not tonight."

She closed her eyes to take in the scent of the Old Spice that she had given him for Christmas. And the buttery-alcohol smell of Wildroot, which he still used even though the other kids mocked him for using hair oil.

Tony pulled her onto the dance floor and glided her smoothly into their familiar position, her arms around his neck, his hands clasped behind her back. Her blouse, which had held up while she was scrubbing the cool church, began to cling. The collar weakened. Her hips swung with Tony's, as did her head and arms and shoulders. When her sock snagged on a nail in the floor, Tony laughed and steadied her. "I guess I better take you home. Isn't that what Father said?" He slipped his arm around her shoulder and turned toward the staircase. She did not move with him.

Tony stepped back and made a show of opening his hands. "OK, OK. Have it your way." Mary Kaye started up the steps, moving aside at the top so he could get the door. Outside, he headed for the parking lot. Mary Kaye paused.

"I want you to walk me home, like you used to."

"And leave my car here? I got to get to work tomorrow."

"You work the supper shift. You've got all day to come back for the car." She didn't trust herself to get in the car with him.

Tony's face flushed. He walked to his car and jammed the key into the lock. "You're playing with me and you damn well know it." He slid into his seat. Always before he had opened her side first.

Mary Kaye walked to her side of the car. She had to get home. "I don't want to give you the wrong idea," she said, opening the door.

"What the hell are you talking about? Get in the car. I'm taking you home. Now."

She hesitated, but got in. Tony sighed. "Mary Kaye, you said you needed time. Just now I thought you had—how did you put it— doped things out." He turned the engine over. Mary Kaye stuffed her fingers down into the seat, groping for a seat belt. Tony pulled away from the curb and she gave up.

She cleared her throat. "I wasn't going to say anything until I knew for sure."

He did not look at her. "'For sure' about what?" He stepped on the gas. "I thought you were upset about the nuns. Isn't that why I'm driving you home tonight?"

"You don't have to yell, Tony. I thought . . . I thought if it actually came down to it, we'd be able to talk."

"If it 'came down to' what?" He blazed through a yellow light on Lincoln Boulevard. There was only the stoplight at Jefferson Avenue between them and Sycamore Lane. "Spit it out, Mary Kaye." He cast her a sidelong look, then slammed on the brakes.

"Shit. That's why you wouldn't take my calls."

"Tony, please, please pull over. We can't sit here. Somebody's going to smash into us."

He hit the gas pedal and swerved toward oncoming traffic so fast that her head smacked the window. He narrowly missed a bicyclist. What kind of moron would ride a bike at night without a headlight?

"You're supposed to be the smartest kid from our class—not just the smartest girl, the smartest kid. But you can't count the days in the month?" Tony pulled into the parking lot in front of Klipper's Toys and parked.

Mary Kaye felt the heat rise in her face. "What do you want out of me, Tony? I wanted to see what it would be like, before going to the convent."

"But you plan everything. Down to the bug spray for a goddamn picnic. I was counting on you."

Mary Kaye looked out the window. "I don't know what went wrong. I made a calendar of the months until I leave, with little x's on the days that are supposed to be safe. I thought I had it figured out."

Tony turned the key in the ignition. "You're not going to pin this on me."

"I thought I had the bases covered. I didn't think it could happen."

She cupped her hands over her face. What had happened to her famous self-restraint? She'd tossed it out the backseat window of a beat-up Chevy with a guy whose idea of class was a chartreuse paint job. The cardinal virtues that had never failed. Prudence, fortitude, temperance. And then three deadly sins. Pride, lust, wrath. Tony reached over, but she batted him away. "You're mixing me up. You're making me feel like I don't know what I'm doing."

He grabbed hold of her wrists. "No shit. Listen to this: You don't know what the hell you're doing."

She leaned against his shoulder and tears started.

He put his arm around her, pulled her to his chest, and stroked her hair.

"What if I'm really pregnant? Not just scaring myself? I can't tell my parents. No way they'd understand."

"Here's what you're going to do." His voice was a whisper. He pulled his handkerchief out of his pocket and patted her eyes. "You have a problem. And you're going to take care of it. I'll talk to my dad. He'll know how to handle it."

"No, don't tell your father. I've been late before." She took the handkerchief from him. "I've got to pull myself together. Not get ahead of myself."

Tony turned the key in the ignition. He checked the rear view mirror and the side mirror. He turned all the way around to check for cars. Cautiously, he pulled back onto Lincoln Boulevard. He murmured, "Max, you're going to need some help."

Nobody but Tony called her Max.

Mary Kaye tapped her fingers on the door. "It doesn't make sense to tell anybody until I know for sure."

3

SATURDAY MORNING MARY Kaye went shopping for convent clothes with her mother. She certainly wasn't up for shopping for anything. And she didn't want to talk with Mom about seeing Sister dead. But the excursion had been on her mother's calendar for weeks and, when it came down to it, she was too grief-stricken to get into it with Mom.

Even if she wasn't pregnant, she was sure that Sister Michaeline was right that she was too young to enter the convent. On most things, Sister Michaeline had been on the money. She was right to overrule Mary Kaye's father and let her watch the TV special on Birmingham in the convent Visitors' Parlor. Dad had insisted it was wrong to encourage the troublemakers—that all they wanted was attention—but she had needed to see for herself. Black kids knocked to the ground by police fire hoses. Boys and girls with police dogs biting and tearing their clothes, lunging at their necks. There was talk that their parents might be arrested for contributing to the delinquency of their children. What a joke. How could it be wrong to claim your right to be free?

Sister had been right about Ravel and right about Satie and especially right about Louis Armstrong, whom she had heard as a girl when his riverboat docked along the Mississippi. She was right to encourage Mary Kaye's friendship with the O'Donnells' neighbor, Judge Engelmann, who introduced Mary Kaye to James Baldwin and Rachel Carson in weekly doses of his *New Yorker*.

And although Mary Kaye found it hard to believe, she hoped that Sister was right that she had the talent to sing professionally. In between choir rehearsals and voice lessons, Sister had pressed her to investigate colleges and let herself get a taste of grown-up life. This was a new idea. Mary Kaye's mother was allergic to new ideas. With enough time, Mary Kaye could, and regularly did, plant the seeds of ideas that sprouted and flowered in such a way that her mother claimed them for her own. But there wasn't time for that now. Mary Kaye had just come to her senses with help from Sister Michaeline. Since Mom's calendar said convent clothes shopping on the morning of the last Monday in May, 1963, Mary Kaye found herself in Daleiden's with her mother.

From the street, Daleiden's looked like a normal store. But inside, atop a globe, stood a life-size statue of the Blessed Virgin Mary, her bare feet crushing the head of a serpent. The statue was Mary Kaye's height, taller than Mom by four or five inches. The Virgin wore a white veil and a gown that fell in even folds under a dark aquamarine mantle. At her neck and waist a brown band molded like putty, its color matching the sliver of hair that showed from under her veil. Under the Virgin's foot, pink flesh ran tellingly all the way down the snake's throat.

Daleiden's was a huge, airless space, a labyrinthine bazaar of cabinets, tables, and display cases, holding thousands of religious articles. There were holy water fonts; crucifixes and crosses of gold, wood, and even plastic; statues in marble and porcelain; rosary beads in all sizes and colors; and racks of holy cards, marking every moment of life from Baptism to Extreme Unction.

There were statues of hundreds of saints, mostly miniatures, like the foot-tall Our Lady of Fatima porcelain that had been stationed on Mary Kaye's nightstand since First Communion. She recognized St. Anthony, in his brown monk's robe, holding a lily and the Baby Jesus. And St. Jude, patron saint of lost causes, in hopeful green robes, ready for backyard burial in case a family wanted to sell their house. And Mom's patron saint, Agnes, holding the lamb signifying virginity.

She and Mom stood next to the statue of Our Lady with the serpent and went down the shopping list. The four white short-sleeved undershirts she had already bought in the boy's department at Montgomery Ward's. The two gored regulation-length black half-slips Aunt Nancy had made on the sewing machine. Now they were looking for a black cotton robe and two full-length nightgowns, white, 100% cotton, yoked high at the neck, full-length sleeves, no buttons or ornamentation—not even a tiny white flower, like the one embroidered on the gown Sister Haraldo had made her take back.

"Flip a coin, honey," said Mom, never much for patience. "What'll it be? Robes or nightgowns?" She'd dressed in high style for the trip:

High heels and capri pants, à la Ava Gardner. Her hair was platinum blonde, pulled in a French twist and set off by the hat of the day, a wild bird's nest.

Mary Kaye fought back tears at the memory of ister Michaeline's hardened body. To buy time, she needed to give Mom a head start. She pulled her ticket out of her purse: the letter from the nuns stating that she would enter the convent in September. Mom nabbed it and disappeared into the room marked "Clerics and Nuns Only."

Drying her eyes, Mary Kaye headed back into the labyrinth, where St. Agnes immediately indicted her. Bypassing Bibles, missals, breviaries, and novena books, more occasions for guilt, she found a copy of *The Interior Life* and turned to the page she had quoted in her convent application. "I will unite myself to the will of God, protesting that I desire and wish nothing more for time and for eternity than what He Himself wishes."

"Do you know what that means?" Sister Martina, the postulant mistress, had asked in her entrance interview.

"Yes, Sister," she had answered. "It means my life will belong to God now. My thoughts and actions will be directed only to Him. All I will ever want is to be united with God in Heaven." At the time, she had meant it.

But things had changed. Tony had wanted her. That had been no surprise. What had caught her off guard was how much she had wanted him. And, even more so, the vividness of the memories. Memory was really too tame a word, as if it were something you took out of a box to examine only when you wanted. She would be in the middle of something, like ironing Dad's shirts, and, without warning, a jolt of electricity would zing up her crotch. With the shirts scorching, she would shift from one foot to the other, feeling the soft slipperiness of his mouth, the hardness of his muscles, the gentle weight of him covering the whole of her. She would smell the Wildroot, and the other smell that came with the searing pain, and with that pain, the feeling of being one. The idea of unity with God in Heaven paled.

The door slammed hard in the back of Daleiden's. Mary Kaye's mother appeared, holding a pile of white nighties in one arm and black bathrobes in the other. "Come on, slowpoke. Are we shopping or not? I'm doing all the work."

"Sorry, Mom." Mary Kaye followed her toward the clerical room. It was hitting her hard. She had wanted to escape from taking care of children. She wanted to read and make music. She wanted time for her own inner life—not like Mom, who snatched afternoons in desperation. (Though better a shampoo and set or a matinee than all those lost days in bed.)

Her choices were sharply limited. Housewife was out. As much as she loved her brothers and sisters, she did not want to spend her days cooking, cleaning, washing, and ironing. If she wanted to stay single, she could become a schoolteacher, a stewardess, a secretary, or a nurse. That was it.

But of the women she knew, by far the happiest were nuns. They were the brides of Christ, which gave them a definite prestige. They were able to do most of the jobs Catholic women could do, but they didn't have to worry about making money or friends. They were free to think and to keep their thoughts to themselves. They could read and study and develop an interior life, which gave them depth to draw from. The nuns had a special freedom, along with an obligation to avoid calling attention to themselves.

She had been looking for a refuge. She felt squeezed by a general feeling that everybody wanted something from her. On the last day of dance lessons before homecoming, all the girls had received dance cards. Sister Donald had given the boys pens, telling them to wait for her signal.

When Sister had finally clapped her hands, Mary Kaye nearly got knocked to the floor. From all sides, boys had shoved and thrust their pens at her. One of the boys had plucked the dance card out of her hand, jumped in the air, and waved it overhead. He had leaned on another boy's back, scribbled his name in slot one, and passed the card on. Boy #3 had snatched her dance card from Boy #2 and so on and so on until all eight slots had been filled. The last signatory was polite enough to fold the card and present it to her with a bow.

Her face had heated in shame when she learned that some girls' cards had only a few signed names and others were actually blank. At home, Mom and Dad had trained her to make sure that each child in the family got the same amount of attention. Her siblings knew about her straight-A report cards, but she protected them from learning that she had won the silver medal statewide in debate. Obviously, she had fallen down on the job at school. Girls were crying and she hated herself. Sister Michaeline thought that all that male attention scared the bejeezus out of Mary Kaye. Not that she pushed her, but she certainly didn't slow Mary Kaye down when she and Tony started getting intimate.

At Daleiden's, in the clerical room, Mom had rolled a half dozen racks out from the wall and was weeding through dozens of robes. The lines on the sides of her mouth tightened as she pulled one off a hanger and held it up to her shoulders. Mary Kaye started at the other end of the rack, discarded one or two robes, but shot the rest of the possibles down the rack in Mom's direction.

"The robes are all alike," Mom said, as if she were issuing a papal edict. "They don't even have sizes. I suppose the cuff on this one's a little wider. Are you sure this is the store Sister said?"

"Yep, this is it. They've got a bigger store in the Loop, but this looks like plenty."

"Put this on, M. K. It's a smidgin shorter. It's got a little more flair."

Mary Kaye bit her tongue, then found courage. "If it's flair I'm after, maybe I shouldn't be going to the convent."

Mom shoved the rack in the direction of a wall, strode off, and returned, rolling a rack of white nightgowns. "Don't start up, sugar pie. The nuns are expecting you. You can't commit to something, then back out."

Mary Kaye retreated to the mirror in the corner and stood up straight, draping a robe over her shoulders, slipping an arm into one sleeve, then the other. The robe had pockets on each side. She didn't know whether nuns were allowed to carry anything in them, but it would be good to have somewhere to hide things, just in case.

"The nuns have no business giving you girls big ideas. Like you could just do what you want. A woman who is fool enough not to get married can be a teacher, a nurse, or a secretary. Period."

"Mom, you forgot. I could also be a stewardess."

"Sorry, honey. You don't have the legs for it."

"Or the face. Remember when you wouldn't let me get my hair cut in a pixie? You said to wear a pixie you had to have a pretty face."

Mom threw the nightgowns over a rack and flopped in the chair.

Mary Kaye sat on the floor. "All I'm saying is: What's the rush? I could go to college for a year or two. Or music school. Even Sister Michaeline said I've got my whole life to be a nun. I should have a taste of what I'm giving up." Desperate, certainly with no thought of anybody's right to be free, she tried her old stand-by, brushing her fingertips over Mom's wrist, curling a finger around a pinkie, and cooing, "Mom, I'm not sure I want to go to the convent now."

Mom pulled her hand out of Mary Kaye's and parked it on her own waist. "Forget it. You know we don't have money for more school. Not with six kids coming up behind you."

Mary Kaye untangled her legs and tried to pull herself up, slipping a little on the edge of the robe. Three Cadillacs in the garage but no money for college. This time, she held her tongue.

As if she didn't know there were six more behind her. For as long as she could remember, it was hold the baby, kiss the baby, tickle the baby. She had watched this nonsense ad nauseam. "Where did Jack get that gorgeous blond hair? Would you look at those eyes? He's got Grandma Mueller's sweet disposition. Don't you know, the girls are going to fall all over him, the little darling." "Look at that little rosebud. Francine's the family beauty. You can see it already. She's got Aggie's perfect skin." "Have you ever in your life seen anything as precious as Meggie? Cute as a button, a little charmer, already the apple of her father's eye, a little fireball—you know what I mean—in a good way."

They fawned. They clucked. They pinched. They jiggled. She wondered at how they could see so much in so little. By the time Patty was born, she had nodded no and nodded yes more often than the puppets on the *Howdy Doody Show*. She was wise to the deal. In first grade, Sister Immaculata had looked at one of her paintings and said, "Why, it's a Nutcracker soldier. Tell me about your little soldier." She had held her breath when Sister responded, "Yes, I see, he does stand straight and tall. He watches everything. He does not look to the left or to the right. He nods when he's supposed to nod. He doesn't waste time wearing a tutu and leaping in the air. What would the younger children do without the little soldier, standing guard, watching over them, keeping them safe?"

Mom had come to school and interrupted that conversation to tell Sister that Mary Kaye would not be returning to St. Patrick's. They were moving to Chicago, which was news to Mary Kaye. Sister Immaculata had rolled up the toy soldier and put a rubber band around it. Mary Kaye and Mom had walked to the car. "Want to look at my painting?" Mom hadn't answered and she had let it go.

Three weeks later, when Mom had tried to hand her the newborn Patty, she had more guts. She looked Mom right in the eye and said, "No."

All around the clerical room at Daleiden's, nightgowns and robes lay discarded. Some lay in piles over the backs of chairs. Some were heaped on the floor. Finally, Mary Kaye had worked up her nerve. She was done with shopping. "You and Dad have three Cadillacs in the garage."

"And?"

"And would it kill you, Mom, to spring for my college? At least the first year. After that I could try for a scholarship."

Mom raised a finger to her lips. "Hmmmm," she purred. "What if you went to the convent, got your education, and then up and left. What could they do to you? Make you give your education back?"

This was not a valuable piece of advice. Mom had given her only one valuable piece of advice in her life and she had not heeded it: "Once a guy gets going there is no way he can stop. They can't help themselves," she had said. "So if you cross a line, it's your own damn fault."

Mary Kaye had managed to get through the entire shopping trip without one thought of blood. Now that was all she could think of. She could not wait to go home to check her pants. And she had to get away from her mother.

"Let's take this bathrobe to the cash register. We'll get a receipt in case we have to return it."

4

SATURDAY AFTERNOON SHE went out to her rock, the granite boulder in the farthest corner of the pasture behind the house, where nobody could see her. She was dead tired. She needed fresh air. Familiar smells turned her stomach: bacon grease from last night's dinner, Mom's Jungle Gardenia, Dad's cigarette smoke. She could smell things she never had before, like the naugahyde couch and the newspapers. She kept feeling she was going to throw up. If this was morning sickness, no wonder Mom had spent so many days sprawled over the bed.

She knew that the people in charge never told you the important things. When the Blessed Mother had appeared to the three shepherd children at Fatima, she had given them a message for mankind. And the Pope had promised to reveal that secret to the world in 1960. But 1960 had come and gone with no word. That chipped away at her faith in the Pope. But not in Sister Michaeline, who wasn't the least bit surprised at the Vatican's silence. The barricade that had contained Mary Kaye's tears all morning crumbled and she wept and sobbed for Sister Michaeline until she could barely breathe. She had been counting on telling her this weekend that she was afraid she was pregnant. Sister would know what to do. She had helped Mary Kaye before with worries that were too heavy to carry alone.

One Friday after school in 1953, when she was eight years old, before they had moved to suburban Crosshaven, Mary Kaye had walked up Henderson Street in Chicago, wondering why the Buick was parked in front of the duplex with the motor running. Sitting on her rock in the pasture, she could see it, as though it were happening again. When she closed her eyes, it almost seemed real that she could tell the whole story again to Sister Michaeline. Mom in the passenger seat. Dad standing on the front porch next to their suitcases.

"Tell the kids we'll be back soon."

"Where are you going? Can you leave me a number?"

"Your mother's flipping out. We need a vacation. I'll call you from the motel."

"What about school, Dad? When will you be back?"

"I don't know, M. K." Mary Kaye saying nothing and Dad continuing. "Look, you know the ropes. If you need something, you've got your friend Johanna across the street. How old is she now?"

"Twelve."

"I thought she was thirteen."

Dad hugging her and the Old Spice smell nearly bringing tears. Standing on the porch, waving goodbye. Mom not turning to look back.

The memory as vivid as if she were watching TV. Patty and Brendan crying, their diapers full. Brendan hitting his head on the china cabinet door that somebody had set ajar. Clarice tearing through the house looking for her pacifier. Meggie running after her. Francine in Dad's chair, in a daze, eating potato chips.

Jack holding a hot pad holder over the gas burner on the kitchen stove, yelling, "I knew Mom was wrong." The hot pad holder going up in flames.

Mary Kaye screaming, "Turn off the stove, Jack," snatching the hot pad holder and throwing it into the sink.

Jack saying, "Mom said they put something on this stuff so they don't burn."

"Asbestos, Mister Wizard. No more experiments while they're gone. Now please go get the chalkboard."

Jack bringing the chalkboard from the basement to the living room. Her writing The Rules in pink chalk. Underlining key words, even though nobody but Jack could read. Trying to keep it simple. Jack had not picked up first grade as fast as she had.

- All doors are locked. DO NOT GO OUTSIDE.
- Do not play with the telephone. When Dad calls, you do not want to be the reason we missed it.
- Jack is my helper. When I am not in the room, OBEY JACK. DO WHAT JACK SAYS!

Mary Kaye turning from the chalkboard and seeing Jack fencing with a pick-up sticks like they had seen on Ed Sullivan. Francine stashing the potato chip bag in the television cabinet and dripping butter pecan ice cream on the couch. Meggie yanking rhododendron leaves out of the planter. Patty pulling Brendan's hair. Hearing Clarice howling, "My pah! My pah!"

Mary Kaye shouting, "Jack, give me that pick-up-stick. Francine. The ice cream carton. Into the freezer. Jack. The mail slot—Clarice hides her pacifier there." Rounding up the kids and sitting them in a circle on the living room rug. Reading them the temporary rules, asking each one, in turn, to repeat after me, "DO <u>NOT</u> GO OUTSIDE" and "Do <u>not</u> play with the telephone," and "Do what Jack says!"

"We're going to do what we always do when Mom and Dad are gone. I make the popcorn. Anybody who's bad has to kneel on top of the popcorn, in the corner. If everybody's good, I melt a stick of butter over the popcorn and we all watch TV."

Francine murmuring, "*I Married Joan.*"

Her feeling like a robot. "That's on Wednesday nights after Perry Como." Thank God, Francine was talking. She could stay mute for days.

Making Friday macaroni and cheese from a box, adding Velveeta to make it special. The kids sitting on the floor, bowls in their laps, watching TV. Telling Jack twice to wash the bowls and put them on a shelf down low so the kids could make their own breakfasts.

Trying to make it a slumber party by letting everybody watch *The Adventures of Ozzie and Harriet* and *The Life of Riley.* Brendan and Patty falling asleep with their chocolate milk bottles; Meggie and Clarice falling asleep hugging their bunnies. Francine nodding off after finding the tag on her blanket that she thumbed to go to sleep. Making popcorn. Watching *Cavalcade of Sports* with Jack and debating whether Rocky Marciano would keep his title as heavyweight champion. Telling Jack, "Too bad the kids didn't get popcorn." His making her laugh. "Make more tomorrow—they won't know the difference."

Waking in the night. The day's TV shows over and only a storm of black and white dots moving furiously on the screen. The set making a loud, scratchy sound that Dad called "snow," what was left after everybody in charge at the TV station had gone home and there was nothing for anybody to watch until the next morning, except the Indian-head test pattern. Turning the TV off. Picking up the encyclopedia, Volume P, bookmarked at the Periodic Table. She loved studying the rows and columns of chemical elements, ordered by their atomic number and electron configurations, by which she could predict the reactions of the elements in relationships. So different from people—especially Mom and Dad—for whom it seemed impossible to construct a model that would account for, much less predict, their behavior.

Saturday was a blur, but Sunday morning they played Mass. Jack was the priest; she was the organist; the girls and Brendan were the faithful. To keep them in their pews, she gave Brendan and Patty their bottles, Clarice her pacifier, Meggie an all-day sucker, and Francine a bag of Cheetos. Jack used grape juice for the wine and Necco candy wafers for the hosts. At Communion, she let the younger kids chew their wafers.

"I don't get the big deal about not letting it stick to the roof of your mouth," Jack said.

"The real Host is stickier. You'll see," she said, "when you make your First Communion."

Jack put the chocolate wafer on his tongue. He had had the sense not to give anybody clove or licorice.

Sunday there had been nothing on TV, so they played with the dials on the radio and moped. She consulted with Jack about what she should tell the principal at St. Ferdinand's about why they would not be in school. They decided the safest thing was to leave that one for Mom.

The phone never rang. Sunday night, after Jack Benny, she tucked Brendan, Patty, Clarice, and Meggie into their beds upstairs. She let Francine stay up for the *Colgate Comedy Hour*, but not for *Fred Waring*. She and Jack got to the part on *What's My Line* when they reveal the mystery guest's identity when Mom and Dad burst in, all smiles.

"School tomorrow," Mom said, pointing to the staircase.

"Everything's OK!" Dad said, setting down the luggage.

Mom beamed. "Your guardian angels watched over you."

Mary Kaye was a sophomore in high school when she and Sister Michaeline first talked about the whacko weekends. It was on the basketball court. In the first place, Mom would have killed her if she'd known she and Sister Michaeline were shooting baskets in the gym, a forbidden sport sure to put muscles on her legs. Sister leapt up for a jump shot, cocking her knee so that its outline showed through her floor-length skirt. For the first time, it hit Mary Kaye that there were legs under those skirts, and, attached to those legs, feet in the nuns' black, lace-up shoes.

"Do you think my folks are bad people?"

"What do you mean by 'bad people'?"

"I mean people who leave an eight-year-old in charge of six little kids for three days—wouldn't you call that evil? Brendan and Patty were in diapers."

"On paper, it's not good."

"If they really loved us, they wouldn't do stuff like that." She threw the ball to the far end of the court.

Sister Michaeline hustled after it, saying, "I don't think it has much to do with love. People do what they know. I'll bet none of your grandparents ever had a babysitter."

"I'll bet they never took off for days at a time without so much as a phone number either," Mary Kaye said.

Sister swiveled and dribbled. "You don't know what you'd do if you were in their shoes, you really don't." She tossed the ball. Mary Kaye missed it and ran downcourt. "Everyone has limits, but it's hard to know what yours are before it's too late. You do something stupid, you learn what happens when you get in over your head."

Mary Kaye wondered why Sister Michaeline was making excuses for her parents. It struck her as odd. What she said, though, was, "Nobody should have kids unless they're sure they can properly take care of them. And don't you think that if Mom and Dad really loved me, they'd be trying to talk me out of going to the convent, at least until I was a little bit older?"

"Your folks wouldn't second guess the Church," Sister said, dribbling the ball to the other end of the court. "Father Moriarty told them you had a vocation. That's the end of it. The way they were raised, they wouldn't stop you. No matter what they thought. Father Moriarty told me your dad was in tears. Especially when he told them we'd cut your hair."

Mary Kaye caught a pass from Sister half a length down the court, pivoted, missed a shot from the free throw line, rebounded and threw the ball to Sister. "That I never would have guessed."

Sister returned the ball. "He's trying to be a good sport."

She leapt for the catch. "At least he tries."

"Maybe they're doing the best they can," Sister said. "And maybe the best you can hope for is that each generation improves on the last."

Mary Kaye took the ball to the other end of the court. "They did let me go on the art study tour of Europe."

"Perfect example," Sister said, catching the throw.

"Mom said they had rocks in their heads paying for me to spend three weeks looking at paintings and statues. But she let me go."

Sister laughed and dribbled from one end of the court to the other. "She might not have if she'd known what we were up to."

In Florence Mary Kaye had come under the spell of *David*. He wasn't a statue—he was sculpture. Even from the other end of the gallery, she could tell the difference. She couldn't take her eyes off him. Treading in the deep end of the parish pool, she had watched Loyola boys hoist themselves up on the palms of their hands, swimming trunks twisted and plastered against seats and thighs. She had seen the outlines of hanging, curving things as they shook their suits from their bodies. *David* made fantasy easier.

Sister Michaeline had come up behind her in Florence and shook her arm. "I remember the first time I saw a Michelangelo. He makes the hair on your arms stand straight up."

In the pasture behind the O'Donnell house in Crosshaven, Mary Kaye slid down from the rock and sat on the earth. She knew that Sister Michaeline knew that there is more to being alive than being Catholic. But as to what that revelation meant in practice, there was so much more she wished she could have learned from her.

5

THE PARISH HELD a wake for the nuns on Saturday night. There was window air conditioning in Our Lady's Chapel—Father Schultz had seen to that—but it was not cool enough to keep the bodies looking fresh. Sister Michaeline's eyebrows had settled into an uncharacteristic frown and the sides of Sister Jane Denise's mouth looked like they were starting to melt.

Mary Kaye felt feverish and disconnected, as if she were standing slightly outside herself. Candles seemed too bright; voices, too loud. She could barely glance at Sister Michaeline's body. Having spent most of the day at home weeping, she was determined to hold it together in public for Sister Michaeline's wake.

One by one, the families of Holy Ghost squeezed past the caskets, which stood head to head in the chapel in front of the altar. The crush of parishioners must have outstripped Father's expectations and there was grumbling that the wake should have been held in the main church, where fans could have been brought in. Mary Kaye overheard Mr. Conlon grousing that Father never missed a chance to show off the window air conditioning. Mrs. Riley confided that it was like Father to underestimate the love that parishioners had for the nuns. There had been a paragraph in the *Tribune* reporting that they had died in a car accident. Mrs. Mahony grumbled that, so far, Father Schultz had managed to embargo further details.

Sister Giles, the sacristan, had positioned the caskets directly behind the Communion railing so those who wished to could kneel to say their goodbyes. Parents had especially loved Sister Jane Denise because she had taken the grade school to the Catholic League basketball championship in 1959 and 1962. The kids had loved her because she was light-hearted and praised them generously, in contrast to her predecessor in the gym, whom they had dubbed Sister Hitler. And Sister Michaeline had brought the parish a shelf of trophies from instrumental and choir competitions, most recently the jazz band competition at the Civic Opera House. But what Mary Kaye mostly heard parishioners whisper in the line for viewing was how much they would miss Sister Michaeline at the holidays. She wondered whether Sister had any idea how many had been lifted up by the choir's rendition of Mozart's *Mass in C Major* at Christmas.

Sister Giles had posted her at the head of Sister Michaeline's casket so she could distribute funeral cards, with the names of the two nuns and their dates of birth. She was surprised that Sister Michaeline had been born in 1916. Sister was forty-seven, seven years older than Mom. Mary Kaye had thought Sister Michaeline was younger.

She held several fussy babies while their mothers knelt in front of the caskets and helped a toddler or two step up on the kneelers to get a good look at the bodies. Sister Giles had instructed her to give flowers to any mourners who would take them. There were so many gladiolas and lilies that the air was thick with heavy scent. Beginning to feel faint, she recruited Lee Mahony's sister Lydia to take over the cards and walked toward the back of the chapel.

At the end of the last pew, in black, a man knelt by himself. He was the only black person she had ever seen in church. And, except for Zenia, the O'Donnells' cleaning woman, and the Pullman porter on the Illinois Central train, the only black person she had ever seen up close. Amos and Andy didn't count.

Thinking of Sister Michaeline, Mary Kaye perked up at the sight of the man. Sister had her reading James Baldwin's novel *Go Tell It on the Mountain.* Then, later, she read Baldwin's essay in the *New Yorker* and began to glimpse the fact that so many black people grew up seeing only dismal prospects for themselves. She had thought they had it like the Irish, who, when they fled the British, were looked down upon in America. It was a real struggle, but many of the Irish grew up with a cheering squad insisting that, with hard work and perseverance, they could rise through the ranks. Baldwin was right. It's hard to imagine a cop mocking an Irish youth the way a policeman sneered at him. As Baldwin headed up the library steps at age thirteen, a cop muttered, "Why don't you n-----s stay uptown where you belong?"

The black man in the pew looked up and caught Mary Kaye's eye. Was it her imagination or had he nodded as well?

She glanced at Lydia, who seemed to be managing well at the caskets. When she turned back to the pews, the man had disappeared.

She dropped the funeral cards on a radiator and, on impulse, darted out of the chapel after him.

Sauntering toward the parking lot, the man looked straight ahead. He was taller than her father, slimmer and graceful, and noticeably older as well. He held his elbows close to his waist, forearms extended and wrists flexed like a pianist's. His strong stride had an athletic grace, at times flirting with a sashay. From the back he looked like Cary Grant. When he got to the foot of the convent steps, he stopped.

Mary Kaye caught her breath, slowing down as she approached. "Sir, excuse me, sir."

As he turned, the glow from the convent porch light played on his skin and she thought of coffee cut with cream. He lifted his homburg, revealing black hair flecked with white. His outfit gleamed in the porch light. He wore a black silk suit with a black satin bow tie and a white silk handkerchief in the breast pocket of the jacket.

"You're here for Sister Michaeline," Mary Kaye said. "Could we talk?"

"Sure, but not here. Not now. I best be off." He motioned toward the parking lot and started moving in that direction.

She followed. "My name is Mary Kaye O'Donnell, sir."

The man turned his key in the car door. "I thought you might be Mary Kaye." He lifted his leg, rested a foot on the running board, and reached into the car.

She eyed his leg. A little row of gold dominoes lined the side of his black sock. They looked like dice, when the game is done and you line them up to put them back on the shelf.

The man emerged from the car and handed her a package, wrapped in newspaper. "Sister Michaeline said if anything happened to her, I should give you her book."

"Who are you? How do you know who I am? How did you even know she died?"

"Maureen—sorry—Sister Michaeline said you had spunk. One way or another, she said, you'd find me."

He was sitting in the car now, the dice under his pant cuffs. In white space on the newspaper, she read his handwriting, every bit as elegant as his attire: "Duck pond. Lincoln Park Zoo. 2 p.m. Tuesday, June 4. Birdhouse, if rain."

She tucked the package under her arm against her side. She was sweating and sick to her stomach. She wondered if the newspaper ink would leave a dark smudge on her skin.

"Read it," the man said. Just before he closed the car door, he looked up. "My name is Lucius."

6

DRIVING DAD'S CADILLAC Eldorado, she headed home from Sister Michaeline's wake, the newsprint-wrapped book resting in her lap. She kept reaching down to make sure it was still there, rubbing the newsprint, as if to kindle an unforeseen hope. Maybe there would be a way to stay in touch with Sister Michaeline.

There were two gated entrances from Sycamore Lane to what Dad called the O'Donnell compound. They were built with the same red brick as the mansion, a two-story southern colonial with a pair of Doric pillars. The house stood atop its own hill, facing south, behind a forest of oaks, between an apple orchard and a stand of hickory trees. There were sundecks on the second floor, off bedrooms on either side.

In front of the house, the forest was so thick that, from the street, even in winter, it was impossible to see the O'Donnells, inside or outside. Behind the rows of hickory trees, which stretched all the way from the east entrance to the goat pasture, a tall thicket of Austrian pines shielded them from the eyes of the neighboring Andersons, whom Mary Kaye's parents had deduced were some kind of Protestant.

The driveways were a pair of opposing horseshoes at the bottom of the hill, joined at the curved middles in front of the house. Like everything else O'Donnell, the horseshoes shared space. The legs of one led in from the street. The legs of the other curved back around the bottom of the hill to the doors of the garage under the house. The kids liked to torment Mom by driving go-carts at breakneck speed through the garage, while she leaned down out of leaded windows in the kitchen, warning them not to crash into cars that might be driving in from the street.

Apple trees ran from the west entrance to the duck pond and stables behind the house. When Mary Kaye wasn't looking after children, reading, or practicing her music, she rode her horse, Lady. Behind the stables, and behind the neighbors' houses, a wide pasture with her rock in one corner ran the length of Sycamore Lane. As a child, she had climbed the apple trees to watch Judge Engelmann and his wife tend their roses. The O'Donnells had no time for roses—not with four acres and seven kids. By 1963, Mrs. Engelmann was dead and the Engelmann roses were gone. Judge Engelmann was spending his nights on the ham radio in his attic, making connections with strangers. He had shown Mary Kaye his amateur radio station, how to tap Morse code, how to talk with people who spoke different languages. And, when Rachel Carson's "Silent Spring" series appeared in *The New Yorker*, he had coached her on how to infuse biochemistry with heartfelt emotion in her thesis for all-state high school debate.

As the Eldorado rolled into the west entrance, she patted Sister's book. What had been a flicker of hope caught fire. What if Sister Michaeline had picked up that she might be pregnant? There might be guidance for her in the book. Maybe she had asked Lucius to give her the book to send her a message. That train of thought led to another idea, more alarming. What if Sister suspected something was going to happen to her? What if she thought she was in danger? Mary Kaye planned to sit in the car in the garage and at least thumb through the book immediately. But she had to contain herself. Not get carried away.

She hit the automatic garage door opener and, as the door rose, came back to earth fast, at the sight of her father's feet, legs, torso, smiling face, then arms waving her inside. How to hide the book? She couldn't leave it in his car, even for a moment. Too risky to stash it somewhere in the garage temporarily. He was walking toward her. She stuffed the book under her skirt and half-slip, into the front of her underpants, and fluffed up her blouse and jacket, knowing full well that she was accentuating the bulge she was spending most of her days trying to hide.

Dad was chipper. "Come on up. I've been waiting for you," he said, steering her up the stairs to the kitchen.

She tried to beg off. "I'm tired, Dad."

"Aw, honey. Who else am I gonna talk to?" He poured an inch of Jim Beam into his Waterford tumbler, an upgrade when they had moved north from Chicago to the suburbs.

Mary Kaye pulled an ice tray from the freezer and knocked the last few cubes into a goblet. She ran the faucet until the water turned cold, refilled the tray—one exasperating square at a time—and slammed it back into the freezer. She was exhausted.

Dad drummed his fist against the teak table. Although his widow's peak was receding and his green golf shirt clung tightly to the spare tire around his waist, he did not look forty. He had the O'Donnell skin, steadily rosy, slow to wrinkle. And he was prone to enthusiasms. If a little Brylcreem was good, a whole lot was better.

She leaned against the sink, making sure the book was secure, then filled the goblet from the tap and sorted through the dishes stacked on the counter.

Her father softened. "We went to a party tonight. She's asleep already. You know the deal. Her nerves are shot."

Listening, Mary Kaye rescued the Porterhouse platter from the sink, but didn't have the patience to drain grease into the coffee can. Waste not, want not. Mother's side was German. They kept everything that might be remotely useful in plain sight. Not so, the O'Donnells. Once, when Mary Kaye was putting away laundry, she had found in her father's drawer a small leatherette box, golden brown and butter soft. Half the snap on its cover was missing. Inside had been a miraculous medal; a rosary from Lourdes, the first trip he and Mom had taken once they had money; the diamond stick pin his old company had given him when he was national sales leader, the year before he went into business for himself; and his discharge papers from the Navy. In the square marked "Immediate Plans," he had written "College." But he had not gone back to school after the war. The kids had come fast.

Until recently, Dad had had confidence in her. Mom had been in the hospital in Fort Wayne with Meggie when he registered her for kindergarten. "You're five, right, Mary Kaye?" he coaxed. "Tell Sister Simon you're five. Mom can't find her birth certificate, Sister, but she's five and I'll swear to it." Mary Kaye had one hand in her pocket, fingers crossed. It was OK for Dad to lie because he did not look Sister in the eye, the way you do when you're telling the truth. At eleven, she'd gone to him for kitchen table advice. "I don't know how to talk to the kids at school. They keep saying, 'Kookie, Kookie, lend me your comb.'"

"That's supposed to be funny?"

"I don't know what they think."

"Don't say nothing. You'll be out of that school in no time. Who's this Kookie anyway?"

"The guy who parks cars on *77 Sunset Strip*."

Her father glowered. "Forget about TV. Forget about friends. Friends don't mean nothing. Keep hitting the books. You grow up, you could be President of the United States. You got the looks. You got the brains. Keep your eye on the ball. Don't get sucked into silly kid stuff."

Dad was in railroad salvage. He could eyeball a wreck and know immediately what was worth saving. He said it was like playing blackjack when you know how to count cards. For any crash within a five-hundred- mile radius of Chicago, Dad would drop everything and drive to survey the damage. Sometimes he pulled Mary Kaye out of school to go with him. Once at Christmas, a freight train derailed near Rapid City and he had rousted her out of bed to be his second driver.

That night, coming around a curve at a hundred miles-per-hour, he'd said, "I'm gonna slow down. You slip over and take the wheel. I'll get some shuteye."

The speedometer had dropped to eighty.

"OK, now. Switch."

She had stayed put. "Dad, aren't you going to pull over?"

"What for? This is how we do it. One guy slips his leg over the other guy's and scoots up onto his lap. You get your foot on the gas pedal while the other guy slides out. There's an art to it. You want that guy out from under you before you hit the next curve."

The night of Sister Michaeline's wake she could tell that Dad was especially wound up. "Listen, Mary Kaye. I heard from one of the fellas at the party that there was a wake tonight."

She froze. Suddenly, she felt he could see right through her and at any moment would demand that she turn over Sister Michaeline's book.

"Yeah, Mel Peterson, he's a what-cha-ma-call-it, heart doctor. Plays with Mom and me in the parish bowling league. He said the guy who runs the funeral parlor told him two nuns had died and they think their deaths have something to do with the racial crap— nuns agitating, visiting Negroes in Cabrini-Green."

This was news. She rummaged through the T-towel drawer, not looking at Dad, bracing for a rant.

"You're not listening to me, Mary Kaye. Cardinal Meyer damn well better get his ass in gear. Mayor Daley better get on the ball. Cabrini-Green's a snake pit for women with no husbands, kids with no dads. Every time I hear the nuns did this, the nuns did that, I ask myself how in the hell did my Mary Kaye get suckered into this bunch of radicals?"

She looked over at her father and plugged the drain in the sink. She opened the spigot, squeezed the plastic detergent bottle, and watched the tops of the bigger bubbles burst, leaving craters on the soap surface.

"Anybody else I know at the party?"

Dad poured a few more inches of Jim Beam, then thumped the bottle on the table. "Yeah, sure, a couple of those folks you babysit for. The guy in the pit at the Mercantile Exchange, you know, one of the guys in the funny coats who jump around making hand signals. I can't stand that guy. Every time I run into him he introduces himself like he's never seen me before. Every time he asks me, 'So, what do you do for a living?' What am I supposed to say? 'You little shit. You know goddamn well what I do for a living. You just want to hear me say it again.'"

Mary Kaye plunged a mug under water and listened to it gulp. She was not going to get into it with Dad that night.

Dad stood, crossed to the freezer, and plunked a few ice cubes into his glass. He walked over to her at the sink and put his arm around her shoulder. "I can buy IBM to kingdom come. It don't matter how much money I make in the stock market. It don't matter how big a house I buy on the Chicago North Shore. I'm a farm boy from Storm Lake, Iowa. Nothing's going to change that." He wiped his mouth with the back of his hand and whispered, "For you, sky's the limit. Forget about the convent. Go get the education. Go get the credentials. Then come talk to me about what you want to do with your life."

He went back to the table and stirred the ice in the bourbon. She stood with her back to him, looking out the kitchen sink window, seeing only herself. In the old days, she could have told him at least something about what had been happening. Until she had graduated from high school, her stock with him had only gone up. He had big ideas for her. He loved the piano, so he'd paid for lessons. She was the next Van Cliburn: she had to have the Steinway; she was headed for a concert tour. And when it had turned out she didn't need a Steinway because singing was her thing, that had been OK too. The next Maria Callas. Then she had given up opera for Joan Baez—and last Christmas he'd bought her a guitar.

Five months later, he had raised a toast at her graduation party and she had been stunned to hear him say, "Here's to my oldest daughter. She can do anything she sets her mind to. She can be a Pan Am stewardess. She can see the world and meet a Notre Dame lawyer. He'll give her the big house, the big car, the big family, everything she deserves." A stewardess? A wife? Somehow, while she had been busy with her music, making application to the convent, growing from a girl into a woman, her stock had crashed.

The telephone rang.

"Oh, hi, Mel. I just saw you. What's up?"

Mary Kaye held her breath.

"No, no, no, no. You don't know what you're talking about. My Mary Kaye's been hanging around the nuns, but that doesn't make her a flaming idiot. No way would she be standing on the convent steps talking to a colored man."

After he hung up he turned to Mary Kaye. "What the hell were you doing talking to a colored guy? I got to get some sleep. And I ain't going to be sleeping anytime soon if you're out there mixing it up having conversations and who knows what comes next, you got to be realistic, there's only one thing on those guys's minds. You've got no business saying boo to any one of those jigaboos, let alone having a so-called conversation. You used to be a smart gal. You better wise up or you're going to ruin your life."

Mary Kaye had heard screeds like this and worse from Dad and her usual response was to say nothing.

That night felt different. Sister Michaeline had known this man Lucius well enough that she had asked him to deliver her book to her. So Dad wasn't just slandering all black men, which was bad enough. He was trashing a man, who, from everything she had observed in that first meeting, seemed a lot more cultured and refined than her father.

In something like a reflex she fired back in defense of Sister's friend. "So black people are good enough for you to sit around their kitchen tables to persuade them to buy things they don't need at prices they can't afford at credit rates that bleed them dry—but not good enough to be partners in an open, genuine, honest, real conversation."

At which, Dad slammed down the Jim Beam bottle and what was left of its contents and bellowed, "And you wonder why Mom isn't rushing to spend my hard-earned money to send you to college? There's too much sass in you already. Now, how'm I going to sleep?" He hoisted himself up, teetering a bit. "Listen to me, baby-doll, there's talk in the parish, something about a colored guy helping some of the nuns. No telling what a guy like that might be up to." His slippers scuffed across the floor. "What the hell! I'm going to bed, darlin'. Don't forget the lights."

She sat for a moment, dumbstruck by her own words. When she was sure that Dad wasn't coming back, she tore the newspaper off Sister's book—carefully saving the date and time of her meeting with Lucius—and went down to the wine cellar to read.

My Particular Examen Book
Examination of Conscience
Saint Francis Convent, Milwaukee

June 1, 1947. Feast of Saint Angela Merici, whose motto was "The disorders of society are caused by those in families."

This is my Particular Examen book. This is where sins and offenses against the rule are supposed to go. Sister Augustine says it's our record of wrongdoing.

But, tell me, God, what counts as wrong? Is it wrong that I didn't tell the postulant mistress that I'm going to use this book to talk to You? I don't picture You keeping a score card. Thumbs up. Thumbs down. Nope. I think You want me to write whatever pleases me. I think You want me to speak of myself to You as I really am. I need a place where I don't have to keep up a front.

I keep losing things. It would be a waste of time to write down every one. Yesterday I couldn't find the white collar that goes over the postulant cape. It goes on a hook on the wall of my cell. The cape is kind of cute, but a pill to fasten. I must have knocked the collar off the hook and kicked it under my cell curtain. Too dark to find it. I love wearing the veil. I love dressing in black. I miss the light and mirror on my old wardrobe.

We didn't go back to the Dormitory until after night prayer, so I spent the whole day without the collar. My penance came to four Our Fathers and four Hail Marys. Sister A. says that if you put things where they go, they will always be there. I wouldn't bet the farm on it. Of course, You already know that I know that and that I did not mouth off to the postulant mistress. I held my tongue. But I wouldn't mind a little sign from You. Is it OK to put acts of virtue in the Particular Examen?

June 3, 1947. Feast of Saint Kevin, whose parents sent him to live with monks at the age of seven.

I lie down to sleep and Michael comes to me. I would put that in the Bad column except that Sister says there is no use pretending I don't miss him. He stands in the doorway, as he did five-and-a-half years ago, tall and lanky, wavy black hair dusted with snow. Flakes shine on his eyelashes. His cheeks are red, redder than when he'd had a few too many. He shakes the snow loose and plays with the part in my hair.

He puts his long arms around my neck and whispers, I enlisted.

They won't take you. You can't see without your glasses.

I wasn't fool enough to wear them. Nobody said a thing.

Does Lucius know?

I made him promise not to tell. Boot Camp starts next week. How fast can you pull together a wedding?

Sunday morning I had never heard of Pearl Harbor. The next week he was gone and I was Mrs. O'Leary.

June 10, 1947. Feast of Saint Margaret, widow, schooled her eight children in Christian virtue.

Sister A. said Mother Isidore may assign me to study music. They can't hear the Billie Holiday in my head.

"A sailboat in the moonlight and you / Wouldn't that be heaven just for two." Scrubbing the kitchen floor. Dusting the Infant Jesus statue in the Visitors' Parlor. Swinging hard, singing in my head against the beat. Keeping time with my shoulders, letting my arms go limp, pushing the volume harder, lagging behind. Uncle Bill on the tenor sax smooth as hot fudge running down the side of a sundae. Lucius two beats to the bar on the bass. Michael, oh, Michael's got the gentlest touch. He sashays, he slides, he pumps the piano tenderly, his touch clean and strong. He shows me how to play with time, keep the melody going, push against the rhythm, rush ahead, lag behind. He shows me how to land firmly on the beat.

Sister A. is thinking "Jesus, Joy of Man's Desire." Maybe Bach will teach me another way to want. Maybe I'll stop feeling Michael's touch when I become a novice and they cut my hair.

June 19, 1947. Feast of Saint Juliana Falconieri, virgin who renounced her inheritance and devoted herself to the Seven Sorrows of Our Lady.

Sister A. had to remind me again that I must lower my voice, the pitch, and the volume. That is hard to remember, even harder than remembering to walk without making a sound. The idea is to call as little attention to myself as possible. The slang has also got to go. A nun doesn't say, "What a drag" or "That was a doozy." I asked Sister about "That's no picnic," and she said that a good nun does not complain.

July 1, 1947. Feast of the Precious Blood of Jesus.

I sang the intonation at Compline this evening. "May God grant us a peaceful night and a perfect end." Was it wrong to admire my voice, strong and clear, piercing the chapel silence? When we chant, every time we bow, I still grasp for my pendant. Michael gave me the citrine with diamonds for my birthday the year we met. I hung it on a gold chain and wore it around my neck every day until I came here. Whenever I bent forward or turned sharply to the side, my hand went up to catch the pendant. By force of habit, it still does.

The pendant sits in a cardboard box somewhere in the Motherhouse, probably in a closet. The day we entered, we went to our cells and changed into postulant clothes. Sister A. had us fold our street clothes and stack them in a box for safekeeping. I was so nervous that I wrote "Maureen Rieger" on the side of the box. Should I have crossed out Rieger and made it O'Leary? Sister said that next year, when we are received as novices, our things will be given to Catholic Charities. My filmy blue-and-white checkered skirt and jacket, the matching sleeveless ruffled blouse, low enough to show off the pendant, the silky underthings, the white pumps and nylon hosiery. After reception, the pendant will go to Sister Stanislaus for making jeweled reliquaries. I asked Sister A. whether she would break up the citrine and diamonds. She said the pendant will stay in the box untouched, so that if I should leave the convent before reception, it would come back to me. After reception, its fate will rest with Sister S. Burying the pendant in the box was the hardest thing I've had to do here so far, harder than watching the other postulants hug their families goodbye. Mine didn't come to deliver me here. You know why.

July 5, 1947. Feast of Saint Zoa, martyr, hung from a tree by a rope of her own hair and suspended over smoky fire until she suffocated.

I should not think ill of Mother Isidore, but the Fourth of July fizzled. No fanfare. Zilch. What do I expect from the Bavarian Amazon? She came to America as an orphan with the German founders of the convent and her war wounds have not yet healed. But would it have killed her to let us have a little Coke and chocolate?

When her feast day comes we'll celebrate Saint Isidore the Husbandman. I looked him up in the *Lives of the Saints.* What a guy! When he was late for work, angels appeared, driving snow white oxen to help him plow the field. He didn't get a tardiness penalty like I do when I'm lost in thought. But then I'll never be a saint. I giggled in the library about his wife, Santa Maria de la Cabeza. When they pray for rain in Madrid, they carry her head in procession. I'd die laughing.

I asked Sister A. if laughing out loud in the library is something I'm supposed to confess. She stood on tiptoes as if to appear taller than me and warned me against scrupulosity. She and her baby-faced smile told me that God wants us to enjoy our thoughts. Saint Francis loved a good laugh.

July 19, 1947. Saint Vincent de Paul, parish priest and chaplain to galley slaves.

It's hotter than Hades in the dormitories. I am not supposed to complain, even in my thoughts, but we are tucked under the dormers in the attic. Oh, for the day after I moved to Chicago, when Uncle Bill took me to the Athenaeum because they had air conditioning at the bowling alley! Michael was in the next lane, throwing strikes and spares. I knew him from the band at the Jazz Emporium but we had never met. It impressed me that he drank beer out of a glass.

Michael stood watching me throw gutter balls, then leaned toward Uncle Bill and me and cupped his hands around his mouth. "If it's all right with you, Bill, I'd like to show this lovely lady how it's done."

He steered me out to the lane—I can still feel the heat of him against me—and centered me in front of the pins, lingering longer than I expected, his hands around my waist, getting my hips right. He came around in front of me, rearranged my fingers and thumbs on the ball, moved them where they belonged. He slipped behind me, rested his head on my shoulder, slid his arm down the back of mine, and lifted the ball up to my chin. "You want to hold it like this for a while. Never let them rush you." I could feel his cheek moving on mine as he spoke. "That's what it's all about. Complete concentration, thoroughly relaxed."

Without turning his head, he shouted, "Go get your jacket from the cleaners or something, Bill."

He whispered to me, "I'm going to swing your arm down and back. That's it, you've got natural rhythm, just like Bill said. Now swing forward. Let me do the rest." I was so discombobulated that I dropped the ball. "That one doesn't count," he said. "Do you want to do it again?"

July 22, 1947. Saint Mary Magdalene, penitent, delivered from seven devils, washed Jesus' feet with her tears and dried them with her hair.

Like it or not, we write one letter a week. I keep feeling I will tell Michael how music soaks our days, from the first intonation as we rise from sleep—"Jesus Lives / Eternal Love"—to the last intonation at night prayer, "May God grant us a peaceful night and a perfect end."

At home I had the hang of it. Michael was dead. Here it's as if he's back in Chicago, waiting for my letter. I catch myself planning to write him and it brings me up short. Don't be silly. He was dead. He's still dead.

August 10, 1947. Saint Lawrence, martyr, broiled on a spit.

I kept talking when the bell rang for Benediction. I finished a sentence. Telling Shirley that Virginia Woolf said a woman needs her own money and her own room to be free to think whatever she wants. Otherwise, how can she disagree with the man who provides support? Franciscans have a different way to skin that cat. We don't earn our keep. We own nothing and have no one to please but You. Shirley asked me where she could find the Woolf reference. I said, "In the library, in *A Room . . .*" and the bell rang. I disobeyed and continued, " . . . *of One's Own.*"

They say the bell is the voice of God. We're supposed to stop in mid-sentence when it rings. That You don't want us to finish the thought, the word, the syllable. The silence is eerie. Everybody freezes as if the whole lot of us have simultaneously been tagged: You're it! I suppose we have been, chosen women that we are.

The silence is absolute. Unless it is marred by a chatterbox doing what I did at the end of recreation. Sister A. said not to get carried away with remorse. It takes a while to develop the habit of obedience. The novices and professed nuns have got the hang of it. And postulants learn faster than the high school girls, the aspirants.

It is preternatural. Like the moment when the doors on the bus close, or the fuse blows and the lights go out, or the symphony conductor punches the end of the last note. Everybody folds hands under capes, lowers eyes, turns to move toward what is next.

The novices come downstairs from cloister and make no sound at all. As if they were spirits floating from step to step, never touching the stairs. The postulants sound like a cattle stampede, but we're better than the aspirants, who thunder like buffalo. I must try harder to walk without a sound, especially on the stairs.

August 12, 1947. Saint Clare.

Every year for the rest of my life I will celebrate this day not as Michael's birthday, which it used to be, but as the feast day of the first woman to become a Franciscan. Saint Francis, the knight, brought Clare to her bridegroom, Jesus. She and her nuns slept on the ground. They didn't wear shoes or socks or even sandals. They never ate meat. They never spoke except out of necessity or charity. Yet we celebrate her day by moderating our own austerity. We live it up, talk to each other at table, and have boiled beef with horseradish, chocolate, and Coke at dinner. Michael would have loved the irony.

August 21, 1947. Saint Jane Frances Fremiot de Chantal, widow, devoted herself courageously to the education of her four children.

After he died, the place where I found Michael was in his books. The page numbers he had written on the inside covers took me to passages he had underlined, marked with an "!" or a "?" or an "*." Our conversation began. I posed my own questions, made my own remarks, said them out loud. I thumbed through the pages, looking for his responses, following his arrows and lines through the text, reading words in the margins. I went back to the inside cover and started again. When he didn't come back from the war, that's how I talked with Michael, until I came here and had to leave his books behind. There were thousands of them, mostly novels, but also poetry and biographies. In philosophy, only Aristotle. Michael lived in his flesh, not his head. I thought I could live without his books, but I'm not sure I can.

There has never been another place, not in the Middle Ages and not in 1947, where a Catholic woman without money of her own could pursue her intellectual interests. Single or widowed, women are consigned to families, hospitals, schools; taking care of and watching over the young, the weak, the needy. Only in the convent can we count on hours of contemplation daily. Reading, meditation, Mass, Rosary, Benediction, chanting the Divine Office. We live in Your presence, and thereby in the presence of our own minds. O Lord, I love the chance to think. But I will miss the chance to have a daughter of my own. How I would love to be able to teach her to sing.

August 23, 1947. Saint Philip Benizi, confessor, gave his cape to a destitute leper who was immediately healed.

Tonight, at night prayer, I moved my lips, but didn't make a sound. I listened to the others chant in a single voice, cutting clearly through the thick silence, so different from the muddle of instrumental voices I remember from the Jazz Emporium. Those guys fell all over themselves to work together. They took turns at solos, but nobody ever called too much attention to himself.

The first time Michael and I argued it was over Billie Holiday.

"You call that singing?" I said. "She can tell a story to background music, but her voice is nothing but another instrument in the band. It's limp. It's got no starch."

"I'm not saying try to sing like Billie. I'm saying there's a lot to learn from her," he said.

"I'm not going to tag along on a song, squeezed in somewhere between the piano and the bass. I'm not a crybaby, or somebody's cast-off whiny cat."

"OK, OK. But I love it when you sit under her picture and watch me play. What's got into you, Maureen? I never saw this side of you."

"It's not a side of me. It's me. I don't want to learn to blend in. I want to stand out."

Michael laughed. "Maureen Rieger's never going to lose her starch."

"What if I get hit by a truck?" When he didn't answer me, I said, "You pulling my leg?"

"Maybe just a teensy bit."

Now I'm trying something different. I had my shot at standing out.

August 28, 1947. Saint Augustine, bishop, confessor, doctor of the Church.

My first serious offense. Actually, two. But not on purpose. Walking through the chapel vestibule after Compline last night I tugged on Ann's cape and whispered, "Tomorrow's my birthday." A good postulant, she didn't twitch. Eyes cast downward, arms folded under her cape, she kept the Great Silence. One of the first things Sister told us when we entered three months ago was that we may never, no matter what, touch another person. I feel chastened and plain old stupid. Actually, I have committed a third offense. We aren't supposed to talk about our past lives. If I have no past, then I have no birthday. Today is no longer my birthday. It is the feast of Saint Augustine and Sister A.'s name day.

August 29, 1947. The Beheading of Saint John the Baptist.

The day after what used to be my birthday. I turned 31, but Michael is still 29. I am older than my older man: husband and lover, but first of all teacher. When Uncle Bill introduced us at the Athenaeum, Michael was reading *To the Lighthouse.* To think that a man would care what a woman had to say. He bought me a copy, his first gift to me, and showed me how to open a book, creasing back each cover, carefully turning page after page, pressing each one against the spine. I can see him, pocket watch chain hanging from his vest, teaching me to write notes in the page margins, to make my own index inside the front and back covers, to record my reactions and questions, to make a book my own.

He didn't talk much about jazz, the music or the business, or how he kept his group together. Jazz was something he lived, like literature. He introduced me to Emma Bovary and Maggie Verver as if they were next door neighbors. He poked fun at Casaubon's scholarship as if he were a friend. He mocked the real Clare College dons who had sat at his table in Cambridge and the men who wore their scarves around their necks instead of stashing the black and gold on a hook in the second bathroom. They knew everything about each other, those men. After he was killed, their black-trimmed condolences arrived one by one. Maybe Michael's greatest gift to me, beyond music, beyond literature, was his confidence that there was a community eager to hear his thoughts, watching for his letterhead, ready to put him up for a month in London or New York, so they could talk about reading and writing. In him I lost my dearest link to culture, but he left me with the idea that I too should find a group. So far, better than expected. In the convent, we are forbidden to speak about our past lives, but that does not include books, which tie me to my old self and to Michael. Never have I known so many people, women, genuinely willing to listen and understand.

September 2, 1947. Saint Stephen, king and confessor, visited the poor in their homes and washed their feet. His right hand has remained incorrupt.

Sister A. told me that Lucius drove up to the Motherhouse for my birthday. He stood most of the day at the street entrance, on the chance that he would see me. He had brought a Whitman Sampler and my old copy of *Mrs. Dalloway*, the one that says Maureen Rieger, Chicago, 1938, with my notes in the margins. Sister told Lucius to send a fresh copy—without my scribbling—and she would put it in the library. Nothing belongs to me anymore. I must keep the rule of poverty. I do not say, even to myself, I want my book. Instead I say, I want the book that used to belong to me. I hate that I'll never get to write in a book again.

The Whitman Sampler, of course, went into the pantry for general use.

I remember Lucius leaning against a street light hour after hour in the old days, waiting to see me. The longer he'd stand there, the less I'd want to see him. The more tender and affectionate he was with me, the more I held it against him.

Which makes me feel sick with guilt. When Michael died, after Grandma S. went back to Dubuque, it was Lucius who pulled me through. We spent hours in Lincoln Park Zoo stuffing ourselves with popcorn and gaping at the animals. He said the tigers reminded him of me, but that—for better or for worse—he was a turtle. When he was a kid he killed a guy, but in the war he didn't kill a single man. Which I consider a failure of nerve. If I were a soldier sent to war, I'd shoot to kill. Not because I'm heartless, but because you have to do what you're sent to do. You better have the guts to do it. Because if your nerves fail, you will never live it down. Other people might forgive you, but you'll never forgive yourself.

Would Sister A. have let Lucius send a copy of what I used to call my book, if she had known about him and the guy he killed? Or if his father hadn't made him take elocution lessons as a child? He doesn't sound colored. If she talked with him on the phone, or if he didn't take off his hat, she might have assumed he was white.

7

SATURDAY NIGHTS MARY Kaye set her hair tightly in two-inch curlers, the orange foam rubber kind that were easier to sleep on. Before Mass on Sundays, she ducked into the downstairs powder room, teased her hair so that it poufed into a helmet, and flipped up the ends in a straight line below her chin and around the back of her neck. She spritzed it twice with lacquer so the flip would hold. The powder room off the foyer was her bomb shelter, equidistant from the girls' wing upstairs and their parents' wing on the main floor, far from the boys' exile-room in the basement. Other than church, it was the safest place to think critical thoughts.

Sunday morning after the wake, she closed the bathroom door and sat down to do her business. Her stomach felt flatter. Tony had said his dad would know what to do, but what, precisely, did that mean? Brenda Halsted had been sent to Our Lady of Lourdes School for Wayward Girls and did not come back with a baby. Tony knew about the School for Wayward Girls. He probably knew about coat hangers too. She had heard that you could use Lysol. She had heard you could throw yourself down the stairs. She had heard you could use an enema.

She coaxed one, then another square of toilet paper from the roll. The roll ran out and she started another. Mom always had a replacement at the ready.

How much longer would she have to worry?

Dad pounded on the door. "Mary Kaye, what the hell are you doing? We're going to be late for church."

She checked the back of each leg and straightened the seams on her hose. The black patent flats went with everything, but they were especially smart with her gray pleated skirt. Mom said she ought to hate pleats because she had always worn uniforms. But those came in plaid or blue and were tacked down from the waist. The pleats on her gray flannel skirt swung freely.

As she left the bathroom, the four younger girls, as usual, thundered down the stairs for inspection. Francine was fifteen. Meggie was fourteen. Clarice was thirteen. Patty was twelve. They were close to Mom's height, all shorter than Mary Kaye. They had strawberry blonde, light brown, blonde, and dark brown hair respectively, cut in pixies—Mom hadn't stopped *them*. Mary Kaye, as she always did, reviewed the girls' dresses and dispensed white gloves, hats, and purses from a shelf in the foyer closet. Brendan, at eleven the baby, slumped against the front door, waiting for Mary Kaye to help him with his tie. Jack made his entrance last, bounding up from the basement, twirling his shoes on the ends of his fingers, sliding in his socks on the black vinyl. Jack was a bit of a card, always ready with a prank or a joke: her confidant, cross-examiner, and court jester. At sixteen, he was taller than their father, with Dad's blue eyes and ruddy coloring.

Patty asked, "Are they going to tell us who I get for my new teacher?"

"You dummy," Jack said. "When your teacher's dead, school's out for you the rest of the year."

Dad cuffed Jack with the back of his hand. "One more wisecrack and you walk. For Christ sake, Mary Kaye, get the kids under control."

"When do we find out how the nuns died?" Francine asked, switching hats and purses with Clarice.

"Father Moriarty said we'll hear it from Father Schultz today," Mary Kaye said, steering the kids down the steps to the garage. It hurt to hear them talk so matter-of-factly about Sister Michaeline. She had cried herself to sleep after starting Sister's book and was dreading going to church, knowing Sister wouldn't be there.

Mom always backed her car from the garage first so the kids wouldn't smudge their clothes, but Dad said they could damn well squeeze their little fannies between a car door and a workbench. Everyone squeezed into the 1959 Eldorado.

Dad loved the 1959 Eldorado. He drove it more attentively than the 1960 white Eldorado Biarritz convertible with the tomato red interior, which was supposed to be Mom's. He drove it far more deliberately than he had the 1957 black Eldorado Brougham, which he had sold on impulse because the air suspension had been a waste of money. And he drove it more devotedly than the black 1962

Fleetwood, because life's greatest joy was watching everybody fuss over the bullet tail lights on the 1959's tailfins.

Week after week, no matter what time the car pulled out of the driveway, the O'Donnells arrived late for ten a.m. Mass. Mary Kaye said the Kyrie and the Gloria in the car under her breath. They missed the Epistle and the Gospel, but as long as they arrived during the sermon they technically fulfilled the Sunday obligation. At the church, all nine of them marched up the center aisle to the front pew, the only spot left.

Mary Kaye rushed the genuflection. She was distracted by the sound of the organ, which belched and spit at the hands of a last-minute substitute for Sister Michaeline, and by Father Schultz. He walked and talked like Andy Devine, the raspy-voiced tub on *The Adventures of Wild Bill Hickok*. He was short and bald, except for a few wisps of white hair plastered to his skull with Wildroot.

"Sister Michaeline and Sister Jane Denise served this parish well. God rest their souls. We were lucky to have them as long as we did." Mary Kaye closed her eyes. The smell of Wildroot incongruously reminded her of Tony. "When someone goes too soon to her eternal reward, it is always painful for those left behind. It is especially tragic when blame for the loss can so easily be assigned: the Sisters were killed in a senseless car accident, on their way home from the Loop."

As he spoke, a movie unrolled in Mary Kaye's imagination. She saw Sister Michaeline driving in rush-hour traffic, edging impatiently toward the inside express lane, a Corvette full of juvenile delinquents barreling into her tail end, the convent station wagon spinning sideways into the median, Sister Jane Denise's delicate head smashing against the dashboard, Sister Michaeline's blessed neck snapping like a stalk of celery. She saw the bodies of the two nuns tangled in yards of black wool, threaded closer in death than either of them had been to anybody in decades. She was surprised that they hadn't looked more beaten up in their caskets.

"I dare say," Father Schultz droned, "Sister Michaeline didn't see the crash coming because she was wearing the Franciscan veil. The nuns' veils stand out a good three or four inches on each side of their heads. The veil is not safe for driving a car, especially not on Chicago's new expressways."

Mary Kaye barely smothered a snort. Sister had been a whiz at managing her head and veil. She'd done fine on the expressway in

February, when she'd driven the jazz group to the Civic Opera House for the archdiocesan battle of the bands.

"There has been talk that the Sisters of Saint Francis will change the veils. But I say leave the habits the way they are and keep the nuns off the expressways. We need them in the parish and in the schools. We need them in the convent praying."

Only Father Schultz could turn the nuns' deaths into a political disquisition on the veil. Other parishes turned the altars around so the priest celebrating Mass could face parishioners. Some had guitar Masses with prayers in English. Pope John XXIII was bringing Catholic worship and practice into the twentieth century. Father Schultz, meanwhile, had never even mentioned the Vatican Council.

The pastor returned to the altar, turned his back on the people, and bowed to the organist's accompaniment. How many ways could the woman slaughter a Bach prelude?

Mary Kaye thought it would be just like Sister Michaeline to speed on the expressway. Sister was always trying to slow her down. "What's your rush to get to the convent?" Sister would say, "A good nun doesn't run away from the world. Get your education, make your way in the world until you feel at home there. Don't run to God until you know what you're leaving behind." But Sister had been no better at waiting, really, than her pupil.

Mary Kaye had to cup her hands over her ears. The organist had moved on to mangle a Mozart interlude.

"You're too young," Sister had said. "You're running away from looking after kids at home. You're running away from Jim Beam and your father's yelling. You're running away from your mother because she can't begin to take care of herself or you kids and she lets your father get away with murder."

Sister wasn't supposed to talk about her life before the convent, but she'd still told Mary Kaye about Michael, her husband who had died in the South Pacific. Mary Kaye had imagined Sister in the thirties and early forties, playing Cole Porter records, tapping her feet in jazz clubs, drinking Bloody Marys. She could see Sister jitterbugging; her reflexes had been incredible. One time during rehearsal, she had leaned first a little too far forward and then a lot too far backward. Sister had fallen off the stage, but she hadn't dropped down directly. Instead, she'd lifted into the air, old-lady shoes leading the way, legs propelling her straight upward. Her whole body had turned as if she were unwinding. She couldn't have hung there for even a second, but Mary Kaye could still see Sister launched into the air, knowing she was headed for the ground, but refusing to concede without a leap, a flourish, and a perfect landing.

Mary Kaye suspected that there was more behind her death than trouble with speed and vision. Maybe somebody tampered with Sister's car. There were parishioners who strongly disapproved of her civil rights activism. Might somebody have been just trying to scare her? Maybe they wanted to stop her from going to Cabrini-Green.

It was time for Communion. Thank God, Sister Haraldo sang "Panis Angelicus" a cappella. No need for the organist. Mary Kaye never knew whether her father would step out of the pew to let the family slide past or kick the kneeler over and lead them to the Communion railing. When he didn't go to Communion, she couldn't help imagining the different kinds of sins he might have committed to disqualify him. Mortal sins: pistol-whipping a guy from the blackjack table, or taking off his clothes in front of some woman, or selling a black family a "good as new" TV set that had got rained on after a train crash.

The kneeler thumped against the front pew and she followed Dad to Communion. She knelt on the cushion, folded her hands on the marble railing, tipped her head back, and stuck her tongue out for Father Schultz. The host was called bread, but the wafer had no taste or texture. It melted so fast that by the time she got back to the pew it was gone.

Thank you, Jesus, for coming to me today. Without Sister Michaeline I feel desperately alone. I can't quite believe she really is dead. I keep thinking I'll tell her this or that when I see her next. I'm crying all the time. It's hard to keep going.

I get that death is a mystery, but Sister's death is different. I don't think it was an accident. Some of the nuns might not either, but they will never speak up. The cardinal, the priests, the parents won't ask questions.

What am I supposed to do? Sister Michaeline was the only person in this world who would give me a straight answer. Maybe that makes me responsible for finding out what happened to her.

I know I've been complaining about taking care of my brothers and sisters, and telling You that I need some time when I don't have to be in charge. So I'm sure I'm contradicting myself when I tell You that I want to take on another job and find out why Sister died.

And I'm trying to be patient but I can hardly stand waiting for my period. If I'm supposed to have kids, maybe it could be later. I'd like to have a chance to be a kid myself. Anyway, please help me figure these things out.

She bowed her chin, lifted her hands upward, and hugged her helmet hair.

8

AFTER MASS, MARY Kaye found her father and Tony standing in front of the convent: Tony talking with his hands, Dad nodding, one hand in his suit pocket—fishing for the keys to the Eldorado—the other waving at her.

"You're excused from the Holloway House brunch. Tony's gonna walk you home."

She set her tan straw purse on the convent steps and sat down next to it.

"Thanks a million, Mr. O'Donnell, but they pay me pretty well at the restaurant," Tony said, trying to hand a folded bill back to Dad, who turned on his heel and headed into the parking lot.

"I guess that means 'bye,' Dad?" Mary Kaye called after him.

Tony unfolded the bill.

"What's with the tenner?" she asked, handing him her purse, ready to push up from the steps.

Tony slipped the purse handle onto his wrist, flicked the latch open, and stuffed the bill inside. He took her hands, pulled her up, and returned the purse. "Let's go to Carson's. How about some chow?"

"What's going on? What did he say? What exactly did you say?"

"Who says anything's going on? You and I are walking to Carson's. We're getting our favorite booth. You're going to get French rolled pancakes with cherries and powdered sugar on top, unless you've got a new favorite. We're going to sit and look into each other's eyes like we used to. Then we're going to finish our orange juice and I'm going to walk you home. We'll take the back way, past our secret hiding place."

She lifted her purse, shading her eyes from the force of the midday sun. Nobody had more enthusiasm than Tony. And only she had a better head for memories.

All month she had avoided taking the back way home. Near one end at Jefferson Avenue, a dirt road brushed alongside Jewel, around the corner from Marciano's. She hadn't wanted to run into Tony, to tear the thin scab that had begun to form over their goodbye. She hadn't wanted to see the prairie smoke sprouts, the needly new leaves of the Arkansas blue stars, the mauve phlomis in flower, the white tulips in bloom. She had avoided the Virginia bluebells, which must have flowered and disappeared without her. The blue meadow sage, soft and hairy to the touch, had been cut down long ago after the first flowering, and grown right back up. Not just the leaves, but also the flowers, which bloomed twice.

Their secret place was deep in the prairie acreage, where someone had planted a stand of spruce trees. They reminded her of the string of oak trees that ran all the way west from Lake Michigan and through the O'Donnells' backyard, which the Iroquois had used as markers for their trail. No one knew who had planted the stand of spruce, but she sometimes imagined it was a new husband who had come from the east coast to build a house for his bride.

She slipped her hand into Tony's. "After breakfast, let's go sit under the trees. I haven't been back. I didn't think I ever would."

The church parking lot had cleared out. No matter how many times Father Schultz insisted in the sermon that nobody should leave Mass until after the final blessing and Last Gospel, families still slipped out after Communion to get the jump on Sunday breakfast. Cars raced in for the next Mass. Tony steered Mary Kaye out of their path. The two of them stopped for a moment at the river, the natural boundary for Holy Ghost. It wasn't much more than a creek, but it was the north branch of the North Branch of the Chicago River, which Tony had often said should count for something.

"You really putting off the convent? Your dad said something like that."

Her mother must have told her father, as she had planned and expected. It was at least a half mile to Carson's and she was getting hungry and thirsty. She had made toast and peanut butter before going to bed the night before, but had only swallowed a bite. And she hadn't had any water yet, even though the rules on fasting before Communion had been relaxed. Grandma Mueller used to tie rags around the faucets on Saturday nights so her kids would remember that they were not supposed to drink after midnight. Even a sip had meant no Communion.

"I don't know if I'm coming or going," she said.

"No kidding."

Mary Kaye and Tony walked along the river, turned at Church Street, and turned another corner at Lincoln Boulevard, where the sidewalks ended. The rest of the way to Carson's they had to pick their way through grass and gravel and dodge oncoming cars. She was glad she was wearing flats.

"I was up all night banging around the kitchen," Tony said. "I kept thinking about us. What it would be like if we got married. The kids we could have. How happy we could be."

"Maybe we should walk single file," she said. "One of these cars is going to hit us."

"Then get behind me. For safety's sake."

She slowed to let Tony walk ahead. A moving van roared past and she yelled, "Can we at least wait to talk until we get to Carson's?" She knew that she should tell him that having kids was the last thing she wanted at the moment, but she couldn't bring herself to say it.

The Marcianos had a houseful of kids, like the O'Donnells, except the Marcianos had not had the sense to stop at seven. Tony was the oldest but his idea of raising kids was throwing babies in the air, ducking under doorways with a toddler on his shoulders, taking training wheels off a bike and running alongside to make sure a kid did not fall off.

Mary Kaye's father almost never played with his kids. When he tried, Mom got scared. When they'd gone out on his first boat, named the Mary O after Grandma O'Donnell, Mom had sat in the back with the fumes, never moving, pregnant with Clarice, holding Meggie and Francine, with Jack clinging to her ankles for dear life. Dad had served on a Navy destroyer during the war. He didn't believe in life jackets. He said the best thing that could happen to a kid was to fall overboard: That's how you learned to swim in a hurry. The next summer, when Mary Kaye had paddled off the back of the boat, she had to remind herself to stay clear of the outboard motor, so she would not get her leg sliced off. Tony might be easier on the nerves, she was in no rush to find out.

The line at Carson's moved quickly. Their usual booth was occupied and Tony accepted another. The waitress slid glasses of ice water across the formica tabletop. Mary Kaye didn't much mind that the water sloshed, but she picked at the edges of a napkin, wiped up the water, folded the paper in half a few times, and squeezed it into a tiny ball.

"We don't need 'em," Tony said to the waitress when she brought the menus.

"I like to take a look," Mary Kaye said, "even when I know what I want."

The waitress handed them each a menu and disappeared. Mary Kaye made a show of thumbing through the lacquered pages, moving her eyes back and forth.

"I thought you'd be hungry."

"I am hungry." She did not look up. "That doesn't mean I don't want to look at the pictures and see what there is."

"You know what there is." He plucked an ice cube from his glass and tossed it into his mouth. "We're here all the time."

"You and my dad have it all figured out. I'd like to hear what the two of you decided." She spread the menu on the table like a poker player sure of the strength of her hand.

"I would have told you already, if you'd stop fooling around with that menu."

"No need to get smart," she said, fanning herself. "It's too hot." Sleeveless blouses were not allowed in church.

"Usually you tell them to turn the air conditioning down. But that's not what's on your mind." Tony grabbed her menu. "Your dad asked me what I knew about you not going to the convent."

"You can't talk to my dad behind my back. I'm mixed up enough without that."

"Give me a chance. Used to be, I'd help straighten you out."

When the waitress returned, Tony ordered his three eggs over easy with hash browns and four pieces of whole wheat toast. The thought of fried eggs lying in grease made Mary Kaye's stomach turn. She made a point not to order the French pancakes. She was not even tempted by the sight of the cherries and powdered sugar on a platter at the next table. She ordered a Belgian waffle with maple syrup on the side, no butter.

Tony reached across the table, took her hands, and pulled them to the middle of the table. "I was pretty rough on you the other night. I've been afraid you'd never speak to me again. I've been doing a lot of thinking. We should work things out."

She slid their hands toward herself. "You mean get back together?"

As soon as she said it, she knew the idea was all wrong. Sleeping with Tony had been much better than expected and it was ever harder to imagine life without men. But, for now, she hated the idea of marriage.

And even if she ever did get married, she certainly wouldn't choose Tony. She didn't admire him. But then she might be pregnant, and he was ready to marry her.

He had said the other night that she didn't know what she was doing. He was right. She was all over the map. She felt like a fool.

Tony clicked their hands together on the table. "I don't see you in the convent, Max. Not with your spirit. I see you married with a houseful of kids. Smart kids, cute and smart, like you."

The tightness in her chest hurt. She was so furious that it felt like a miracle that she did not erupt in dragon fire. Fighting not to lose her cool, she reclaimed her hands and leaned over the table. "Thank you, Tony, thank you, Dad." She heard herself speaking too loudly and too fast. "You've got my life tied up in a bow. I guess that's the end of that." She leapt out of the booth and bolted toward the exit. Tony whipped his wallet out of his pants pocket, threw a five on the table, and raced after her in time to snag the space behind her in the revolving door.

"Take it easy, Max. Slow down."

She charged down the side of Lincoln Boulevard toward the intersection with Sycamore Lane. "I'll bet you blabbed to your dad. That would be just like you. I'll bet you told him my whole story."

Suddenly silent, they turned up Sycamore Lane, walking, heads down, on the right side of the median. The houses had plenty of space around them. They were so far apart that you had to go out to the mailbox in the median if you wanted to run into anybody. She needed elbow room. There was nothing wrong with that. Passing the Mahony house, she started to calm down. Lee Mahony had once given her a pink rosary in a plastic heart. Lee would never have gotten her into this mess.

"I didn't exactly tell my dad the whole story." Tony reached for her hand, but she hid it in her skirt pocket. "But he did tell me something big. There's a new test to find out if you're going to have a baby."

Mary Kaye stopped abruptly, in front of Judge Engelmann's mailbox, at the place where the back acres of the O'Donnell pasture were visible from the lane. "If I get married, my life is over. Cooking. Scouring. Waxing. Vacuuming. One baby after another. Bathe them, feed them, change them, put them to bed. I'll never read another thing, unless you count the missal at Mass on Sunday or the back of an aspirin bottle. OK, maybe new recipes for fish on Friday. Or crochet patterns for baby booties.

"If I don't become a singer, there is so much else I could do. Sister Haraldo says I could study American history. I could figure out how we got to be a country where only a hundred years ago people owned other people, where you could whip a slave until her back bled and still go to Communion in the morning. I can't stand to turn on the TV. You don't know what you're going to see, riots at universities where black people want to study, policemen turning fire hoses and dogs on blacks in Alabama. I could write about what's going on. Not now, but someday, if I got serious about what I wanted to do, and stuck to it. But if I got married, I'd never write anything. I'd probably never even read another book. In three months my head would rattle when I walked. By this time next year, everything in my brain would have fallen out."

Tony stepped in front of her, blocking her view of her pasture and her rock. He bent down so their faces were level and rapped the hair on the side of her head.

"Stop," she cried. "I'm trying to tell you what's on my mind."

"I'm trying to knock some sense in your head, if I could get anywhere near it through the hair spray. One way or the other, maybe we should get married. That's what I've always wanted anyway. If we don't get married, you know what they would call you?"

She closed her eyes and clamped her hands over her ears. He was lecturing her. As if she didn't know what she would be. "A girl in trouble," she said. "An unwed mother."

He locked his arms around her and rocked her back and forth. Very softly he said, "You know, Max, it would get a lot worse than that."

John Riley's new sedan flew past on the other side of the lane. Zippy, the German shepherd, leaned out of the back seat, his head reaching into the wind, tongue wagging.

"OK, OK, everything is going to be OK," Tony whispered. "Here's what my dad said. You put some Number One in a jar and then he's got a guy at a lab who knows what to do with it. He puts the

Number One in a test tube with something or other from a rabbit. In a week or so he can say."

Tony turned and walked backward in front of her, motioning her to follow him across the lane, through the west entrance into the O'Donnell side orchard. She said nothing until they had crossed the street.

"You mean I'd know for sure?"

He stopped and looked back, as if scanning for more traffic. "He didn't say that exactly. He said, 'What else is she going to do? In the old days the rabbit died. Tell her she's lucky she doesn't have to kill a rabbit.'"

She flopped down next to the lily bed on the side of the horseshoe drive, inside the brick entrance. "Oh, Tony. I don't know. I get out of bed and I feel like I'm going to puke. I go to the kitchen and the smell of bacon grease makes me gag. Why don't I wait, like Mom always did? I should know soon enough."

"You and everybody else, Max. Maybe you could use some wiggle room. Maybe you want to know before the rest of the world knows too." Tony stood and pulled her up by her hands. He started to walk in the direction of the house. It was hard to keep up with him. Would he blow his top? "Things could go different ways. The last thing I want is some stranger raising our kid. I won't stand for it. My dad is dead set against it."

His words electrified her. She stared at him in a rush of regret. She had not figured on Mr. Marciano. How could she have believed that he wouldn't have involved his father? What was she doing telling Tony everything, thinking out loud about herself before she knew what she wanted? She should have gone first to Judge Engelmann for one of their kitchen table conferences. Like Tony said, things could get a whole lot worse.

Tony was still talking. "If there's a child in this world that belongs to us, that child should grow up with family. We don't want some free-for-all where he winds up with strangers and never even knows his own folks." He picked up a couple of twigs and walked along a row of miniature pear trees, brushing the twigs against the bark. "You know, there are other ways to go. If you don't want to raise a baby, my dad also has a guy to take care of that."

So much for keeping her cool. She ran up behind Tony and swatted his arm. "I told you I'm not going to get ahead of myself.

One thing I learned from Sister Michaeline is that you've got to take one step at a time. Keep a steady beat. That's what we said Friday night."

Mary Kaye stumbled across the drive into the cool and dark of the front woods. Tony followed. "All right, all right, don't blow a gasket, babe. Maybe all this commotion's for nothing. Maybe you're not even pregnant."

Tears trickled down her face. "There's nothing I can do. Absolutely nothing," she sobbed. Tony reached in his pants pocket. He shook out his handkerchief and wadded it up in her hand. She took her time patting her face dry.

Tony put his hands on her shoulders. "Listen to me, Max. I'm way ahead of you on this one." He reached into his other pocket and handed her a small glass jar.

"What am I supposed to do with this?"

"It's a jelly jar. Mom uses them for canning. It's sterilized and everything, just like my dad said. All you have to do is pee in the jar, screw the top on, and my dad's guy will take care of the rest."

"What kind of jelly?" She looked toward her house.

"Really, Max. Who the hell cares?"

Mary Kaye turned her back on Tony and the house and faced Mrs. Templeton's across the street. There were no cars coming. She twisted the jar's lid.

"I can't get it open."

"Give it here. How're you going to pee with a dress on anyway?"

"Take my purse. Go somewhere so I can do my business." He walked a couple of yards. She squatted in the brush under the trees and steadied herself against a smooth birch. She let her underpants fall to the ground and slipped the jelly jar under her skirt. The pleats opened like an accordion. What was it Sister Michaeline used to say? "Hang loose, kiddo." The pee hesitated, then got bolder.

She stepped over to Tony and handed him the jar.

He screwed the top on, put the jar in his pocket, and patted his pants. "Atta girl."

Mary Kaye wasn't sure if he was talking to her or the jelly jar.

9

THE TRAIN WAS late, so Mary Kaye took a cab to the far end of Lincoln Park, across the street from a skyscraper. It had been hard to get going that morning. The papers had been full of the news that Pope John XXIII had died and she had lost time cutting out a full-page picture of him to mount on the dresser in her bedroom.

Halfway out the door, she ran back to check Sister's book. She was deliberately reading as slowly as she could, trying to hang on to the fresh access to Sister as long as possible, but she wanted at least to know what year the book ended. To think that when Sister met her husband Michael he had been reading *To the Lighthouse*, one of her favorite novels. In the days since Lucius had given her Sister's book, she had returned to Virginia Woolf's image of "a scrap of china in the hemlock," treasuring every snippet left of Sister Michaeline's life then past. She bookmarked the passage in which Sister regretted that she would never have a daughter whom she could teach singing and wondered whether that was why Sister had wanted Mary Kaye to have her book.

And there, at the Lincoln Park Zoo, was Lucius. Right where he'd said he'd be, standing in front of the wrought iron fence between the duck pond and the flamingoes. She had the harder task, sidling next to him, making the exchange look benign. A black man could not walk up to a white girl and start a conversation unless he was a Pullman porter or a waiter. People's thoughts turned to robbery or rape.

Flamingoes were pecking at the dirt, at each other, and at themselves. Vicious fights arose out of nowhere. One bird spread its wings and charged at another's neck. Seeing the flamingoes squabble suddenly reminded her that she should take care. She had trusted Sister Michaeline entirely, but she knew almost nothing about Lucius.

"I'm reading the diary. Actually, it's a Particular Examen book. Did you know nuns keep track of their sins and offenses against the rule?"

"Nope. Can't say as I did." Lucius nodded in the direction of the next exhibit. There was nobody there. The sign said that Andean bears ate fruits and roots and insects. She left about a foot and a half between Lucius and herself. She watched the bear paddle, paying particular attention to the ring of yellow fur around his eyes and his cream-colored snout. The bear pulled himself out of the water and lay down under a tree. The bottoms of his feet looked soft, like Indian moccasins.

"About Sister Michaeline," she said. "Father Schultz told the whole parish she died because of the veil. But I've been on the expressway with her. She knows how to use the mirrors."

"'Course she can—I mean, she could. More than likely she would drive when we'd go to Joliet to see my son."

"You mean the prison? Sister Michaeline went with you to the prison?"

"Yeah. We go way back."

"You come up in the book, but you probably know that." Mary Kaye looked at Lucius expectantly. "You must have read it before you gave it to me."

Lucius said nothing.

She tried a different tack. "How long is your son going to be in prison?"

"Hang on to your hat," Lucius replied. "Twenty years."

"That long? What'd he do?"

"Anything to make my blood boil. But it wasn't a typical B&E."

"What's a B&E?"

"I forget you're not a city kid—breaking and entering."

"But twenty years for a burglary?"

"There's more to it than that. But what gets under my skin is that it's his own damn fault. Pardon my French. I'm talking to you like you're Maureen, you know, Sister Michaeline."

Mary Kaye paused for a moment. "I don't think Sister's death was an accident."

"Oh?"

"I don't know what happened," she said. "She was such a good driver. I don't see her just crashing the car. I figure the nuns don't want to know what happened. The priests don't want to know. The last thing the parents of the school kids want to know is what really happened. All I know is something must have happened. I mean something more than the steering went out or the brakes failed. I feel like I'm supposed to find out. Maybe you could help me."

They were quiet, watching the Andean bear sleep.

Lucius turned to Mary Kaye. "I can put my buddy Stan on it. He's got a cop friend who can track down the car. Chop shop or junk yard, Stan'll find out if the car had anything to do with it."

"Great!"

"What's been on my mind has been making sure you got Maureen's book. I wanted to get the dope on you anyway. Who is this gal she talked so much about? She told me about your singing a solo from Handel's *Messiah* at Christmas. She was not easily impressed."

"'He Shall Feed His Flock'?"

"What I remember is the look on her face when she described the timbre of your voice—plush and radiant. I teased her that she must have heard herself in you, but she wasn't joking around. 'You've got to hear her,' she said. 'You'll know exactly what I mean.'"

"Sister Michaeline took me under her wing. You see why I want to find out more about her death?"

"Then how 'bout you meet my son. I checked the prison records. Maureen died on her way home from visiting him. Chances are he knows something. Seems to me Maureen would want you to meet him."

Mary Kaye was not sure why Sister would want her to meet an inmate. But Sister was her teacher and she was used to following her, even when she did not know where they were going.

"What do you say you meet me in the Loop on Saturday?" Lucius asked. "In the morning, 'round about ten? Leave your car in a garage. I'll be looking at newspapers at Michigan and Randolph. You sally up to the bus stop and make believe you're waiting for the westbound bus. I'll get the Nash and pick you up. Got it?"

"Got it."

"Wear something to cover your skin. You don't want to call attention to yourself. You know what I'm talking about."

"Yeah, nothing to make me stand out."

Lucius grinned. "See you there." He spun around and strode away.

Mary Kaye stayed a little longer, watching the groundskeepers sweep dirt around the trunks of trees. Finally, she started away in the opposite direction from Lucius toward the cab stand, passing a small boy in shorts. He looked a little like Jack at that age, dropping leaves, one by one, down the storm sewer.

10

THE NUNS STILL thought she was going to the convent, so Mary Kaye didn't hesitate when the parish superior, Sister Florence, called to ask whether she would accompany Sister Haraldo on Thursday to the church near Cabrini-Green. Nuns were not supposed to go anywhere without another nun and, by virtue of her expected entry as a postulant in the fall, Mary Kaye counted as a suitable companion.

Any number of times before, waiting for Sister Michaeline, Mary Kaye had stood in the large entry to the parish convent, peeked down a corridor off the entry, and seen the little parlors for visitors. The rest of the convent was cloistered—off limits to anybody who wasn't a nun. But after she was accepted for entry at the Motherhouse, the parish sisters had welcomed her as one of their own. When Sister Michaeline had given her a tour of the parish convent, she had been struck by the simplicity of the Danish furniture, the peaceful pale brown wood, the soft lamp light in the large common room, where each Sister had a desk.

Sister Michaeline had put a finger to her lips as they had walked up the back stairs to the chapel, Mary Kaye on tiptoes, trying to imitate Sister's silent step. The chapel had seemed slight—a few rows of pews in the same Danish style and wood, but no stained glass windows, no statues, no shrines, the altar bare, except for the gold tabernacle holding consecrated Hosts. Sister had explained that the nuns had morning and evening prayer and weekday Mass in the chapel. They could use the chapel anytime, but, in practice, many preferred to pray in the parish church, except when they were ill, when Father Schultz gave them Communion in the convent from the chapel tabernacle.

The nuns' life looked tantalizingly unencumbered. Altogether as a group, they cleaned the entire convent every day in twenty minutes. Mary Kaye had seen their "daily work" boxes, each marked with the name of a room, outfitted with aprons, dust clothes, waxes, and whatever cleaning materials were needed so that each nun could go straight from getting dressed in her cell to daily work, and, from there, when the bell rang, directly to morning prayer. They were a family working together, but not a typical family where a woman had to be a jack-of-all-trades doing housework night and day.

She and Sister Haraldo met on the convent front porch. Thanks to the two-inch-stacked-heels-old-lady nun's shoes, Sister was tall enough that she could look Mary Kaye in the eye. Dominating her face was a pointed beak that in American history class seemed to run a straight line from the end of her nose, through her raised arm, all the way up the pointer to the blackboard. She was precise and incisive, and, at the same time, even-handed. If Sister Michaeline was a speedboat, bouncing straight ahead, Sister Haraldo was a gondola, swaying from side to side, on the one hand, on the other. Mary Kaye guessed that, like Sister Michaeline, she might be of mixed Irish and German stock, but that in Sister Haraldo's case the German had taken over. She was not pretty like Sister Michaeline. Her teeth were tea-stained and crooked. But she was brilliant. She had written her dissertation in American history at Catholic University on the controversy surrounding Pope Gregory XVI's 1839 condemnation of slavery.

Sister Haraldo pulled out of the parking lot in a new station wagon, which had been donated after Sister Michaeline's death by a parishioner who owned a Chevy dealership. They headed east toward Lake Shore Drive. Mary Kaye smiled at the thought of herself as a small-time double agent. She and Lucius wanted anything they could find on Sister Michaeline's death, but before she drove with him to Joliet Prison she also wanted to check out Lucius.

"Does it feel funny not driving on the expressway anymore after what Father Schultz said about nuns driving blind?" Mary Kaye asked. "No surprise, I guess, he blamed the veil."

"How about the part when he said that we should stay home and pray?"

"Yeah, nuns are a menace to themselves and everybody else," Mary Kaye said. "But Father Schultz made it sound like she just crashed into the median. I mean she was a better driver than that."

"The police are investigating whether the brakes or the power steering went out."

"But if the steering went out," Mary Kaye said, "wouldn't Sister have been strong enough to keep the car on the road? She would have slowed down and—whatever it took—she would have made it at least to the exit ramp. If the brakes had failed, why would that happen at that particular time on that particular day?"

"Why not? It could happen any day. And anyway, I'm not thinking about Father Schultz or the car," Sister Haraldo said. "I'm thinking about Sister Michaeline. You know we don't have special friends, of course, but if I had a special friend it would have been her. She spoke out of a deep well of lived experience. She knew her way around.

"It was my turn to go to Cabrini-Green—well, their parish church—that day. Sister Jane Denise and I alternated going with Sister Michaeline. Sometimes we'd go out to Joliet for the prison ministry too. More often Sister Michaeline would go out to the prison by herself."

"That day, why didn't you go to Cabrini-Green?"

"I've asked myself the same thing. I had work at the convent, getting our books in order. But it wasn't that. I guess I had a bad feeling. The last time she came back from prison ministry, Sister Michaeline was upset. I've never seen her like that. Crying and sobbing so hard I had to drive. I kept asking her what was wrong, but it was like she was in her own little world. Nothing I said got through. It rattled me to see her fall apart."

"But we're going today. You seem OK. More than OK."

"Yeah. But, we're not going to Joliet. Sister Florence said Father Schultz hadn't known we'd started a prison ministry. I guess he really put his foot down. We don't belong on the expressway, imagine what he thinks of us teaching convicts. Sister Michaeline was teaching jazz. I had a class on civil rights. For me, it wasn't that different from teaching anywhere. I can tell you those young guys were all ears when I told them what Martin Luther King is doing."

"But weren't you scared? Even a little bit?"

"There were guards in the room. And there was a black man who helped out at the Cabrini-Green parish—Lucius—who went with us sometimes. Maybe I should have been scared, but I wasn't."

Mary Kaye decided not to say anything about Lucius yet. Instead, she said, "Do you think Sister Michaeline's death was an accident pure and simple?"

Sister Haraldo sighed. "You mean Sister Michaeline and Sister Jane Denise. Don't forget they both died. It wasn't just Sister Michaeline."

"But do you think it was an accident?"

"Nothing's ever plain and simple. But what else could it have been?"

"I don't know. It's just a feeling. You know how good a driver Sister was. How many people knew about the prison ministry? There are plenty of folks who think nuns shouldn't get involved in civil rights. Maybe somebody tried to sabotage her."

"Maybe. But that's all beside the point now. Father Schultz has pretty much cut off that line of thought."

Mary Kaye tried another tack. "Will this Lucius guy be at the parish today?"

"No telling. Sometimes I see him there. Sometimes I don't."

"You know anything about him?"

"Odds and ends. His car is something else. He said he bought it from a GI who enlisted right after Pearl Harbor. Sounded to me like he goes to confession every Saturday, goes home and washes the car, goes to Mass the next morning. That kind of man. He's a bass player in a jazz band. One time it was hot and Sister Michaeline was asking him about his breathing. It came out that he got gassed in the Argonne during World War I, and, not to turn this into a history lecture, but you asked, he was part of a regiment the Germans called 'black devils' because they fought so fiercely in France."

"American blacks fighting in France? I've never heard about this," Mary Kaye said.

"They were black American soldiers, but they used French weapons and their top commanders were French, which made the whole thing possible since the French were more tolerant. They even let them have black officers. But it was their bravery they were known for. That and the bloody battles. American armed forces wouldn't let blacks and whites mix."

Mary Kaye looked at Sister Haraldo. "You know how engrossed I was in biochemistry last year when you were coaching me for the debates? When I hear you speak like this—you have so much from the past at your fingertips that bears directly on our lives today—it makes me want to study history."

"I could see you going either way," Sister Haraldo said.

Mary Kaye had no idea what to expect of the Cabrini-Green neighborhood, but the drive along Lake Michigan was comfortingly familiar. They passed the Baha'i Temple, Calvary Cemetery, and the apartment buildings on Sheridan Road. They turned unto Lake Shore Drive and glimpsed the Edgewater Beach Hotel and the skyline to the south. The O'Donnell family made the same drive every Christmas on their way to Marshall Field's, where, after lunch in the Walnut Room, the kids would sit on Santa's lap. Sister Haraldo turned onto the Inner Drive and drove west on Division Street, near the Esquire Theatre, where the O'Donnells had seen a Charlton Heston movie the past year.

How bad could Cabrini-Green be? Mary Kaye thought. The streets were not immaculate, but they were as clean as any thoroughfare in Crosshaven. One row house after another on Division was embellished with intricate ironwork and stone carvings, such as she had seen at the Art Institute. Each house seemed like a work of art in its own right. And they were almost at Cabrini-Green. What was Dad worried about? There was nothing unusual about the people in the street. If anything, even in the June heat, many more men were in suits and more women wore heels than in downtown Crosshaven.

The change didn't happen all at once, but it happened fast. She barely registered the sight of the first broken liquor bottle, maybe a Jim Beam, then a Smirnoff's, and a Seagram's half-pint. Then the dilapidated houses with porches falling down. Broken windows. Missing doors. A ratty-looking mutt dragging a Kentucky Fried Chicken bag off the sidewalk into the dirt. No grass, no flowers, barely a tree. Those houses still standing with clotheslines strung between them.

Rising up from the mess stood a lone skyscraper. If the building were turned on its side, the balconies would look like a serrated knife. "Just up here," Sister Haraldo said, as they passed a toilet sitting in a vacant dirt lot. A couple of men in overalls stood on a crumbling sidewalk, staring at the ground, smoking who-knows-what.

"I guess this is what my dad calls the slums."

Sister Haraldo pointed ahead. "There. See, those buildings are what they call the 'reds.' I wanted you to see them. That's where some of the parishioners live."

Mary Kaye shook her head. "What gets me is they had the nerve to name this place after Saint Frances Cabrini. If Mother Cabrini were in charge, she'd have this place running like a top."

Sister parked the station wagon in an empty lot across the street from the church. A little girl with pink ribbons in her hair ran toward them and tugged on Sister's cincture. Mary Kaye followed them to the rectory. While Sister did the parish's bookkeeping, she sat with the little girl. Her name was Thelma. Mary Kaye had brought *The Little Engine That Could* as a gift for the parish and read it aloud until Thelma fell asleep in her lap.

When Sister finished her work, she had to wake them both up. Mary Kaye waited to speak until they were out of the neighborhood.

"How can they stand it?"

"How can who stand what?"

"How can the people who live just a few blocks away stand to live in luxury while other people live so close in squalor?"

"Well, it's not as simple as that."

She knew that if she pressed Sister Haraldo, her "on-the-one-hand, on-the-other" reflex would kick in. Sister Michaeline would have given her a straight answer, even if it made her sick, but Sister Haraldo rarely came down squarely on one side in any question.

Maybe it was true that there were questions for which you could find no definitive answers, but Sister Haraldo didn't even try. Mary Kaye thought that, on this issue, she must do better. She must try. Which made her miss Sister Michaeline all the more. And made her all the more grateful that she had not told Sister Haraldo about Lucius and Sister's book. Or thought to confide that she might be pregnant and in need of real advice.

11

THAT SATURDAY, MARY Kaye wore the same navy blue shift and pearls that she had worn to the wake, but threw on her mother's black linen stole to cover her arms. In the parking garage, she locked the Eldorado and turned to see Lucius loping up the ramp, looking cool in khaki pants and a long-sleeved white shirt. He must have spotted her car from the bus stop. She adjusted her sunglasses and a broad-brimmed straw hat bought for the occasion and followed him at a distance to the Nash, head down.

The Nash was a maroon two-door sedan. Its interior was impeccable. Lucius had redone the seats in butter-soft leather, the color of coffee with a teaspoon of cream. Another teaspoon and the upholstery would have matched his skin. She tried not to stare, except at his arm when he shifted gears. She liked the rosiness of her own arms, but next to Lucius's smoothly toned skin, her freckles looked unsettled.

Her stomach was uncertain and her throat burned. It could be morning sickness. She didn't want to throw up all over the Nash. She asked Lucius to stop at Walgreen's to get saltines and tea towels. When he returned, he picked up his straw fedora from the seat between them, tossed it to the middle of the back seat, and flipped the radio on. They set off for Joliet Prison.

Lucius said that Sister Michaeline had talked so much about her that he felt as if he knew her.

"So how about you?" she said, with more force than she intended. She wasn't as calm as she had thought. "Have you always lived in Chicago?"

"You might say you're posing two separate questions: Has my residence always been in Chicago? And in Chicago have I always felt alive? What did Sister say in her book?"

"I'm only part way through. You really haven't read it?"

"Right now I'm broken up. Maybe you'll let me read it later."

"Of course. Anytime you want."

The seat didn't go back very far in the old Nash, but she tried to relax. The city limits were behind them. They were out on open highway.

"Yes," Lucius said cordially, "I'm from Chicago. But my great-grandfather had a plantation in Mississippi. My grandfather was his son and his slave."

"Oh," she said, her voice still higher than usual.

Lucius told her that after the end of slavery his white great-grandfather had arranged a job for his grandfather with a doctor in New Orleans. His grandfather learned what they called "medical arts," played piano, and married a school teacher. "Black as coal, they said she was. My parents came north at the turn of the century so I wouldn't have to live under Jim Crow."

"Was it bad?"

"Not 'was,' 'is.' You know, I was in a band with Sister's husband, Michael. We toured together. We'd play half the night in these swanky hotels. Then, the show'd be over and they'd pack off the Negroes to a colored motel on the other side of town. Maureen—Sister Michaeline—used to come with us."

"You can call her Maureen. I get it." She could feel herself easing up. "How long to the prison?"

"An hour, give or take."

"Good. I want to hear the rest." She tossed her hat back, next to his fedora.

"Glad to tell you. I adored my mother. She put me in the Catholic school where she worked. I was five when she died. Those nuns didn't miss a beat. They scooped me up and took care of me like I was one of their own. My grandparents moved to Chicago and lived with us, but without the nuns I'd have been up a creek."

Her stomach felt less queasy but, to be on the safe side, she opened the box of crackers.

Lucius extended his hand. "I wouldn't mind having a few of those myself, one at a time."

They crunched for a while.

"All my father talked about was advancement," Lucius continued. "He went out of his way to learn to cut white hair. He wanted me to stay in school and become an accountant. He said I could keep track of time and money, just about anything. He had me shining shoes in the barber shop, which is how I got into music. This guy took a liking to me, I must have been eleven, twelve. Turned out the cat ran a couple of theaters. He had me cleaning up between shows, scraping gum out from under seats, stuff like that. Those were the days of silent movies. I got chummy with the accompanist and he started me on the trumpet."

"I thought you were a bass player."

"I am, but I started out on trumpet. Then, after the war, I was hanging around Lincoln Gardens, picking up this and that, listening to Jelly Roll Morton. The white guys started coming to the South Side to hear what we were doing. They called them the Austin High Gang. After the show whoever was left would play around, white guys, black guys, didn't make a difference. We egged each other on, made quite a rumpus in the twenties, not just the music, but the whole idea of us mixing like that. After World War I, after the race riots in 1919, that just was not done."

"Didn't Benny Goodman and Gene Krupa get started here?"

"That's what I'm talking about. Chicago jazz. Black, but also white."

She turned the radio up. "Is that a voice? Is it human?"

"No, child, that's Louis Armstrong, using a plunger mute."

"It sounds like cats: Me-ow." She turned the radio down. "So what'd you do next?"

"I heard Earl Hines and Louis Armstrong do 'Weather Bird' at the Sunset Café. 1927. Louis was bouncing along being Louis, but Hines refused to play good boy. He rippled, he mixed ragtime and stride. He was no accompanist, that's for sure. I was floored. I told my father about it and he said, 'Go to college and become an accountant.' Guess you could say I did, sort of. That's what the bass player does. Keeps count. Keeps the beat. The other players, they go where the spirit moves them. They improvise. I keep them on the straight and narrow. I bring them back home."

He turned up the radio. "You've got to hear this, 'Blues in My Heart.' That's Chick Webb's orchestra. Hear how the woodwinds play off the brass. Chick doesn't get a chance here to explode on the drums. Maureen used to sing this one, with Michael on the piano."

He turned the volume up further and yelled, "Benny Carter wrote this song. My boy's namesake. Benny Carter's trumpet could bring me to tears. I decided that if I ever had a son, I wanted him to be named Carter or Benny, I'd let my wife take her pick." He paused and said sheepishly, "Sorry, sis, I'm back talking to you like you're Maureen."

"I'm having the time of my life," Mary Kaye yelled back. "Sister Michaeline never told me she sang on the road."

"Sure as shooting, I bet there were lots of things she never talked about once she got to the convent." He turned the radio down. "But there's something else on my mind. My boy's a loose cannon. There's something I don't want him to spring on you today. I want to tell you myself—the worst thing I ever did. It's kind of a long story, but the only way for me to get through it is to tell it my own way."

Mary Kaye studied the dashboard. Under the radio knobs was a little lever that Lucius used when he shifted gears.

"They say I killed a man." He looked at her. "I guess you could say I did."

How different that sounded than when she had read it at home in Sister's book. Suddenly, out in the middle of nowhere, she felt a flicker of serious caution. Lucius was like family to Sister for half her life. But if he were a con-man criminal, would Sister have known? Sister saw only the best in people. Sister Haraldo was impressed with his weekend confession and Communion and washing the car, but her judgment might not be any better. Nobody knew where Mary Kaye was, not Tony or Jack, who could bail her out of anything. Or was she just being a nervous Nellie?

"That's Bessie Smith singing, with Louis. 'Restless Blues.' Nobody does heartache like Bessie."

Mary Kaye folded her hands in her lap. She couldn't make sense of Bessie's words, but the singer could wail and she could feel it.

They rode in silence, past fields of corn stalks sprouting sharp-edged leaves in the June sun. She stuck her arm out the window and, feeling the hot air slap her fingers, closed her hand in a fist. She couldn't hear Bessie, or Lucius, or anything except the snap of wind as a laundry truck passed. She pulled in her arm, rolled the window halfway up, and tried to get into Bessie's groove. She told herself that she believed in Sister Michaeline, so she had to believe in Lucius, so she had to believe it was OK to go on a trip to Joliet with him.

The lines in Lucius's face deepened.

"Long time ago I was a prizefighter. I was in this fight. Don't know what you know about boxing, but I had two inches on the other guy. And fifteen pounds. In 1913, I was mostly muscle. The other guy came out of his corner coiled around like a snake, head down, neck down, like he was bowing to me. For some cockamamie reason, I thought he knew the fight already belonged to me and, out of the goodness of my heart, I was supposed to give it to him. I was eighteen years old. What did I know? All I could think was, 'Who do you think you are?' Like he could unwind himself, and, by some miracle, stand up and be as big as me. I didn't register at the time that he was vulnerable. He was submitting and I didn't even know it.

"Close the window, child. I can't take the dust." She rolled up the window. Lucius was coughing and gasping. Sister Haraldo said that he had been gassed in World War I. No wonder he was having trouble breathing.

"He's jabbing, he's crossing. He's a punching machine. I'm thinking, the guy's all heart, give him that, but he barely moves his feet. He's got no smarts. Bobs and weaves. Then pow. The machine explodes. Left jab to my shoulder, right cross to my chin, left hook to my head over the ear. I'm awake now. My legs feel like they're getting longer. I pivot on the back foot, get spring, shake it off, like I'm bouncing up and down on a trampoline.

"The bell rings. We're back in our corners. My trainer Stan, I told you about him, God bless him, my best buddy, he slaps my face. He pours cold water over my head. He knows the other guy's a four flusher. He knows I got the size. I got the footwork. I got the left hook too."

Lucius turned up the radio. "You know Miles Davis? Sister Michaeline must have put him in the Basic Music class."

"Maybe. I'm just now studying jazz seriously."

"Then, seriously, hear how the cymbal puts the pressure on. Listen to the backbeat on the high-hat."

They rode with the music. She cracked the window.

"Round after round, I take the punishment. Usually I waited for the other guy to wear himself out. Not with this guy. He cuts off the ring. He puts me in a corner. He gets me on the ropes, back so far I'm in my sister Lillian's lap. The ref slides a hand in between us. 'No holding, fellas. Break it up.'"

She turned the radio up some more. "What's this one?"

"Miles called it 'So What.' OK now, listen up."

"I didn't mean to interrupt."

But she had meant to interrupt. Acid burned her throat and she felt like she was going to vomit, maybe from morning sickness, definitely from nerves. Fight or no fight, to out and out kill somebody, even if you're doing what you think you're supposed to be doing, wouldn't the church say that's wrong? Even in a boxing match, it must be wrong. Unforgivably wrong.

"Weight was all they talked about. How about arms? I had a reach of seventy inches, darn near as good as Sugar Ray. I'm slipping and swaying, parrying and blocking. Small fry's got no grace, no style, no sense of the art. But, God darn it, he's *strong*. He could knock me out. It's not just my pride because I'm better than him, I'm mad as hell. I've never been knocked out. How'm I going to make music if I get my brains knocked out?"

Mary Kaye reached down to fetch the cracker box, which had slipped between the door and her seat. Hanging on to it seemed to help.

"I've got grace. I've got style. But I've got to knock this guy down. Right uppercut to the jaw. Sweat sprays off his face. Left hook to the other side. He holds his arms up over his face. He's my speed bag. He goes into his snake coil, moving in for a clinch. 'Break it up, boys. Enough.' The bell rings. He's bought time.

"Mostly, the crowd is elevator music. All you hear is silence. And your own people. My sister Lillian yells, 'What's the matter with you, Lucius? Take this guy out.'"

Lucius shifted into second gear at the foot of what seemed to be the only hill between Chicago and Joliet. She tore the waxed paper off a cylinder of saltines, picked up a couple of crackers and stuffed them into her mouth.

"I'm in my corner, scared, eyes closed. I don't hear Stan. God bless him, the snake has got heart. Lillian's right. It's him or me. Get me out of this, Jesus. I'll never fight again.

"Bell rings. Snake raises his head. I'll play with him till I'm good and ready, then I'll knock him flat. A right hand lead. Nobody does that. You leave yourself open to a humungous jab from the left. That was me at that age, hit him with the insult punch. Bring him down in disgrace. 'You're nobody. I can do anything I want with you. Nothing you can do about it.'"

She felt faint. There was too much noise, the crackle of stones flying against the road, Miles Davis' rhythm section marking time, bass strings tolling, piano intoning, Lucius's baritone scraping the bottom.

"I didn't know my own strength. The guy was garbage. He was in my way. Another right. I was going out in style, the last punch of my career. But there was nowhere to go. The guy was already on the floor. Out cold. 'One. Two. Three. Four. Five. Six. Seven. Eight.' Not a twitch. Come on, man. Don't lie there and be all still.

"I kneel next to him, like I'm a little kid saying night prayers, leaning over the side of the bed. 'Now I lay me down to sleep . . . If I should die before I wake . . .' I can't talk straight. I'm crying like a girl. 'Please God, don't let him die.'"

The hand she had been holding over her mouth dropped to her lap. There was no danger that she would speak too soon. She could barely breathe.

"The whole place went hushed. Now it's my head that's bowed. Not a sound but me, weeping and wailing. I killed him. I can't believe it. I actually killed him. They'll be taking him out to a coffin. All I want is to wake up in the morning, see blue sky and warm sun. Never think about the guy in the cold, hard ground."

They drove for a few minutes in silence, except for the music. Lucius seemed lost in another world. Her thoughts darted here and there. Catching one was like grasping a firefly. How come Lucius didn't know his own strength? Yet if you felt you were the underdog or the victim, maybe you shouldn't blame yourself for hurting the other guy. You would be trying to protect yourself.

"What was his name?"

"John Coltrane," Lucius said, glancing at the radio. "He played tenor sax with Miles before he started his own group."

"Not the music, the other guy. What was the name of the guy who died?"

"I can't say it. I still can't say it without breaking up."

They drove without a word. She paced her breath to Ella Fitzgerald. She had missed two periods. She counted the days again, wondered how bad morning sickness could get, how long she could hide that she was showing, and what, for God's sake, she would do with a baby.

He wiped his face and blew his nose. "Maureen said to me, 'Lucius, when are you going to stop making yourself sick over this?'"

She looked up at him, dazed.

"Isaac. His name was Isaac Sheinfeld."

Mary Kaye hung her head and rubbed her face with her hands. What would it feel like to kill someone even though you didn't want to? She would never get over it. She would cry every night for a year, and then on the death day start crying for another year again. She had given no thought to names. She didn't know what the due date would be. She didn't even know whether to think of the life inside her as already human. Sometimes she felt that she was carrying a little somebody who would someday grow into a person. Sometimes she felt that something was standing in the way of life as she wanted and that maybe the thing to do was to get rid of it.

If she had a baby now, it would be the end of music. No more lessons. She would be an amateur. A dabbler.

"Now I'm going to tell you something you can't tell anybody. My own secret."

"I'm with you."

She took a breath. "I might be pregnant. If it turns out I am, my boyfriend's talking about getting rid of it."

Lucius turned the radio off. He tapped the steering wheel with the heel of his hand and rolled his shoulders back. Silent.

"I know it's a mortal sin. I know it's illegal. But I can't stop thinking about it. Tony's father has connections. They know the nuts and bolts of it."

Lucius pulled the car into the prison parking lot, found a space, and turned off the engine.

"All I had on my mind today, child, was we got to see Benny. I kept worrying what's he going to say about me, what's he going to say about Sister Michaeline. To think you've been sitting here listening to me talk about something that happened to me forty-some years ago with all this on your mind."

She was limp as a tired shirt.

"Let's sit for a while." He fiddled with the radio until he found Hank Jones playing "Nobody Knows the Trouble I've Seen" on the Saturday afternoon Gospel Hour. He strummed the steering wheel, as if he were keeping time on the bass. They listened to "Go Down, Moses" and "Swing Low, Sweet Chariot."

"Wish my grandfather were here," Lucius said. "He's the one who performed the medical arts."

He reached across her, opened the glove compartment, and handed her a manila envelope marked "*Chicago Sun-Times, November 2, 1962.*"

"You asked me what Benny did. He's got my big hands. He's got my nimble fingers. I wish to hell he would put them to better use. Don't look at this now. If you're still up to it, let's go see my son."

12

JOLIET PRISON LOOKED a lot like the Motherhouse. They both covered several city blocks, were built around a courtyard, and had bars on the windows. But the bricks at Joliet were cream-colored instead of dark brown and the prison yard was empty, a scrubby expanse of crabgrass. The convent courtyard was a labyrinth of paths, winding through gardens and orchards, with shrines and grottoes and an entire section devoted to the Stations of the Cross. And, as Father Moriarty had explained when he took Mary Kaye and her mother to visit the Motherhouse when Mary Kaye was in fifth grade, convent windows had bars, not to keep the nuns in, but to keep the world out. She signed the visitor log after Lucius, admiring his Palmer penmanship, and copying his spelling of "Benny Claremont."

Two guards, revolvers ready at the waist, escorted them to a small steel compartment with two doors, a table, and three chairs. There were no bars because there were no windows. The taller guard looked like a Sumo wrestler she remembered from a grade school geography unit on Japan, except that instead of a diaper he was wearing a khaki uniform and was white. He blocked the door through which they had entered, while the leaner one seated them facing the other door. She played with the latch on her purse. She had seen guys in the clink on TV and in the movies, but nobody under security like this, except maybe Burt Lancaster in *Birdman of Alcatraz*. He had been in for murder. Whatever Benny had done, she figured it must have been a whopper. She stuffed her hand in her purse, fishing for the envelope with the newspaper clip.

A door banged open. She looked up and there was Benny, stooping to clear the door frame. He was all hair and lanky limbs. He wore an orange jumpsuit. His hands were cuffed behind his back. He nodded, keeping time with the clank of leg-irons, and scuffed toward them. His skin was light like his father's. In certain circumstances he might have passed for Italian or Greek.

The guard pushed Benny into the chair facing Mary Kaye and Lucius, released the hand cuffs but not the leg-irons, and stationed himself directly behind the prisoner. Benny stared at the table and swiveled his feet back and forth, pushing the grit on the floor to make a raspy rhythm. He tapped his fingernails on the tabletop.

"One man jazz band," Lucius said. "That's my boy."

Mary Kaye cleared her throat.

"Wassup, daddy-o? Who's this? She ain't Queen Elizabeth paying no respects. She ain't no headshrinker either. I seen all kind of headshrinkers, they all mean as hell. They got a law in this state headshrinkers be butt-ugly. Nobody be looking at them, how they supposed to get inside your head? Ain't nothing in my head, never was, never will be, you done taught me that, Pops. Don't give me that look. I know you love it when I talk jive."

"This is Sister Michaeline's music student. Her ace."

Benny picked up the pace with the grit on the floor, brushed his hair across the table, and raised his head slowly, grinning. "Thought I be Number One."

"I've got news, son."

Benny closed his eyes and held his breath. He leaned forward, tapped a passage on the table, and whispered, "You bring music for 'Dead Man Blues'?"

"You know what he's talking about, Mary Kaye? The twenties, 35th and State, Jelly Roll Morton." Lucius turned, nodded toward Mary Kaye, then toward Benny, who was still drumming on the tabletop, rapping triplets, four to the bar.

"You talkin' like Blackbird she give me the heave-ho?" Benny's voice was pipsqueaky and singsong.

Without thinking, Mary Kaye ran her finger under her pearls from one side of her neck to the other.

"Will you quit with the Briar Patch baloney, Benny. This is for real. You know she's dead."

"What you think I be talking about, dumb-ass. Folks poking around where they got no business."

Lucius glanced in the direction of the guard behind Benny, as if to warn his son. "Watch your mouth, son. You've got enough trouble."

The guard stood stock still, legs planted squarely, arms akimbo.

"What you think I be, Pops, boy grow up, no mom, no home, nothing but an auntie and a big-shot pops out fiddling on the road?"

"Look here, son, you can bad mouth your old man to kingdom come, but you're not going to sit here and bad mouth your Aunt Lillian. You know damn well she did the best she could."

Benny switched to a Nat King Cole velvet. "And the tooth fairy be leaving pennies under pillows. You messing with my head, you know Lillian got nothing to do with it." He threw back his head and intoned, as if in prayer, "Sing a song of sixpence, a pocket full of rye."

Lucius eyed the guard again. "Jelly Roll was a fussbudget. He could improvise his head off, but, in the end, he wrote everything down."

Benny cut Lucius off with a drum flourish on the table. Locking his hands behind his neck and bowing his head, he solemnly chanted, "Old Mother Hubbard went to the cupboard to give her poor dog a bone."

Lucius turned to Mary Kaye. "I don't just mean for piano, for clarinet, for trumpet. The guy actually composed lines for the bass. Wrote them down. Nobody writes music for the bass."

She had not intended to speak, but it felt like Benny was using some kind of code. She had no idea what he was trying to tell them, but if Lucius had enough time, maybe he could translate. She just had to keep the talk going.

"We did jazz in Basic Music," she said, looking around the room at no one in particular, then looking at Benny. "Sister Michaeline was my music teacher too."

Benny made a point of looking directly at Mary Kaye. "So you had private lessons like I did."

She was struck that he spoke to her in plain English, no sing-song, no rhyme, no jive. It felt to her like he wanted her to see another side of him, perhaps to open the possibility of conversation. But she wasn't sure. Perhaps he was just trying to send a message to his dad.

"Little Jack Horner sat in a corner," Benny said, looking back and forth between Lucius and Mary Kaye with great earnestness.

Mary Kaye said, as if it were a sensible reply, "Sister Michaeline had a set of old records and some of them had Jelly Roll. The guy had a diamond tooth and a pearl-handled pistol. His people came from Haiti. You know, they have voodoo there."

Suddenly, the guard jerked Benny's chair from the back and knocked his shoulder. "Time's up, folks. The doorman will show you to your car. No hug, no pat on the back, no handshake."

"We just got here," Lucius objected. "I mean, we came all the way—"

"Don't give me any guff," the guard said. "The kid has been pulling funny stuff since the minute you walked in. I'm going to make a report to the warden."

Mary Kaye was determined to act cool. She was so nervous that phrases like "See you later, alligator," and "Catch you on the flip side," ran through her head before she settled on "Nice meeting you." They had called too much attention to themselves.

Lucius started the car and turned the radio off. He waited until they cleared the parking lot to speak. "You were on to it. Benny was trying to tell us something. But what?"

"I hope I did all right," Mary Kaye said.

"Not to worry. I've been dealing with Benny's mumbo-jumbo all his life. Though I can't say it gets any easier."

"Do you think Benny was playing with us right from the start, talking about Blackbird?" she asked. "I thought of Sister Michaeline, of course."

"Let me take a stab at it," Lucius said. "You know that rhyme 'Sing a Song of Sixpence'? Benny chanted the first line as if to say, 'Listen up, folks, here's the story for today.' The next line is 'Four and twenty blackbirds baked in a pie.'"

"Right," she said. "So we know he's talking about Sister Michaeline and it ain't good."

"The next rhyme is something about Old Mother Somebody. I don't know that one."

She burst out excitedly, "Old Mother Hubbard went to her cupboard to give her poor dog a bone." She ran through the rest of the nursery rhyme in her head and, when she got to the verse she was sure was Benny's point, she nearly shouted, "And when she got back the poor dog was dead."

"You got it," Lucius said, clearly pleased. "Other people have dictionaries and encyclopedias on their shelves. I need a slew of Mother Goose books to talk to my son."

"There's one more rhyme," she said, enjoying herself. "What's with 'Little Jack Horner'? You know 'Little Jack Horner'?"

"Little Jack Horner lived in our house. When Benny was little he had a constant refrain. He didn't give a hoot about the Christmas pie or the thumb or the plum. It was all about shouting the last line, proclaiming, 'What a good boy am I!'"

She laughed. "That's no mystery. He just wanted you to tell him he was a good boy."

It felt odd that she wasn't afraid that she had got ahead of herself with excitement. People had been telling her all her life she was too serious, but when she would let go and say silly stuff, or things she was trying on for size, she got nervous because then people brought her to heel. But she felt safe with Lucius and they could play. A few hours ago, she had barely known him. The only link between them was Sister Michaeline. Now they could joke around, dead serious about getting to the bottom of Sister's death, but joke around because, despite the difference in their ages, and the obvious difference in race, it felt like they were in tune. Just off the highway, she spotted an A&W root beer stand. It did not feel the slightest bit forward to suggest they stop for a root beer float.

"A&W's my favorite too," he said. "During the Depression they used to have gigantic root beer barrels on the roadside. You walked up and took a swig. Now it's all drive-ins. I could sure use a bite to eat. Got time for a hamburger?"

"A cheeseburger would hit the spot."

As they sat munching their burgers and sipping their root beer floats, she said, "There are a couple things I don't get."

"Shoot."

"We think Benny was playing with us from the get-go. Was he trying to tell us that he knows something about why Sister Michaeline died?"

"Maybe so." Lucius folded the hamburger wrapper over and over until it was a tiny square. "What he said about poking around. He could have been saying he thinks somebody had Sister Michaeline killed because she knew too much, whatever that means, and that he's afraid somebody might kill him too."

"But why would he make a point of insisting that he's a good boy?" she wondered.

"Who knows?" Lucius said. "The kid is fearless. He's clowning around like he always does, playing with voices. Then out of nowhere he throws a bomb. Did he seriously think the guard wasn't listening?"

She slurped the root beer. The ice cream was melting fast. She dabbed the napkin on her mouth. No lipstick left. "The main thing that came through to me is that he had something important on his mind. Something that's bothering him. Maybe something that's scaring him."

"I'm sick and tired of fox-trotting my tail off trying to decode his word games. If he's got something to say to me, I wish he'd just talk like a regular person."

Mary Kaye bristled. The words and the music. She felt that Benny was intent on getting through to his father. Desperately intent. And she admired his ingenuity in trying to get some kind of message to them past the guards.

Lucius stood up, slid his chair under the table, and rocked it back and forth. "What we need is a change of pace. You ever been to the Art Institute? Maureen and I used to hang out there. It helps me get perspective. Maureen felt it unleashed her imagination."

"I've been busy with school and kids and meals and cleaning house," she said. "When I haven't been researching DDT and how it's poisoning everything that grows near the roads we've been travelling today. Except for the time I went on an art study trip to Europe with Sister Michaeline, I've never had time for anything fanciful like art."

Lucius smiled. "Time we did something about that. How about we meet at the Art Institute on Tuesday, say, two o'clock. I'll show you some of Maureen's favorite paintings."

"Great idea. Imagination is frowned on in my family. My folks think that with so many real problems to be tackled, it's a waste of time to make things up." She did not mention the irony of Lucius encouraging playfulness in her, moments after sneering at Benny. His son was in prison, but, even so, it didn't make sense to her how little warmth he seemed to feel for him.

They walked back to the Nash in silence. Lucius turned the radio on. She paced her breath to the clarinet solo from Peggy Lee's song and listened to the words to "Waiting for the Train to Come In."

She read and re-read the newspaper clipping that Lucius had given her in the car before they had visited Benny. The same thing started happening as had been happening when she read Sister's diary. Suddenly she got dizzy. On some point, she would disagree with Sister as she was disagreeing now with Lucius, a word or phrase boring into her brain, eating away at her wish that she could unquestioningly believe in them. She kept hearing Lucius mock Benny's rhymes and word games. And she kept finding there was no getting away from her feeling that Benny was determined to get through to his dad and that she saw some things differently from Lucius.

COP IMPERSONATOR ESCAPES FROM JOLIET
Serving 15 years in Gold Coast Break-in

Joliet, November 2, 1962–An 18 year old black man, convicted of impersonating a Chicago police officer in March, escaped from Joliet Correctional Center around 11 p.m. last night. Benny Claremont is at large and considered dangerous. Anyone with information should contact the sheriff's office. The escapee is light-skinned, 6 foot 2 inches and 160 pounds. He was last seen wearing his hair in a striking mound of curls, but he may have shaved his head.

It is not known whether other inmates aided Claremont, but none have been reported missing. *Sun-Times* sources suggest that, given his long history within the criminal justice system, he may have had help from prison staff. Officials are investigating.

Claremont was serving a 15-year sentence in connection with the attempted armed robbery of a 46-year-old socialite in her Gold Coast home in January. Wearing a Chicago police department uniform and armed with a concealed Smith and Wesson .44 Magnum revolver, Claremont surprised the woman in her bathtub in the late afternoon and left when he heard her scream. Less than an hour later, Claremont was spotted by Police Sergeant Robert Casey on an 'L' platform in Englewood. He did not resist arrest.

Court records describe Claremont as a professional criminal who got his start pickpocketing on city buses as a youngster. Authorities described him as having "magic fingers" and an "uncanny" attention to detail. But he was not precise enough in January. Casey said that he surmised that the suspect was not a police officer because Claremont was wearing the six-pointed Chicago patrolman's badge that was phased out by Police Superintendent O. W. Wilson in his recent overhaul of department policies and procedures. Otherwise, Claremont's police dress was appropriate and included the new hatband with patrolman's two rows of blue and white checks.

At the time of the break-in in January, Claremont apparently believed the residence was empty. He gained entrance to the three-story brownstone by picking a complicated set of rear door locks. Police found sophisticated lockpicking equipment in Claremont's shoulder holster. Officer Peter Mikulsky said at the time, "This guy was no amateur lock picker like you see in the movies. He had a pick gun and torsion wrenches you don't see every day. And somebody must have bought him that powerful revolver."

Claremont's attorney, Walter Klein, suggested at the sentencing that Claremont may have been backed by a fence with known underworld ties. "Claremont may even have been set up," he said at the time. "What he expected to be a routine burglary turned into attempted armed robbery. He had the sense not to draw his weapon or remove property from the residence. Once he realized the job was not going as promised, he fled." Chicago police have been increasingly careful in their handling of home robbery suspects since the shakeup in the department related to the 1960 Summerdale police scandal, in which eight officers were accused of operating a large-scale burglary ring.

Claremont was tried as an adult in March, but he was well known to juvenile authorities over the last decade. He began his career by lifting purses from the backs of chairs at Loop restaurants and knifing purses off the arms of women outside Marshall Field's, especially during Christmas season when shoppers were loaded down with packages. Juvenile officers remarked that, as a boy, Claremont seemed to enjoy the added challenge that went with robbing people in high profile places in broad daylight. As a teenager, he also picked pockets wearing a suit and tie, pretending to be a Moody Institute Bible salesman. He is said to have developed his lockpicking skills playing pinball to enhance his reflexes.

A prison official remarked Thursday, "When the story of Claremont's escape is told, it is sure to be a doozy. He's like Houdini, except he uses his fingers."

Try as she might, Mary Kaye couldn't help but feel that Lucius wanted her to read the story so that she would understand what a difficult child Benny had been. She couldn't quell her own reaction. She wondered what Lucius was really trying to prove. She curled up against her door, pretending to sleep until they pulled into the parking lot in the Loop where the Eldorado waited.

By the time she roared into the east entrance of the O'Donnell driveway—in the last round of a summer storm—the Colorado blue spruce at the foot of the hill was holding steady, but the weaker firs on the sides of the porch were half-standing, arms straggly, limbs limp in the wind. They reminded her of prizefighters on the ropes, buying time before the storm's last punch. She drove past the path that led up to the porch and stopped near the weeping willow tree. It was making creaky, achy noises. How could Lucius have killed a man? How could anybody kill another person? If she had to kill to save her own life, would she be able to do it? Willow tree wood was soft. It grew too fast to claim its strength. It was weak, the worst thing that could be said about anybody. She was so weak that she didn't even know her own mind. And then when she did, she felt bad about it. It was time to read Sister Michaeline.

September 5, 1947. Saint Lawrence Justinian, bishop with the gift of tears, power over devils, and prophecy. On his deathbed he refused to be moved to a feather bed, preferring to die as Jesus did on the hard wood of the Cross.

There are no mirrors here. Sometimes, on a Wednesday evening, when the light is right, and we are leaving the Refectory late because we've had second supper, on the way to chapel for night prayer I can see my reflection in a tall glass door to the Visitors' Parlor. I must ask Sister A. for forgiveness. I have gotten into the habit of deliberately trying to see my reflection, instead of keeping custody of the eyes, which requires me when we are walking in the corridors to look not to the right or to the left, but at the floor directly in front of me. That's how I know that, without Michael, I'm still alive. Last night I was lost in prayer, but when I turned the corner I was startled to see a face. What a beautiful face, I thought, as if I were looking at somebody else.

What would Michael think of my going to the convent? He would forgive me Gabriel. He would forgive me Lucius. But the rest he would not forgive.

September 17, 1947. The impression of the Stigmata upon Saint Francis of Assisi, the wounds of crucifixion marked on his flesh.

I'm doing better keeping custody of the eyes but my mind keeps wandering. Grandma S. takes me to the World's Fair in Chicago, where we stay at the Edgewater Beach Hotel—was it actually pink?—so we can walk to Uncle Bill's. He's got us in stitches imitating Grandpa S.: "You're not going to amount to anything, Billy, playing saxophone in Dubuque. The only one who can stand that gol dang 'Weatherbird' is your mother. Take that blasted record and find yourself a jigaboo who knows how to play coon music right. Here's a one-way ticket to Chicago. Now get out of town." We hung around the Jazz Emporium and I promised myself that the minute I graduated from high school I'd come and live with Uncle Bill.

September 18, 1947. Saint Joseph Cupertino, confessor, suffered bitterly at the hands of his own superiors.

I should be satisfied with breakfast bread, but I'm not. I miss my toast. This morning at the sanitarium, serving the senile nuns, I lifted the steel cover off a plate of scrambled eggs and toast. The eggs stuck together like jello. I wiped the water off the cover, but it was too late. Cold, soggy toast.

Grandma and Sister Perpetua toasted bread over the fire when they were little. Sister P. was fifteen when she entered the convent, less than half as old as I am now. Unless you count the soggy excuse I brought to her this morning, she may have gone six decades without toast. I can imagine taking vows of poverty, chastity, and obedience for the rest of my life. I cannot imagine going the rest of my life without a piece of toast.

September 21, 1947. Saint Matthew, apostle to whom Jesus said, "Follow Me."

Sister A. says the well-heeled parishes have toasters for the nuns. Mortification of the senses does not extend to toast.

October 3, 1947. Saint Therese of the Child Jesus taught the Way of Spiritual Childhood.

A letter came from mother. It was postmarked Sept. 9, nearly a month ago, what with mail coming from Dubuque and having to sit on Sister A.'s desk until she blacks out the objectionable passages and delivers it on a Sunday. Can't remember when I've been so upset. There's no one to tell except God and He already knows the whole story, which, if I can calm down, might actually become a comfort.

Mother knows that I was Grandma Stickelmeier's favorite, yet her letter went on and on about herself and her grievances, as if Grandma hadn't died and I hadn't missed the funeral. Grandma got me started on the piano. She gave me the McGuffy readers and *The Imitation of Christ*. She read the Bible, both the Old and New Testaments, and she read novels like Goethe's *Elective Affinities*. She and Michael were two of a kind. They loved literature and they loved music. She got a kick out of showing Michael the spot where the riverboat docked in Dubuque when she took Uncle Bill and me to hear Louis Armstrong.

You would think that, for once in her life, mother would have seen things from my point of view. Never mind that I am on the outs with her. She didn't think I should go to the convent, given what happened after Michael and Gabriel died. Now she thinks I've been getting what's coming to me, sitting here in the Motherhouse, not even knowing Grandma was sick, much less what she died of. Grandma Friedie was 72, but when I saw her in May she was the last person on Earth who looked like she would die anytime soon. And to think she was already dead when I served Sister Perpetua breakfast in the sanitarium and when I wrote mother asking her to tell Grandma about it. It's upsetting, looking back in my diary, that she died on the day I looked at myself in the glass.

I have one thing to cling to. I know Grandma's death day. Sept. 5. Maybe by Visiting Sunday I'll be calm enough to ask mother exactly what happened. Who sang at her funeral, who played the organ, whether Sister Perpetua was allowed to leave the sanitarium to go to her own sister's funeral. You'd think mother would have asked the nuns whether I might accompany Sister Perpetua so she could take the Milwaukee Road train down to Chicago and transfer to the Illinois Central for Dubuque. But I should know better. Mother didn't want me at the funeral. She didn't want to see me crying real tears while she stood there, cold and composed. Her Daddy's Prussian princess.

Sept. 8, 1947
Dear Maureen,

Your Grandmother Friedie died peacefully at home on Sept. 5th. I cannot say that I will miss her. She was very fond of you, much fonder of you than she ever was of me. Some of this you ought to know by now, but I will tell you again in the hope that you will finally get it through your head. She never forgave me for wanting to leave home. She took to her bed in the attic and said that she was not well enough to go downstairs. So I had to stay home and take care of her. I brought her meals three times a day on a tray, plus tea and cake at 4 p.m. I washed and ironed her clothes and brought her books back and forth from the library. I got a Victrola and played whatever classical music I could borrow. She gave me a devil of a time, but I managed to find piano works by Bach and Beethoven. I could never find Chopin and she never forgave me. She was so upset by my "threat to abandon her" that she didn't go down to the parlor and play her piano. This went on for about a year, during which time I went to 7 a.m. Mass and Communion every day looking for guidance.

I met your father at an ice cream social at St. Mary's. He was there with his mother, the former Fiona McDonald. She always said that was the end of your father and the Catholic Church because once we got married, he stopped going to Mass, which everybody said was bound to happen because if Fiona McDonald had wanted her children to stay practicing Catholics why in God's name did she marry a Lutheran, and expect him to turn into a Catholic when the only reason he converted was to marry the prettiest girl in Dubuque. The Riegers knew how to deal with people who insist on what they think they're entitled to, and they sure did get me out of a spot with my mother.

Your father proposed marriage and I took it as a sign from God that He wanted me to move up in the world by marrying the son of the president of the German Savings Bank. Grandma Rieger became my real mother. She insisted that you be named something that was obviously Catholic and showed that, although you were German, one quarter of your blood was Irish. She took my side when I didn't want to have more children because your father was running around. She backed me up even though she knew the way I went about it was a sin. She put some sense into your father's head on more than one occasion, like the night he marched down Peru Street with the Ku Klux Klan and the time I didn't know what to do about that business with Mrs. McGinnis. In my book, Grandma Rieger's only blind spot was marrying Karl Rieger, but who am I to talk since I married his son for about the same reason.

Anyway, my own mother always had a soft spot for you and I knew you would want to know she died. It's too bad you were not here for the services. I hope that when the time comes you will at least be able to attend mine. I enclose the holy card from the funeral.

Love, Mother

I slid my finger in the envelope, thinking that the funeral card might have got stuck. I knelt down on the floor near my desk and looked up and down the study hall under all the desks to see whether in the excitement of opening a letter from home I might have sent the funeral card sailing. Then I remembered that we do not have personal possessions here. Sister A. must have confiscated the holy card. Another good reason to hide my mother's letter in the Particular Examen book. I know that I'll have this book at least until I'm received as a novice in June. If Sister A. collects them, I'll say I lost it and hide it in the bottom of my trunk.

I'm surprised Sister A. didn't black out more of the letter. She ran a fine pen through the part about knowing it was a sin to prevent more children, but I could easily decipher it.

October 4, 1947. Saint Francis of Assisi. Founder of Franciscans, troubadour of divine love, beggar among beggars, nature's great friend.

When Michael left for boot camp, I closed his apartment, but kept his clothes. I carried them in stacks to my apartment. I threw out some of my clothes and made room in the drawers for his. I cleared space on a shelf for the shirts I had bought for him for Christmas, crisp and white, folded the way they do in the store, straight pins holding the shoulders in place, cardboard half-moons positioned to make the collars stand straight. I lay in bed wondering what married life would be like.

If I am getting over Michael, why last night did I lie there wondering which is sadder, the clothes I washed and pressed for his homecoming or the Christmas clothes he never wore? Why am I thinking about clothes on Saint Francis Day when we celebrate our Franciscan life of joyful poverty?

October 11, 1947. Feast of the Motherhood of the Blessed Virgin Mary.

Do I have to report the bad things I do in my dreams? The lucky-duck novices were on retreat again, so we were subbing in the laundry, right off the power plant, generators and boilers hissing and spitting, the heat so stifling I could hardly breathe. I was feeding linens into the mangle. All of a sudden, one of the sheets rose up out of the basket, spread itself tall, and stood up on its corners like a Halloween sheet. I screamed and yelled. No Daddy, don't scare me. What are you doing in that sheet? I ran to the folding table, knelt down, and pressed my face into a pile of bath towels, just off the clothes line, stiff as a board. They scratched my cheeks.

I peeked back at the sheet. It was still standing as tall as Daddy when he came in from the Peru Street parade, the Halloween point on its head drooping into a Dairy Whip swirl, like the picture in the *Herald* when Coolidge let the Klan burn a cross in Washington on the Capitol steps.

In the dream, I punched the sheet. Let's go to the Dairy Whip, Daddy. I hit as hard as I could but the sheet wouldn't give. It swooped me up, wrapped itself around me, and went through the mangle with me inside.

In real life, at the house in Dubuque, I sat on the landing and watched Daddy stagger in. He was lit and he was wearing a sheet. He dropped into a chair and shouted at my mother to bring wieners and beer.

She started right in on him. "Your mother was right. Fiona McDonald told me not to marry a fallen-away Catholic, even if his dad was a mucky-muck at the German Savings Bank."

"Get your head out of your ass. The sheet doesn't mean a thing. We got to stop the labor unions cuz I need a job. It's me or some spade."

"You should've stayed at the bank. Instead of dilly-dallying with that shanty-Irish floozy."

"You're a wet blanket, as bad as the nuns. Maureen can play piano till the parlor rug weeps. If they think she's the big cheese, let them pay for piano lessons."

In the convent yesterday, in the laundry, not in the dream, I didn't care what God wanted. All I could think of was I've got to get out of the heat.

October 13, 1947. Saint Edward, king and confessor, so pure that he maintained virginity while married.

Beyond the black wrought iron fence, I see maple trees flaming along the boulevard. Leaves fall in our courtyard. We rake them off the pathways of the Stations of the Cross. In my cell in the Dormitory, the water in the wash basin gives me the shivers when I splash my face. I haven't felt this cold since Michael died.

Mother's letter said it was too far to come from Dubuque to sit around the garden for two hours with a bunch of other families on Visiting Sunday. I should be sorry they didn't come, but I'm not. I stashed myself in Saint Chrysostom at the piano. Sister Victoire says that if I learn Bach on the piano, playing it on the organ will be a snap.

I keep looking for Michael to walk through the door. He is all legs. He doesn't walk. He slides his feet smoothly across the floor, working like the devil to make it look like no work at all. His finger brushes a strand of hair from my eye. His hand fastens my veil. I turn a corner and he is there, walking the corridor in his raincoat. All day long he plays the piano in my head.

I try to play the piano like him, but my attack is too strong, my tempo too fast. I'm trying to get rid of the Catholic bounce, the early Louis Armstrong bounce. Louis had the Catholic smile, relentlessly coercive. Everybody be happy, whether you like it or not. By the time we heard him in Dubuque, he had let his sound darken. His vulnerability came through. Funny that it takes so much practice to sound natural. Sister A. is a smart cookie. She doesn't think I should work to get Michael out of my system. She knows he is part and parcel of me. I must relax into that.

October 15, 1947. Saint Teresa of Avila, doctor of mystical theology, esteemed among women in the Church.

I still can't believe I wasn't at Grandma S.'s funeral. She was the first to arrive in Chicago when Michael died. Mother came late and the day we buried the little box at Rosehill she took the first train back to Dubuque. Grandma stayed for months. She didn't want me to give up the jazz group because Michael was gone. She thought a pregnant woman needed family, all the more so as a widow. Grandma helped me choose which of Michael's books to put in the little box and helped me take the seat off his piano stool, which she had needlepointed for him after we visited Dubuque. We wrapped *The Golden Bowl*, *Dubliners*, *The Good Soldier*, and *To the Lighthouse* in newspaper stories about the war and tucked them under the piano seat.

Mother hadn't seen the point of a cemetery plot since Michael's body was lost at sea. I know that Michael died in the Battle of the Coral Sea. I like to imagine that parts of him floated every which way in the Pacific and that, over time, molecules that used to belong to him found temporary residence in the bodies of fish or ocean plants near Australia and New Guinea and even Hawaii, so that something of him still lives. How much of what used to be him lies anywhere in particular I'll never know. But about the contents of the box I am sure. Piano was part of Michael. James and Joyce and Ford and Woolf were part of him.

I gave Michael's books to Grandma S. for safekeeping when I went to the convent. We planned that, before I was received as a novice, she would give them to the Motherhouse library. Now they are in my mother's hands. If she gave them to the order, Mother Isidore might put them in the Motherhouse library and I could read them while I'm in training. Then again, Mother Isidore might disperse them to the mission sisters. I might never hold them again.

I see Michael, spanking new books in hand, doing his getting-acquainted routine, opening each page, starting with the front and back covers, creasing the pages carefully, back and forth, until the book limbered up, ready to rest in his hands, ready for notes he wrote in the margins, the index of reactions and his own ideas, in columns by page numbers inside the covers, and on the title page.

After he died I was always searching. Day after day, I lost something of mine, my keys, my glasses, my hat. I wandered around looking for it, until suddenly I remembered I had put it in some place special to keep it safe. I ran to find it. In that moment I was cheered. I had not lost everything. But the grief flooded back. It's not Michael I have found. It's just a hat. A hat that I hid so I could search and find it and pretend for a second that I could get back what I want.

October 17, 1947. Saint Margaret Mary Alacoque, who overcame the misgivings of her superiors.

Sister Augustine meant no harm putting me at the front of the procession. She did not know I am numb from too much emotional mountain climbing. Not that I didn't hold the Infant Jesus statue steady. Small victory. My arms still ache. The other postulants intoned the Litany of the Saints. Holy Mary. The novices and professed nuns responded. Pray for us.

Back and forth, I hear our sixty-two postulants chanting, Holy Mother of God. Hundreds of nuns responding, Pray for us. Holy Virgin of Virgins. Pray for us. Saint Michael. Pray for us.

Up the chapel aisle, out the vestibule, through Motherhouse corridors, upstairs, down, through the cloister, past refectories and dormitories, music rooms, sewing rooms, recreation room, visitors' sitting rooms, portress station, back to chapel, down the aisle. Not a habit or veil in sight, everyone in the convent walking in procession behind me.

We are forbidden to talk about life before the convent. But suppose I can stay here, safe in order and quiet, and still have my own thoughts. Maybe I do not have to renounce all my interior gear.

One foot in front of the other. Saint Gabriel. Pray for us. As much as I have read about the men who explored the South Pole, I know better than to step into a crevasse, but it's like I'm walking on a glacier. It cracks open and I go down the chute of lost time. God forgive me, help me stop dwelling on it. Saint Gabriel, my boy's saint. Archangel second only to Michael, my boy's dad. Both gone. So much for everything staying in its place.

Why didn't I know Gabriel was sick? Maybe because he was always warm and moist, working up a sweat. Even in the womb he was always moving. We made a game out of it. I rested a wash cloth on my big belly in the bathtub. He kicked it off. I read Virginia Woolf in bed. He kicked the book off too. The boys played loud at the Jazz Emporium. He jumped in time with the music, like he couldn't wait to get out and be a part of it. For me, he wasn't a part of it. Gabriel was it.

Every time he fed I had to peel him off like adhesive tape, as if trying not to open a wound. The little fatso. I put him over my shoulder and rubbed his back until he burped or spit up on the receiving blanket. What a sight I must have been, kneeling on a rubber mat, diaper pin hanging out of my mouth like a cigarette, blowing on his tummy, patting his bottom, dusting him with baby powder, all dry, all dry, except no matter how dry, dampness clinging in his warm folds, clinging to my hands, the smell of warm bread dough rising. Baby powder caking in the sweaty folds of his neck and the creases above his thighs. The yeasty, powdered-sugary smell of Gabriel in fresh diapers.

You don't want to smother him, my mother warned. He needs to breathe. He needs fresh air. He needs to go out in the buggy every day. He needs the hood on the buggy down so he can get sun.

I should have known his red skin wasn't from the weeds in the backyard. And that because a couple of days had passed everything wasn't necessarily OK. Michael was dead. There was nobody to ask about the red marks flowing into each other, down Gabriel's cheeks, around his neck, down his arms and chest. By the time the doctor got to the house, the red rash was all over him. Beet red, except for the palms of his hands. They were white as a sheet. Gabriel pounded the piano with those hands. Like his daddy. His fever was 105. His tongue was a strawberry. He did not move.

I hate the Infant of Prague statue. I have to dust it every morning for daily work. Getting it ready for the procession, dressing it in its little outfit, is the worst. Somebody went to a lot of trouble to make the statue lifelike, all the satin clothes like priest's vestments and the suntan glow. The day of the procession I looked hard into its face. It was stained pale gold.

The statue's gold face looked like Gabriel's skin. Not his skin when he was kicking the blanket off in the buggy, or playing peek-a-boo with sheets on the clothes line. Like the palms of his hands when I held him in my arms and he didn't move. While he was losing human warmth. Getting dry and cold. While his white palms were turning waxy yellow. I could almost see through the skin. As he got stiff. It took about an hour or two for the waxy glow to set in. These have been the hardest times. Holding Gabriel in my lap while his body changed from him to it and holding the golden Infant Jesus already stone cold.

13

THEY MEANDERED FROM one gallery to the next, Mary Kaye bent on judging each painting, Lucius gently inviting her to forget about voting the contents up or down and instead see whether anything jostled her. On a Tuesday, they had the European works mostly to themselves.

"Depends on what you mean by 'jostle,'" she said. "This Picasso woman in the red chair is looking forward and sideways at the same time. I like her better than the Gris, with the guitar and the glass sliced thinly in softer colors. Yet, neither of them do anything for me, one way or the other."

"My point, exactly," Lucius said. "I've always loved this Monet. He has a whole series of hay stacks, but I'm partial to this one. After Benny was arrested I spent hours eyeballing this pile of wheat. The way the brilliance of the royal blue sets off the hay stack, beached in the flow of the snow on an overcast day. Somehow it's a comfort."

"I can see that. Makes me think of Rachel Carson. You know her work? She exposed the harm caused by chemical poisons in our food. Cancer, genetic damage. I spent my senior year debating against DDT. I can't help longing for a simpler time—like Monet's."

"You must be a whiz at science."

"It came easily so everybody says that's what I should do. Everybody except Sister Michaeline. She kept urging me to do what made me feel alive. Not to worry about practicality, but to let myself try things. With the idea that I might discover what feeling really alive feels like."

"And?"

"Right now it's music. I feel alive when I'm singing."

"Sounds good to me."

"Oh," she said. "Over there, I see one I want to sit in front of."

"You mean the Gauguin? It's called *Arlesiennes*."

"The woman leading the procession looks numb with grief. Maybe it's a funeral. She could be Maureen carrying the Infant of

Prague statue through the corridors of the Motherhouse. I just read that part of the book and I couldn't stop crying. Losing a husband must be pretty awful, but losing your child, that may be the worst. Do you think it was her fault that Gabriel died?"

"She certainly thought so. And blaming herself changed her dramatically. I always told her it wasn't her fault. But if she had had a clearer head, she might have got him to a doctor. Maybe he would have died anyway, but I don't think the blow would have crushed her to her core."

"Why do you say that?"

"Because, with Michael gone, it all fell on her. And because of who she was before. Come, see for yourself. In the next room."

They walked silently into the adjoining gallery. Her legs felt particularly heavy and she was relieved when Lucius guided her to a chair.

"Over here. Never mind the sign says Edgar Degas, *The Café Singer,* 1879. Meet Maureen Rieger, Chicago, 1938. Have you ever seen anybody so joyous, so alive? Throat wide open, belting out a song, stealing the show. Scarlet flowers in her hair. Arms upraised, as if to say, OK, everybody, I made it. I arrived. Here's the back of my hand to anybody who says otherwise. She was a shooting star, confident as all get out.

"When Michael died, she faded some; but when Gabriel died, she cratered. All the life in her went underground. She became subdued and cautious, as though her own survival depended on playing it safe. I tried to help her, but it seemed like everything I tried just made it worse. You're probably reading about that in the book.

"Hey, I didn't mean to cut you off. Mary Kaye. Is there more you want to say about Maureen losing Gabriel? You want to go back to the Gauguin?"

Mary Kaye was carrying a great resonance with Maureen and her experience of losing her baby, but, for the time being, she wanted only to draw comfort from the strength of Lucius's voice.

"I don't know what I'm doing," she said. "I wish I could be the girl in this other painting across from us. She's trying on hats and she's utterly serene. You could say I'm trying on hats right now—what do I want to do, who do I want to become—but I feel more like the painting next to it—half of one lady's head is a horse and the other lady's eye sockets are burnt out."

Lucius laughed. "That's the difference between Degas and Dali."

"How did you get into art? You know so much about it."

"That's a long story, goes way back. I was about your age in France, during the Great War. My captain took a liking to me. He saw me cleaning my rifle and pulled me aside. 'Look how you massage that weapon with oil,' he said. 'We've got a chef who needs an assistant. This may be war, but this is France. The chef is a big part of building morale.' Captain Georges had figured out that I had no interest in killing anybody. I was shooting over the heads of the Germans. I was afraid he would have me court martialed. I told him and he understood. I was amazed. No more Isaac Sheinfelds. So I became a chef.

"Georges had one guy tutor me in French, one in French cooking. I tutored both of them in boxing so they could teach the troops how to box with bayonets and knives, hand-to-hand fighting, you know. My French was pretty good. Hey, I grew up with my grandparents, the ones from New Orleans. I didn't think Georges needed a translator in Paris with the Americans, but he said he could use help with the slang. Years later when we met in New York for an art show, Georges told me he got a kick out of the look on the American faces when they saw his colored assistant. The French always treated us like we were one of them. When we came back to the States we went back to being nobody. No wonder there were race riots in 1919."

"And did you learn art from Georges?"

"Holy Smoke. I learned everything from Georges. Like you with Sister Michaeline. It's like it was yesterday. I turned the corner in Paris and walked up Rue Lafitte. Sacré Coeur, a beacon on the hill. Cafés, patisseries, English bookstores. And the art galleries. On my first trip to Paris Georges pulled me toward a gallery. 'You see that old man heading up the street, that's Degas,' he said. 'He's still got a studio in Montmartre.'"

"You mean the Degas that painted this lady here trying on the hats? The guy who painted Maureen Rieger, 1938?"

"Yeah. Georges knew him and he knew Rouault, who was a Degas protégé. Rouault and Degas were about as far apart in age as you and me. Georges and I would peek into Rouault's studio and watch him use sandpaper, acid, anything at hand, to put depth in his engravings. I've been haunted by his prints ever since. Black, white, and gray. Images of suffering and death. The Art Institute has the

entire series of *Miserere et Guerre*. I owned one print myself—I'd
bought it for Maureen after Gabriel died and it came back to me
when she went to the convent. Not that I had enough green stuff.
Between the horses and the poker table, my bank account's been hit
and miss."

"I miss Sister Michaeline. Especially hearing you talk about
Georges. I'm not sure what I want to do with my life altogether. I'll
go to college and maybe then graduate school. But I'm not ready to
choose. What I'd like to do now is sing."

Lucius was quiet for a while and then he said intently, "If you'd
let me, I might be able to give you a hand. It wouldn't be the way
that Sister Michaeline would do it, but if you're game, I'd like to give
it a try. Come on down to the Jazz Emporium Friday night and see
what we're up to. Then you and I could get together two weeks from
that Saturday and run through some songs. My place in Hyde Park.
See what happens."

"I'd love that," she said, heartened by the gentleness of his voice
and the power of his quiet strength.

14

TONY'S CAR WAS a mess. Mary Kaye had complained about the chartreuse exterior and he had compounded the error with a cheapie spray paint job. The Chevy looked like it had been slathered with lemon, lime, and orange sherbet and left in the day's heat. He was half an hour late, but she bit her tongue. No point in starting the evening with a squabble. She did not want to spoil her first time hearing Lucius perform. Lucius would lift her spirits.

"Great dress, babe. Get a load of those Grace Kelly shoulders." Tony handed her the fake ID that his father had given him last spring.

She had let herself be coaxed into using it for special occasions, but it was about time she kept it in her possession. God knows why Illinois had raised the drinking age for women to twenty-one. Girls were more mature than guys at eighteen and the old drinking age had reflected that.

She patted the hood of the Chevy. "Far out." The most charitable words she could muster.

"Why the hell are we going to Coontown for a night out?"

"Hey, watch your language! You're talking about where Lucius lives."

"Oh, give me a break. You know what I mean." He opened her door and ushered her into the stale cigarette stench. "Look, Ma. No butts. Check out the ashtrays. I cleaned up the whole shebang for tonight."

He swaggered to his side of the car. She kicked through the nest of papers underfoot, Bun Bar wrappers, the scent of milk chocolate, McDonald's bag, the smell of grease from the fries, *Sun-Times* sports section with names of horses circled for races at Arlington. She knew she was probably pregnant. She could smell everything, even sweat on the Chevy's leatherette. The top candidate for barf bag would be the newspaper. It looked like Tony was getting gambling tips from his father.

When had dating him stopped being a lark? He had always cut corners. The rules never had applied to him. But it hadn't bothered her until this summer. She had been conscientious enough for the two of them. Sitting in the cigarette smell and the garbage, she wiped the corners of each eye with a Kleenex.

"Enough with the water works. We're going to the jazz joint. But next time I get to pick."

She had come a long way since their first official date, when he had backed out of the horseshoe drive with barely a glance at the rear view mirror and she had been impressed. "Sure you know how to get there?"

"Do I look like a dunce? What's wrong with you tonight?"

"I'm thinking about Lucius and Sister Michaeline. Sister sang at the Jazz Emporium in the late thirties. Her husband was the piano player."

"Don't you think that's kind of kooky? A man letting his wife do something dumb like that? Bad enough he let her work, much less in Coontown."

She looked out her side window, frowning. "You know you're not on the expressway yet, Tony. Last time I checked, the speed limit on Jefferson Avenue was still thirty. And, please, stop calling it Coontown." She reached for the radio dial. It was sticky. One more thing he had missed in his big cleanup.

Tony turned on to the ramp and floored the gas pedal. "Hang on to your girdle, girlie. We're going for a ride."

She turned the dial, searching for a grown-up voice. "Nothing new today in the murder of Medgar Evers, the thirty-seven-year-old Negro civil rights activist, who was shot in the back this week in Mississippi. Evers was an NAACP field secretary who made a lot of enemies when he helped desegregate the University of Mississippi. Earlier this year, there were two attempts on his life. A Molotov cocktail . . ."

Tony turned the dial to WLS. "Don't be a drag. I got to get you in a good mood. I say Dick Biondi." Little Peggy March was singing the last chorus of "I Will Follow Him." Then Biondi broke in. "It was only a couple weeks ago when a teenager from New Jersey made her debut on *American Bandstand*. Now she's at the top of the charts: Lesley Gore, with 'It's My Party.'" Tony clicked her seat belt open and put his arm around her shoulder, pulling her in close.

Mary Kaye kidded her self into thinking she could relax. "I think I can find the station that plays jazz. Lucius showed me."

"Use your head, Max. I agreed to tonight, but you're in way over your head hobnobbing with this guy Lucius."

Irked, she leaned closer to him in silence.

Even before Sister Michaeline died in the crash, she had hated the expressways. If you wanted thrills and spills, go to Riverview and ride the Bobs or the Flying Turns. Think of all the homes that had to be demolished, railroad tracks torn apart, businesses and churches lost, graves that had to be dug up and moved to make way for these highways. For the longest time, there had been a great gash in the earth. Thousands of people's lives ruined so hotshots like Tony could race around town. Whole neighborhoods destroyed and nobody gave a hoot.

They sped past the neon Magikist lips sign. Tony turned the radio down. "Hey, babe, how about a kiss?"

She pecked his cheek, half-heartedly. She hated that sign. Tony released her shoulder. She slid back to her own side and snapped her seat belt in place.

A single raindrop plopped on the windshield. "Not rain," she said. "I don't want to be late."

One drop followed another, lickety-split, the rain turning to sheets.

"Don't knock the rain. It's so hot I can hardly stand it."

Tony slammed on the brakes, barely in time to avoid rear-ending the Volkswagen in front of them.

She muffled a yelp.

"They say those little cars squish right up," Tony said. "That's why they call them VW bugs."

Around the bend, ahead on the expressway, toward the city center, red taillights snaked as far as she could see. The road looked as slick as a mirror. Next to her, on the side of the car, rain pelted and pierced a puddle. How could something look so dazzling, so mesmerizingly smooth when it was far down the road, and look so blown to smithereens up close?

They sat on the Edens, waiting for the traffic jam to unwind.

She said fervently, "No matter what happens with the rabbit test, I don't want to get married."

"Give me a chance. We haven't even talked." He put the gear in park and revved the engine.

"We've got no business getting married, and you know it. We're nowhere near old enough." She stuck her arm out the window and slapped her hand on the roof of the car. "There's nothing to talk about. I'm not getting married."

"You may change your tune when you actually hear what the rabbit test said."

She was not going to cry. Frantically, she tried to calculate in her head. It would be nine months from April 7th. Or did you start counting from your last period? She switched the radio off.

"I bet I'm pregnant. How long have you known? I thought you'd tell me right off tonight if you had results."

An ambulance roared up the shoulder of the road alongside them, siren wailing. No wonder traffic wasn't moving. A car had crashed not far away, on the other side of the median, going the other direction. In her mind's eye, she could see the ambulance, its back doors wide open. She could see inside. Somebody was lying on a stretcher. She could not help but wonder about that person. She couldn't see him or her and she might not ever know the identity of that person, but he or she, or maybe it was they, had become a part of her life, and at the moment, they were holding up her life. She wanted them out of the way. She felt that clearly. She was numb, but her thoughts were not in a jumble. It was a little cooler after the rain, but the vent kept bringing in exhaust and soot. The air did not feel clean. Traffic began to inch forward.

"Let's go someplace and talk."

"I don't want to go *someplace*. I want to go to the Jazz Emporium." Sister had trusted Lucius enough to give him her book, and she was going to put her faith in him too. She had a big problem but she did not need to be alone with it.

"How did I get roped into driving in a colored neighborhood? Trying to please you again. I could care less about jazz music."

"Well, then why don't you drop me off and drive home! I don't need you to hold my hand and complain about the music. I can get back on my own."

"You think I'm going to leave you alone in this jungle? You gotta be kidding."

"I'm not kidding. I've had it with the snide remarks and the Mr. Big Man performance."

"Watch your mouth, little lady. You're pushing your luck."

She could not stand the sight of him. How could she have gotten mixed up with a guy who had scored a C in algebra, flunked second grade, barely finished high school? Whose father was connected with shady people? For God's sake, at the age of nineteen, Tony even had his own bookie.

They drove in silence for a long time, until she could stand it no longer. "Tony, you're not watching the signs! You've got to get off at 47th Street."

He cut across two lanes of traffic, nearly got rear-ended by a moving van and skidded on to the exit ramp. "You say you don't want to get married. So what's going to happen? I'll be goddamned if I'm going to stand by and let a stranger raise my child."

"It's not about you. I'm the one who's going to have a baby. We're not talking about what you're going to do. We're talking about what I'm going to do."

"I'm trying to talk sense and you're stuck in la-la-land. Typical girl. Doesn't give a damn about me. It's my baby too, you know."

She bit her tongue.

He turned the radio on again. Dick Biondi took them through "Walk Like a Man," "My Boyfriend's Back," and "Can't Get Used to Losing You."

They drove down 47th Street, Mary Kaye reading the street numbers aloud.

"Slow down," she said. "You're going to pass it."

"You know what?" he exploded. "I don't need this bullshit. Have it your way. You keep treating me like I'm an idiot. I'm not going with you. I'm not going to listen to that god-awful music. I'm going to drop you off and then I'm driving home. See how you like going in there all by yourself."

"Watch me." He had rattled her, but she was not going to back down.

When they pulled up to the club, she got out of the car and slammed the door in the middle of Andy Williams. She could hear that Tony had not pulled away from the curb, but she kept walking. She followed a group of couples to the vestibule. A young black man dressed to the nines held the door for her and she followed his date into the darkness.

15

SO THIS WAS the Jazz Emporium. She was too furious and too shaken up to look for the place under the photo of Billie Holiday, alongside the Steinway. She grabbed a chair at the end of a row of tables and swiveled to check out the crowd. Blacks, whites, and mixed couples bowed over cocktails, reading newspaper reviews of Chicago jazz greats laminated on the tiny tabletops.

Early arrivals had nabbed raggedy brown leather loveseats along the walls, under photos of Armstrong, Goodman, Krupa, and Hines—familiar faces from Sister Michaeline's class. Some perched on the sassy hot pink leather and rattan stools around the mahogany horseshoe bar in the back. She wondered how many others had got in with phony IDs. The white pianist intoned the first bars of "It Could Happen to You."

It didn't sound a thing like Dorothy Lamour's song from *And the Angels Sing*, but she tried to stay with it. The trumpeter was playing with a mute. That she knew from Lucius, whom she glanced at only long enough to see that he was plucking strings on the bass. Suddenly, the saxophonist broke in and ran off with the music as if he were in some kind of a pout. She lost track of the melody. The piano picked up the tune again and she was back on track. She hadn't expected live jazz to be so brash, one player grabbing his turn from the other, cutting him off, hijacking the melody for his own use. They had not got to that in Sister's class. This must be improvisation.

So she was pregnant. Of course. She had been kidding herself for weeks, but she had known, hadn't she?

The Jazz Emporium was a foreign place. People around her—it did not seem right to call them the audience, they were too involved to be an audience—were not sitting, hands folded, like at a concert. They were nodding up and down, not just once or twice when something struck them in particular, but in time through the entire piece. Not just with their heads, but with their entire bodies leaning forward from the waist, over and over, up and down. Their legs, bent at the knee, bobbed up and down, heels tapping the floor gently, like when she ran the sewing machine, except that when she ran the Singer, it was exacting work and she tensed up to get it right in the tight stretches, like around an armhole of a sleeve. Jazz wasn't at all like that.

During the Mozart Mass at Christmas, the choir folded hands in front of choir robes. In the allegretto passages, she had been tempted to move her fingers in time, maybe a thumb against a pinkie finger, at worst, a hand keeping time, up and down, from the wrist. Everybody knelt, stood, and sat in church, bodies close in the pews. They were using their bodies to keep time, but it was mechanical time, lockstep, everybody doing the same thing at the same time.

It was different here. The music was in their bodies. They were moving together with the beat, but each separate body moved in its own way, as if listening and responding in its own style. The lady at the next table moved with her eyes closed. Where did she go? To her own solitary place perhaps, but she did not seem removed from the other listeners. That's what was so striking. The lady was keeping time with everybody, but she seemed lost in thought in a world of her own.

She darted from one to another strange sight, trying to get the visual gist of the jazz club, the furnishings, the people. She missed what the trumpeter said, probably the title of the next number. The opening sounded like piano and trumpet or saxophone, maybe both, definitely cymbals. It sounded like bells tolling. It was time to stop distracting herself. She closed her eyes and fell inward. Piano and cymbals, maybe the trumpet tolled again. "Slut." That's what they would call her. "Bastard." That's what they would call the baby.

She hated the way the saxophonist broke in, grabbed a turn, spitting out snatches of notes, each louder than the last, as if he had a chip on his shoulder. The first time it sounded defiant, maybe petulant, as if he couldn't have what he wanted, and was making a point of it. The second or third time she tired of it. Stop complaining. What is it you want anyway?

About big things in life, you are supposed to know. In advance. You shouldn't actually have to go through them in real life to find out what you don't want. Only a few months ago she had been sure she was called to religious life. She was looking forward to order and calm, time to think her own thoughts and develop her music, life with no husband to look after, no kids to tend. One night with Tony and all that was out. What was wrong with her? She missed a period and there she was dancing with him, playing with the idea of getting married and having a kid. Now she'd missed another month and marrying Tony seemed every bit as absurd as becoming a nun.

So much smoke had wafted onstage that, under the lights, the musicians looked like Michelangelo figures playing in Sistine Chapel clouds. The trumpeter and saxophonist were standing, hands at their sides. The piano dropped out. The drums faded. Lucius quietly strummed melody on the bass. There was no telling what would happen.

"'Moanin.'" The trumpeter introduced the next number. The piano intoned, the saxophone responded. They were talking to each other, tossing melody and its variations back and forth. They were pacing each other, rhythm and melody in one stroke.

All five players wore white shirts, charcoal gray slacks, and navy blazers, but each had adapted the outfit to his own taste. The saxophonist wore his jacket double-breasted and his shirt open at the collar, likely in concession to his obvious girth. He was very dark. Sweat glistened on his face and on his goatee. He stood strong and straight and when he drew a deep breath his belly shimmied. The toes of his shoes curled up and she saw a thick white stripe along the end of the soles where the polish and the leather had worn off. Too bad he couldn't afford new shoes. He slumped in a chair for a while, like a ragdoll that had lost its stuffing, but he kept tapping the beat.

Hold your horses, she said to herself. Sister Michaeline always tried to get you to stop jumping to conclusions. His shoes are worn down because he's tapping his feet.

The drummer was gray-brown. He had Clark Gable ears sticking out from the sides of his head. The pianist was the only white. His blond hair was straight and long enough that it fell over his forehead. His jacket looked like it had been thrown in the wash by mistake. Hair and tie bounced with the force of keyboard attack. He had the biggest hands she had ever seen.

The trumpeter was the one with the looks. He had huge Henry Fonda eyes and a fine nose. His mouth was fuller than a white movie star's but beautifully proportioned. His black hair was slick as a whistle with a part cut high on the side. He was much lighter-skinned than the saxophonist or the drummer. He wore his shirt open with wide cuffs and cufflinks. A red handkerchief flared in his jacket pocket. He had the slim angularity of a teenage boy. He was, as Dad would say, almost too good-looking for a man. When he bowed over his trumpet, eyes closed, he looked like he was in prayer.

She had looked closely at everything and everybody in the Jazz Emporium except Lucius. In every number she had listened for the bass. The thought of looking at him made her face hot. Why should she be ashamed? How could it be bad to carry a baby, give birth to a baby, simply because the baby's parents weren't married? The baby would be like her brother and sisters, the kids she babysat, all tiny babies. They can't do anything wrong or right. You can't judge them. The shame isn't about the baby. It's about her. But not about having sex before marriage, not about getting pregnant without a husband. That was wrong but wasn't the shame of it. The shame was that she took on the biggest responsibility of a lifetime and she wasn't able to deliver.

What a horrible way to put it, she said to herself. I can't deliver. I can't give my baby what it deserves, which is to feel that he or she is the most important person in the world. Not that the baby belongs to me, but that I will be there for a person who can breathe only when I breathe, eat and drink only when I do. How can I turn my back on somebody who depends on me like that? Whose little moves I will soon start to feel? I'm heartless. Ruthless. Brutal.

I've been kidding myself that I could put the baby up for adoption, disdainful of Tony when he said he couldn't stand the thought of somebody else raising his child. Tony was willing to let the baby live. I can't stand the thought of worrying every day for the rest of my life. Should I try to find the baby? Make it up to the baby? Explain to the baby that I was only a kid myself? I want to settle it once and for all, so I can tell myself there's nothing I can do about it, no need to worry ever again. For the baby it's life or no life. For me it comes down to escaping from worry. I'm a coward. No wonder I can barely look at Lucius.

Instead, she had been fixed on the trumpet player who, when he was not playing, sat on a chair on the stage across from her, dangling his trumpet between his legs. Glimmers of light blinked at her. The bell of the trumpet flared with light and the long shaft flickered like a lighthouse sending messages in Morse code. She wished Sister Michaeline would send her a message.

The music stopped and all around her people were standing, looking around, heading for restrooms. Lucius came down the stage steps, walked straight to her, and guided her by the shoulder to the foot of the stage. "You got to meet the guys. What do you say? Was it like you expected?"

"Better," she said, sounding to herself hollow and low, as if underwater. It took effort to look Lucius in the eye. The drummer was on stage laughing with the pianist.

"Mary Kaye O'Donnell, Kurt Olafsen. Kurt stepped in for Michael O'Leary and has been our piano man ever since."

Up close, his hair looked more gray than blond. "Glad to meet you, Mr. Olafsen." She was beginning to come back from the deep.

"The man on the drums is another old-timer, Billy Knight. That's Tubbs Hathaway over there on the sax." She nodded at the saxophonist, and waved in the direction of the drummer. As she turned she saw, at eye level, the trumpet player snaking his way toward her along the side of the stage. Long and lean, he moved languidly, making her think of Sister Michaeline's Michael: as if he had all the time in the world, confident that he would never have to break a sweat. He caught her eyes and held them.

She fell back into the deep, casting about for a life vest, seizing on her particular rendering of the story of Maureen and Michael. This was how Michael had walked, as if life held no struggle, as if he were free of the torment that besieged her, the mental weighing and measuring, sifting and sorting.

It was good that she had not flinched when she'd left Tony in the car, that she had not turned around and begged him to come into the club with her, that she was on her own to let real live jazz wash over her freely. These guys and their music and their freedom to make it up as they went along might help her to reclaim what Sister Michaeline had begun teaching her. Worry bled the life out of you. She had to stop worrying or she would lose her mind.

"Mary Kaye O'Donnell, I'd like you to meet Reymundo Conway."

Up close Reymundo's face had more angles. High cheek bones rose above his jaw, which squared off at the corners. She extended her hand. He bent her fingers inside his, bowed toward her, and pulled her hands to his lips.

"The pleasure is all mine," he said, and she thought from the way his mouth curled into a grin that they both knew that wasn't true.

She thought of a blackbird she had seen in Lincoln Park, in blinding sun, with a magnetic blue neck that looked emerald green when it turned.

During the second set she did not take her eyes off him. When he blew the trumpet he closed his eyes. She knew he was making it up as he went along. When he took his solos she was sure he was playing for her and her alone.

Reymundo drove her home in his black Jaguar. Lucius had looked surprised when they left together, but said nothing. She would have gone with him no matter what Lucius had said. He tuned the radio to a station that played Johnny Mathis. "Crosshaven, 1500 Sycamore Lane, between Sleeping Bear Road and Lincoln Boulevard," she had said when he'd opened the door for her. Beyond that, they drove the whole way without looking at each other, without making small talk, without so much as a touch.

At Touhy Avenue he cranked the window down all the way. The air was cooler than earlier in the evening, but it was still warm and close. The wind blew her hair into a tousle, having its way with the bouffant, as though it had never been sprayed tight.

She felt wrapped snugly by the wind, the heat, and the melodies of Johnny Mathis. At this hour, with the road to itself, the Jaguar flew, unencumbered by other people. She leaned into the curve at the Jefferson Avenue exit and decided it would be too soon to let Reymundo kiss her.

"Thank you, Reymundo," she said, as he pulled into the horseshoe drive.

"Once more, my pleasure," he said. "I'll be in touch."

Upstairs, in the dark, she dropped her clothes on the bedroom carpet, the red strapless dress and bra, the cream-colored half-slip, the garter belt and nylons. She didn't bother with a nightie. She wrapped herself in a sheet, praying that, if it were tight enough, she might hang on to the free feeling of being with Reymundo and the invulnerability she hoped she could borrow.

16

ON WEDNESDAY A linen envelope arrived, addressed to Mary Kaye O'Donnell. She picked it up at the mailbox in the lane, but did not recognize the handwriting. It was an ostentatious and firm hand.

She ripped the card out of the envelope and fingered the gold trim.

> *Meet me in the lobby of the Prudential Building*
> *June 27th, 4 p.m.*

There was no signature, but she was sure it was from Reymundo. She knew immediately that she would wear the white satin sheath that Mom had vetoed for prom because it was too low-cut. It was snug now, but she had time to let the waist out a bit. She tugged the emerald green waistband up under her breasts to give the dress more of an empire look. She had to practice walking in the three inch white leather pumps she had worn only at graduation. She might have tripped then, except that she had given herself extra room by wearing the full circle skirt under the gown. This would be trickier. The dress held her tightly at the knees so that she walked like a geisha girl, even in bare feet. The foot-long envelope purse matched the shoes. Maybe he would bring a flower. There was no place to pin one on the dress because the spaghetti straps were too thin but she could stow it inside the purse. She needed a hand free for whatever might happen.

Something had to be done about her hair. It was an unfamiliar feeling, but she wished she had a girlfriend to help. There had never been time for girlfriends, as busy as she'd been, taking care of kids. She brushed the curl out of her hair so she could rat it, or—as Aunt Nancy had once corrected her—tease it. Painstakingly, she lifted each lock of hair away from her head, pulled a tightly-toothed comb down to the scalp, then pushed and patted, smushed and molded it into the shape of a beehive, like Audrey Hepburn's in *Breakfast at*

Tiffany's. She pulled her hair up and pinned it on top of her head, tugging wisps out on the sides and wrapping them around a finger to curl. Mom called it the bedroom look. After weeks of worrying herself sick, it was a relief to be excited and just fuss with her hair. She hoped the height of the hairdo wouldn't make it harder to keep her balance.

About the Prudential Building she knew nothing, except that it was the tallest building in Chicago. Dad had promised to take the family for a view of the city from its rooftop, but never made good. She arrived early with the idea that she would need time to get her bearings, but Reymundo was already waiting at an elevator, the steel and chrome glister setting off his gray silk suit. In the light of day his skin looked creamier. His teeth gleamed. He was holding a single gardenia. Had she been wearing anything other than the white satin sheath, she might have let herself run to him. Not that she intended to play hard to get, but it was better that the skirt and the pumps held her back.

He handed her the flower and scooped her into an elevator, the express. The smell of the gardenia made her woozy and she held it behind her back. She was flooded by a dizzying champagne feeling, half elated, half sick, as the elevator shot up. When it stopped at the top, she was brought up short. She wasn't sure what it would feel like. Mom and Aunt Nancy always said theirs were unmistakable. She was too nervous to count the weeks. But she had thought it was too early for the baby's first kick.

An enormous circular ebony bar lay at the center of the rooftop. Brass on the top and sides of the bar made a circle so smooth that it was difficult to see where the bartender might get out if he wanted to. Waiters in tuxedoes ferried back and forth between the bar and one section of the observation deck, where groups of cocktail tables, also round and brass, clustered.

Reymundo spoke to the bartender directly, asking for "his usual." The bartender put flutes of champagne into their hands and sent double martinis to a table facing south over the city.

"Vodka, shaken, very cold. Ice from the shaker on the side," the bartender said, pointing to the table.

"You've got to see this," Reymundo said, steering her to the edge of the roof. "That's the Pittsfield Building, that's the Art Institute.

That greenery right there is Grant Park. Look all the way south. Over there, that's the Field Museum, the Aquarium. Even if you can't see it, say you do. That's what you do when you're at the top. Above everything."

She felt that bubbly feeling again. Could it possibly be kicking? In the fourteenth or fifteenth week?

All she knew about Reymundo was that he was Lucius's trumpet player and that he had been kind enough to bring her home when Tony had let her down. She had hated herself sitting alone at the Jazz Emporium and Reymundo had lifted her up. Whatever they wound up doing tonight would be OK. There was nothing to worry about but, if she were honest with herself, she was nervous. The guy was moving at a pretty fast clip.

She felt his eyes running over the sheath, the spaghetti straps, the fitted bodice with little silver spangles sewn into the front, the emerald green band under her breasts, the hipline that clung. His eyes raced back to the neckline. When she had bought the dress, even with the push-up bra, it had showed no cleavage, but in the last months her breasts had swollen. Standing in the sunlight, laughing with him, she felt them bobbing over the top. He put one foot on a low railing, cocked his knee, and leaned in close. She stared at the band shell in Grant Park and wondered if the building far away on the left was the Aquarium or the Field Museum. He lifted a single spangle. She had nothing to lose. Virginity was gone. She was already pregnant. She could do whatever she wanted and if she deliberately stood still while Reymundo looked down the front of her dress, there was really nothing wrong with that. He dropped the spangle back in place.

"You have the softest looking skin. I can hardly stop myself from touching you."

An electric thrill ran through her. She felt her nipples rise. She shifted from one foot to the other. "What a lovely tie. The black sets off your eyes."

He spoke so low and so softly that she found herself bending closer. He could have nibbled the spangles one by one. "You know Cliff Smalls? He did backup for Earl Hines. I know you know who Earl Hines is. Lucius and Earl go way back. Cliff had a number with Ella. They called it 'I Hadn't Anyone till You.' That's your song, Mary Kaye. I knew it when I first saw you. They say that once in a lifetime you meet your other half. You know it. How do you know it? You just do."

She pulled away. "For a guy named Reymundo, your English is awfully good."

"Great ear, love. My real name is Chuck. What were they thinking in Altoona, Pennsylvania? I go by Reymundo, but you can call me Rey. It sounds better for jazz. I tell people I'm a Cuban refugee, that I came over with Operation Pedro Pan. When I get through telling them about the mercy mission, I start on the Bay of Pigs."

"I'm glad you leveled with me. A girl can't be too careful."

He took her hand and led her back to the express elevator. She dropped the gardenia. "Leave it. I'll get another one. My mama always said, you meet the right girl, you got to treat her right. You and me, we got to be real."

The elevator door closed.

"This is such a silly thing to say," she said. "I took the train so I wouldn't have to worry about parking. I was wondering where you parked your car." She was nervous but did she have to sound like a lamebrain?

He stood behind her, his long, angled arms twisted around her waist, one finger fiddling with the folds of the band under her breasts. "Friend of mine, he's in the parking lot business. You see his lots all over town. He gave me a sticker. Not that I need it. I can leave my car about anywhere. I got a guy on the force who fixes tickets. My car gets towed, I call him. He takes care of it."

Tony had said the same thing about his dad's cars, but when Tony said it, he sounded cocky. Reymundo sounded self-assured.

"You seem to know everybody. You been here all your life?"

"Nah, just a few months. Doesn't take me long to figure things out."

"Then where did you grow up?"

"Who says I grew up?"

She laughed too hard as the elevator door opened. She could feel his eyes on her breasts. "I had to grow up fast. Always taking care of younger kids. I guess I never got to be a kid myself."

"You're sure no kid now, not the way you fill out that dress."

They walked hand in hand on Randolph, the lake breeze at their backs.

"Thought we'd take a cab over to the Pump Room. They've got a great old mahogany bar there. Slim makes a first-class martini."

"How'd you settle on the trumpet?" The cab screeched down Michigan Avenue, turned at Ontario and came up State Street. He had one arm around her shoulder and the other hand on her knee.

"Grow up. Settle down. You talk like an old lady. You're right, you are too serious. You need a fellow to show you how to let your hair down." One hand was feeling its way down her dress. The other was playing with the strap on her garter belt. "You ever been to the Playboy Club? Next time I'll take you there. The wave in your hair kind of reminds me of a bunny I ran into the other night. That's not all you have in common with that gal. You know the score. You know what I'm talking about."

At the stoplight, a car pulled up next to the cab. She pulled his hand out of her dress, but let him keep toying with the garter. It felt good and it was out of sight. "Be serious, Reymundo. I want to hear about your music."

"No, it wasn't that bunny, it was Jane Russell. You ever see her in *The Outlaw*? A miracle they released that movie, you know, problems with censors." He tipped the cab driver an extra five and the doorman opened the taxi door. "Welcome to the Ambassador East."

"I thought we were going to the Pump Room."

"This is the Pump Room. It's inside the hotel." He led her through the revolving door. "A good Catholic girl like you, what do you know about clubs?"

She knew that if she kept on pushing the revolving door, she could be back on the street in a flash. She could buy some time to think. "When I heard your name was Reymundo, I thought you might be Catholic too."

"I am Catholic. I knew you'd spot it."

They stood in the lobby. She raised her hand and touched his shoulder. "More than anything, I want to be a jazz singer. Tell me how you got to know Lucius, all that stuff."

"We've got the rest of our lives to get to know each other, sugar. That's not where we're at right about now." He led her through the lobby, past the entrance to the Pump Room, past the conversation area with the overstuffed sofas and brass chandeliers, past a couple making out on a tiny loveseat, to a bank of elevators.

All the way up in the elevator, she went over the story of Maureen and Michael in her head. Maureen knew she loved Michael from the moment she saw him walk across the room. He didn't walk like other people. He glided across the floor, as if he were sliding on ice. It looked effortless, the way he moved, how did Sister put it in her book, like hot fudge sliding down an ice cream slope.

Her thoughts whirred. There was no number on the door. Maybe that's how they did it with the penthouse. Maybe people who had money knew these kinds of things. She dropped into a pink swivel chair and started to cross her legs, but the sheath was too tight. She wound one ankle around the other, then, feeling silly, unwound them.

He threw his jacket over a chair and stood behind her, his hands massaging her shoulders. "You're driving me crazy, baby. You're the most beautiful woman I've ever seen."

She kicked off the white leather pumps, snagging a heel on the shag carpet. She stood, arms around his waist. He freed himself, knelt before her, tugged her half-slip down from under her dress. He stood, whirled her around and unzipped the sheath, whistling as he pulled the dress down over her hips, knees, and ankles. He gave her a push that she took to mean he wanted her to step out of the dress. He tossed it in a corner. He unhooked her stockings, rolled them down, and slipped them off, along with her panties and garter belt.

"You kneel down too. Unhook your bra and let it slip off. Yeah, that's how I like it." One at a time he cupped her breasts in his hands, licking, kissing, sucking them, going over every inch slowly with his tongue and lips. "The minute I saw you, I've been waiting for this."

She was breathing hard. He stood, unzipped his pants, and dropped them to his feet. The belt buckle clinked on the brass waste basket next to the chair. She closed her eyes, then opened them. It was OK to look. His legs were hairy and spindly. How could somebody so sure of himself walk around on hairy toothpicks? She wanted him to take off his shorts. He pitched his tie toward the dresser, unbuttoned and pulled off his shirt.

With Tony it had been in the car. Reymundo took her to the bed, which was good. She could hear his shorts sliding off. When it happened it wasn't all that much. He lasted longer than Tony but not much. It didn't hurt like with Tony, but it didn't exactly feel good.

She consoled herself that when she got to know him better, when he was playing trumpet and she was singing, when they were travelling and playing in Paris and Amsterdam, she would have other chances. Maybe a chance every night for the rest of her life.

He rolled off her. "I hope you're not going to get pregnant. Usually the ladies bring something or make you go out and buy it."

She sat up, stung, and pulled her knees under her chin. "I'm already pregnant."

He got up and leaned on the bed on the palms of his hands, squinting and scrunching up his face. She looked at him, nearly certain that he would feel sympathy for her, but not at all sure what his judgment would prescribe. She studied the inside of his left arm. A row of red dots ran toward his elbow. She wondered if he gave blood.

"Next time," he said, "I hope you'll have that taken care of."

"You're not serious, are you?"

"It's got to be just you and me, babe. Next time we're going to take it slow. Really get to know each other. It would spoil everything, thinking there was something between us."

She sat stunned.

Knees under her chin, she watched him pull on his shorts and socks, hustle to the chest of drawers for a fresh shirt, throw it on and button it part way up. "You take your time here, love. I got to get to the club. Where's my jacket? Lucius makes me wear that damned blue blazer if I'm going to play. He can't stand it when I'm late." He kissed her on the top of the head. "You shower. Take a nap. Do whatever you want. I'll be back late. Stay here tonight if you like. Or go home. Whatever you like. Leave your telephone number so I can call."

The latch on the door when it closed made the tiniest click. She sat on the bed staring for what seemed like an hour, but which turned out to be about five minutes. She ran water hard in the bathtub and fluffed the hotel bath gel into bubbles. She hid under the bubbles as long as they lasted, from time to time feeling on the verge of coherent thought. She did not know what to think. She did not examine too closely the idea that it could be the kind of thing that you looked back on after years of marriage and marveled how comfortable you were together, no pretense, no putting on an act for each other, right from the start. But she knew it wasn't what she had expected.

She dressed, staring at the blank TV screen. Garter belt, stockings, panties, bra, half-slip, sheath. One stocking had acquired a run. The sheath would not zip all the way to the top. She turned her ankle getting into the shoe that had got caught in the rug.

Once she was dressed, she called Jack to come downtown to pick her up. On the way out the door, she threw an unopened champagne bottle into the waste basket to see if it would break. When she hit the street outside, it seemed odd that it wasn't even dark. Jack would not have to tell her that it was time to check in with Sister Michaeline.

October 25, 1947. Saints Chrysanthus and Doria, martyrs, husband and wife buried alive in the same sand pit.

There is no right way to pick an apple. You follow the shapes of the trees. Some were low enough in the orchard today that I hoisted myself onto a branch and climbed from limb to limb, pulling off apples like dandelion tops, without thinking, slipping them into a canvas bag hanging from my shoulder. Sometimes I slung the bag over a branch and shimmied up a tree trunk, sat in a V at the center, reached in all directions willy-nilly, popping apples off like popcorn.

Some apples gave up their stems willingly. Others hung on for dear life to stem and leaf. One way or another, they all go into the same bin in the Motherhouse cellar. High in the treetops, leaves rustling, it was like the Jazz Emporium, breeze playing with my veil, sun blaring on my back, bark scratching the canvas bag like a snare drum brush. Heaven.

Then we rode the bus back. Tidy Wisconsin lodgings were sprinkled without plan around Kettle Moraine. By the time we reached the outskirts of industrial Milwaukee, the houses got in line. Sensible bungalows on reasonable lots. The closer we got to the Motherhouse, the more I felt the measuring rod.

The sight of the Motherhouse buildings gave me a shock. Not the facades, which seemed less imposing than they used to, but the scary-looking wrought iron fences, narrow black bars topped with pointy spikes. Sister A. is a sucker for Judy Garland songs. We sang "Somewhere Over the Rainbow." On the last verse I wondered how many bluebirds tried to fly over the rainbow and got themselves impaled on the wrought iron spikes.

Mother Isidore got her apples. The postulants got a gorgeous day out. Why do I put this in the Particular Examen?

I want time to stop. And that is wrong. We are not supposed to question what God sends us. Sister A. has told us that before we are received into the order in June, Mother Isidore will send us home for two weeks to say goodbye to our families. After that we'll be novices, cloistered at the Motherhouse for a year. I will do as I'm told, but if I had my druthers, I'd go back to the orchard and frolic in the trees. I am not supposed to have druthers, which is why on the best day in years this belongs in my list of offenses.

I don't want to go "home," whether that means Dubuque and my folks, or Chicago, Lucius, Bill, Bobby, and the guy they've got playing piano after Michael. I would unravel if I saw Benny.

November 1, 1947. All Saints Day.

While we were in the garden yesterday, saying the Rosary in procession, children in Halloween costumes ran and squealed past our gate. One was dressed in the habit of a nun. I forget how scary we can look.

November 4, 1947. Saint Charles Borromeo, cardinal, reformed the Church and slept on bare boards.

Standing in line for Communion this morning, I felt Michael with me. I brushed sleet from his hair and marched him to the polling place. We stood in line and I watched the water drops play on his eyelashes. I was too young to vote in 1936 but Michael hadn't voted either.

"Fess up, Maureen. You're here to make sure I vote for Roosevelt."

"Somebody had to get you off your duff. I can't believe you've never voted."

"You can't stand the idea something might be going on without you."

November 10, 1947. Saint Andrew Avellino repented for telling a lie in his work as an attorney and joined a religious order. When he returned in darkness from preaching in a downpour, rays of light emanated from his dry body to guide him home.

Sister Cornelius is an old buzzard and I am not sorry I said so. I did say it under my breath.

I finally told Sister A. about the accident. I had told Michael, but I never did tell my family. They never would have let me keep riding Pop Rieger's horse. I bought aspirin with babysitting money and scrounged from the medicine chest.

Here, I'm stuck with Sister Cornelius. She runs the infirmary, but she's not really a nurse. She had me running to the infirmary for medicine four times a day. Every time she saw me huffing and puffing, she clucked her tongue. A good nun does not call attention to herself.

Sister A. told the buzzard how I was by myself as a ten year old, riding Clover when he fell to the ground and rolled all the way over with me in the saddle. How I turned my neck the way he was rolling and tucked my head under his mane alongside his neck, prickly and wet on my cheeks, how the weight of him crushed my chest, how the roll was over in an eye blink, but I couldn't breathe even after he righted himself and went back to loping along, me still in the saddle, correcting my form, heels down in the stirrup, shoulders centered behind his ears, not able to breathe until finally my lungs didn't exactly expand, but the crushing pressure began to ease and, little by little, air coming through my mouth started to seep down inside.

Sister A. told Sister C. to give me a week's supply, twenty-one tablets, so I could take them when I hurt. This morning I tapped on the door of the infirmary, waited and waited, and started to walk away. Sister Cornelius pulled the door open with a scowl. When she saw it was me, she went back to her perch and tossed a small bag at me. I did say buzzard and I still mean it. Sister A. said Sister C. thinks I'm making up stories because nobody who was crushed under a horse would even be walking, much less spending the first three months of the postulancy with nary a peep and suddenly coming up with a tall tale, smelling of sainthood, insinuating that she had the fortitude and perseverance to go months in silence bearing that kind of pain.

I don't know why it hurts more. I wouldn't like to think it was climbing the apple trees. Maybe it's all the kneeling, the marble floors and wooden kneelers. Or the saggy mattress. Maybe it was riding in the bus over country roads. Or maybe I'm letting my guard down enough that I am starting to feel pain.

November 19, 1947. Saint Elizabeth, princess of Hungary, a widow with three small children, joined the Third Order of Saint Francis to devote herself to the poor and infirm.

A single crow stood like a statue under an elm tree. Our rosary procession disturbed her. She extended her neck as if to stretch, opened her wings, and took flight. I told Sister A. I am sorry I called Sister Cornelius a buzzard. My penance was to wipe down the infirmary. There were cobwebs in the corners, covered with dust. It's time I wise up. She's old. I think I'd rather die young than shrivel like her or my great-aunt.

December 8, 1947. The Immaculate Conception of the Blessed Virgin Mary, who was saved at the moment of conception from the threat of ever committing sin.

Another holiday celebrating Jesus' mother. We said the Litany of the Blessed Virgin. "Holy Mother of God, pray for us. Mother of Christ, pray for us. Mother of divine grace, pray for us. Mother most pure, Mother most chaste, Mother inviolate, Mother undefiled, Mother most amiable, Mother most admirable, Mother of good counsel, Mother of our Creator, Mother of our Savior . . ." I will make a litany of my own good things as a mother.

1) I did the most important thing anybody can do. I gave Gabriel life.
2) I carried him until he could breathe on his own and live outside.
3) I felt my blood bring him food and water. Keeping him alive kept me alive when I was dying of grief.
4) I was the first person to feel his bouncing-up-and-down energy, his round-the-clock joy.
5) I mashed his sweet potatoes and ground beef when I was falling asleep on my feet.
6) I found his bunny every time it fell out of the stroller.
7) I pushed him on the swings and caught him on the slide when I was so sad that all I wanted to do was drink cocoa and eat graham crackers with Grandma's jam.
8) I endured. Michael died but I stayed alive.
9) I taught him how to hand me the clothes pins, knob-side up, so he could help me hang the wash.
10) I held him tightly when we sledded down the embankment near the L tracks.
11) I told him about the smell of rain.
12) I showed him how to make bells out of hollyhocks.
13) I said "Atta-boy," even though he missed his mouth with the spoon.
14) I showed him how to blow bubbles. He couldn't do it. I said, "Don't worry, it will happen." But it never did.
15) I showed him the lion's mane and the tiger's stripes in his picture book. We never got to the zoo.

16) I got to hold him, but I would have liked to have held his daughter too.

I started this list so I would stop complaining, but it looks like that's something I cannot do.

December 13, 1947. Saint Lucy, virgin and martyr, died by the sword after refusing to renounce the faith and being set on fire, which did not burn her.

I love the stories that have come down to us about the saints. But I don't think we should take them all literally. They stimulate the imagination and help us distill some meaning, some inspiration. If they have been embellished a bit in the telling over hundreds, sometimes nearly thousands of years, so be it. There is something deeply satisfying in being part of a family of people who have lived and died—whatever the exact details—for the same belief in God and devotion to bettering life for His children.

New daily work assignment this morning, the kitchenette off Mother Isidore's study. It hurt finding a Whitman Sampler box. Was it one Lucius brought for me? What hurt most was seeing the empty columns and rows. The little white curves, the thin empty papers. Michael used to tease me that the only way I'd let myself eat a box of chocolates was if it had a map inside the cover, so I could count the columns and rows and figure out what was inside before I took a bite. Lucius would have reminded me, had Sister allowed him in.

I opened the box. The sin of curiosity. I wanted to know what happened to my chocolates. Not that I would have eaten one. I could not bear being on my knees in Sister's office again, as if I didn't know that nothing anymore belongs to me.

December 16, 1947. Saint Eusebius, bishop and martyr, exiled for defending the divine nature of Jesus.

My mother won't give Michael's books to the Motherhouse library. She thinks I'll come to my senses and leave the convent, not go home to Dubuque necessarily, but to Chicago and the Jazz Emporium to sing with Uncle Bill, Lucius, and Bobby, even though Michael is never coming back. Holding his books is not like holding him, which was the worst part of his death because when Gabriel was dying at least I held him in my arms, but when Michael died all I got to hold was the telegram that I know by heart: THE SECRETARY OF

THE NAVY REGRETS TO INFORM YOU THAT YOUR HUSBAND MICHAEL O'LEARY SEAMAN SECOND CLASS US NAVY LOST HIS LIFE IN THE SERVICE OF HIS COUNTRY ABOARD THE USS SIMS WHEN THAT VESSEL WAS TORPEDOED AND SUNK IN THE CORAL SEA NORTHEAST OF AUSTRALIA.

The bell rang for Michael in an explosion of silence, and that was that.

There is no one but God to talk to about Gabriel and Michael. I put myself in His presence. I start writing and the memories flood. I get deranged.

I know grief in all its shapes and colors. Fiery red grief with jagged edges. Why, why, why was Michael assigned to that destroyer? So many other men came back from the war. We had the wedding. I kissed him good-bye. I never saw him again.

I know the hollow sphere of black grief. I'm inside Gabriel's beach ball, shimmying up the curve and sliding down. No ledge promises a foothold. No window invites escape. No door opens to the other side. He's gone. There's only emptiness inside.

I know the dingy-brown watery grief that has no shape. It sucks everything inside. Lucius gave and gave and gave and gave. Everything he gave dissolved inside me. The only thing that sticks is hunger.

I know shallow grief, aluminum-gray and flat. I touch nothing. Nothing touches me. Days repeat themselves in stunned silence. Morning Prayer, meditation, Mass, Rosary, Benediction, Night Prayer. The seams are smooth. Nothing happens, which is fine with me.

I know the rusty-brown scabby patches of itchy grief. I scratch and scratch but everything keeps itching. The back of my neck where Benny dug in his fingers. The top of my foot where he tugged my shoelace. The inside of my knees where he clung to my skirt. The insides of my ears, "Go, go, go," when I stared into space and he pushed me to keep reading.

December 21, 1947. Saint Thomas the Apostle, to whom Jesus said, "Blessed are they who do not see and yet believe."

It is Advent. There is no conversation in the Refectory. Paula was ladling rutabaga soup at the head of our table. I tried to catch her eye and shook my head back and forth, as if to say, Easy on the soup for me. Good postulant, she never looked up. I cleared my throat. Still no response. There's too much onion in the rutabaga soup. It upsets my stomach. Yet I'm supposed to eat everything without comment. You would think I could do that, particularly since soup is the only thing we don't measure out for ourselves.

In desperation, I tapped the side of Paula's shoe with my toe, and made a sound, "Psst." I don't know which is the more serious infraction: trying to get Paula's attention or saying to myself what a dummkopf she is for missing my signals.

December 22, 1947. Saint Frances Xavier Cabrini crossed the Atlantic twenty-five times as a missionary, despite her fear of water, died in her hospital in Chicago, and was canonized last year, the first American-citizen saint.

Sister Augustine changed my daily work station again. No explanation. I am to clean a music room. I have a gift for music and am to take graduate courses in choral performance and composition. I am to make a mark for the Franciscans in liturgical music. Just like that, my dream of Holly Springs goes up in smoke. I came here to get away from music. I want to go on mission to the South. Maybe when I have learned liturgical music, Mother Isidore will let me go to Mississippi to serve the colored people. I want to atone for walking out on Benny and Lucius. Maybe Mother Isidore purposely put me where I would find the empty Whitman Sampler box. Maybe whatever I do, I will find my punishment.

December 24, 1947. The Vigil of Christmas.

In Saint Joseph's Workshop, I made an ornament to hang on the postulants' Christmas tree. There are workbenches in the Motherhouse basement with paper and glitter, boxes and icicles to cut and decorate. I picked up a cornmeal box, sawed off a few inches, and rocked it back and forth on the workbench. I must have stood there staring at the thing for fifteen minutes. It could have been a candle. It could have been a cradle. But the longer I stared at it, it could only have been Gabriel's Christmas rattle.

For his first Christmas, I made him a set of teething rings, snips of old socks braided into tiny wreaths, and a rattle out of an oatmeal box filled with lima beans, perfect for kicking. On Christmas Eve, Lucius came over and made oyster stew, except there weren't any oysters, so we made it with oyster crackers. He gave me a string of pearls.

"I can't accept these. They're too much. I would be happy with a card."

"But I wouldn't. Humor me, Maureen. See how beautiful they are, how they hug your throat."

"That's why they call it a choker."

"How come it's always a joke?"

But I wore them for Christmas dinner at Uncle Bill's along with Michael's citrine pendant. Aunt Beulah asked me where I got the pearls. I got flustered and said, "Don't worry. They're not real."

The bell rang in Saint Joseph's Workshop. Forty-five minutes down the drain. I'm not sorry, but when I tell Sister A. I will kneel on the floor and bow my head in contrition.

December 25, 1947. Christmas Day, the Birth of Our Lord.

The best thing about being in the convent at Christmas time is that there are no gifts to buy. We have nothing, so we have nothing to give. I hated shopping. Picking out things and hoping they would be right. How can you know what anybody wants? You pretend your way into feeling like other people and imagine what would make them happy. Good luck. People are either happy or not and there is nothing you can do about it.

My mother always insisted that she would be happy with anything I got her. I could always tell that she was not. I don't think she disliked the blue chenille bedspread I gave her last year. I think she was simply unhappy. If I had one piece of advice for parents it would be this: the best gift you can give a child is your own happiness. Otherwise, the little muffin is always worrying what has he done to make Mommy unhappy. A mother should do everything she can to please herself and to avoid doing things she does not want to do. If she is happy, the little one may have a fighting chance.

17

LUCIUS LIVED IN Hyde Park on the top floor of a three-story ivory brick building above the first of five entrances arranged around a grassy courtyard. The shrubs and gardens were as elegantly trimmed as Lucius himself. As he buzzed Mary Kaye into his building, she admired the late-June lilies and bustled up the stairs, singing "Bye Bye Blackbird" under her breath. The smell of herbs and baking bread filled the stairwell.

The door to Lucius's apartment was ajar. She pushed through, singing the first line of "Blackbird" in a big voice.

"Ever hear Sarah Vaughan do 'Blackbird'?" Lucius shouted. Off the hallway, in a black-and-white embroidered sport shirt and gabardine slacks, he stood at the stove in the kitchen, stirring a huge pot. "But first we're going to have lunch."

"Smells luscious," she said, smoothing the floral skirt on her sundress and looking at the art on the entrance walls. "We just saw this horserace at the Art Institute."

"Good eye, my lady. On your left is a print of Manet's *The Races at Longchamps*. The original is in the Art Institute. On your right is Cézanne's *The Card Players*. That's in London. My grandparents' blood pressure went down after I hung the prints. They gave me cash for this place, but they tied the money up so I could only use it for rent. At first, I thought they were joking when they gave me the prints, but they had the dope on me. They wanted my temptations to chastise me coming and going. Hey, I don't need to babysit this cassoulet. Let's have a look around."

Sunlight flooded the apartment, from the street in the sunroom at the end of the two corridors, as well as from the courtyard windows that lit Lucius's study, bath, and bedroom. The sunroom, a cozy bay area with windows on all sides, extended out toward the street. It had a maroon tile floor that set it off from the golden oak and Oriental rugs of the adjoining living room and dining room, which together spanned the width of the apartment. The ceilings were much higher than in the O'Donnell house. The kitchen and a tiny room with a bathroom were off the second hallway. Cheek by jowl with another apartment building, these rooms had almost no natural light. Their windows had thick bars and Mary Kaye could see the drop to a narrow gangway lined with garbage cans. Lucius did not mention which room had been Benny's and she decided not to ask.

The living room was dominated by an ebony Steinway, and, in a corner, a group of string instruments, including the bass, and a stereo set with large speakers. A black leather sectional sofa framed the fireplace. Open shelves on either side held sheet music. Bookshelves covered the far wall.

"Do you have a TV?" she asked.

"In the closet. I'll wheel it out for the World Series or if there's a presidential debate next year. Or the Kentucky Derby."

She carried the mixed greens and vinaigrette, along with bread and butter, to the dining room. Lucius had set the table with linen tablecloth and napkins, silver and china. He ladled the cassoulet into wide bowls and poured the rosé into crystal goblets. They sat down to lunch, Mary Kaye facing the sunroom and Lucius.

"I sipped beer when I was two years old, but I'm just getting started on wine," she said, spooning the cassoulet. "Delicious."

"I've kept learning about wine all my life, but it all builds on what Georges taught me. The age you are now. That's when everything makes an impression. Doesn't this beat plain old bean soup?"

She studied the art across from her on the dining room wall. "Is that the Rouault you told me about? The one you gave Maureen after Gabriel died?" A portrait, perhaps in charcoal. It had a luminescent blackness—set off by pearl and oyster grays—that gave it a power far beyond its small size.

"Actually, it's a copy. The hardest part was getting the tilt of their faces, parallel and close, his so small, hers so much bigger. *Mother and Child.* Where one ends and the other begins, that's always the question."

"But you have the original. Why would you make a copy?"

"I had to sell it, but that's a story for another time. Georges told me that in his late years he went back to copying Titian and Delacroix, the old masters. People think that to be original you have to dream something up out of nowhere. That's not how it works.

You need some talent, of course, but after that it's what you do with it. You copy and copy and copy the masters. For you it's been Sister Michaeline. Now I'm going to show you Sarah Vaughan. At some point—you'll feel it when it happens—you begin to improvise and your own style takes off."

"From my chair here I can see your Rouault, dark and brooding, and, in the sunroom, these airy pastels. They look like Degas' young women getting out of the bath."

"Exactly. I copied Degas' style. Those are all from the years after Maureen left for the convent."

She hesitated, then said, "It looks like you used different models."

"I guess you really want to know. I went through a phase where I was trying to replace Maureen. Blondes, brunettes, redheads. Some of them really took a liking to Benny.

"I was always looking for a win. Got that out of my system, not that gambling was much of an improvement. You would think that my faith, my art, my music would be enough. In my old age, I've decided I'll never get over losing my mother when I was five. My grandparents were great. The nuns were great. But inside is a terrible emptiness. Only thing that tides me over is a young woman's joy."

"Just so you know, I'm not interested in being a model for a portrait or anything like that."

"Of course not. I took that for granted."

"Me too, but I thought maybe I should make it clear."

Lucius stood up and started to stack dishes on a tray. "I've said this before. You and I are like Georges and me or like you and Sister Michaeline. I thought of that when I saw you leave with our trumpet player the other night. Maybe I should have stepped in to protect you. He's quite the ladies' man."

She flushed. Embarrassed, she turned her head and said nothing. Lucius knew. She saw it in his face. She bit her tongue lest she lash out with the first hurt reactions that sprang to mind: What's with all these white women in your life? And, why haven't you said a word all afternoon about your son, Benny, who should be your priority number one? Instead, she put her elbows on the table and cradled her face in her hands.

"Does any of us make sense, even to ourselves?" she said after a minute or so. "All the work I did on *Silent Spring* for the debates. I spent most of last year arguing that it was wrong to kill weeds along the highway with DDT. And here I am still not sure what I'm going to do with this baby."

Lucius set the tray down. "Easy now. In your own time, you'll know." She stood and he steered her into the living room toward the piano. "How about Sarah Vaughan and 'Blackbird'?"

Lucius scooted forward on the piano stool. She looked again at the copy of *Mother and Child*, gave Lucius a quick hug, and then walked toward the fireplace and started thumbing through sheet music. No wonder Lucius loves that charcoal, she thought. It's not just Sister Michaeline. It's his own mother.

"I'll play the record for you later, but first you got to get into your Sarah Vaughan mood. Give it a try. Like the punch in the first line as you were coming through the door. Play with it. Whisper it. Shout it. This song's been done to death, no pun intended. You can't make a mistake with it. Can't tell you how many times I told Maureen that."

She could hear the song in her head. She tossed the sheet music on a cocktail table.

Lucius turned back to the piano and scampered up and down the keyboard, warming up. "Skedaddle over here, Sister, before this train leaves without you."

They went back and forth, running through "Blackbird," a dozen or so times, each time Mary Kaye adding more spunk and more sass, each time Lucius shouting out encouragement. She dropped herself on the sofa. Lucius rolled the piano stool over.

He looked down and smiled at her. "What's on the table, kiddo?"

She leafed through the sheet music. "How about 'They Can't Take That Away from Me'? What you said before, that I can't make a mistake, makes me think of Sarah singing about singing off key. She actually sings that line off key. She's got the guts to do that. I'm trying to let myself be playful like that."

He scooted the piano stool back to the piano. She followed and stood beside him.

"It's all right to steal from Sarah," he said. "It's not only all right. It's what you do. Copying. Pick up a little from Ella, a little from Sarah. Not Billie Holiday especially. I've come around to Maureen's point of view on Billie."

"How come you keep Billie's picture at the Jazz Emporium if she's not one of the idols?"

He parked his hands on his knees and moved them back and forth, in and out. "I keep it there for Maureen. I still can't believe she's dead." His voice quivered. "After all those years she was back in my life, and then she was gone—just like that."

Mary Kaye handed him the score for "They Can't Take That Away from Me." He put his hand on her arm.

They ran through the song at the piano a half-dozen times, each time Lucius showing her how she could do more with her voice, accentuating a word, trying phrases differently from either Ella or Sarah, each time Mary Kaye trying to infuse new meaning by playing with timing and tone. She did steal Sarah's off key sound in the line about singing off key and added her own whimsy by slurping the "s" in the line about sipping your tea.

When they came up for air she stationed herself on the sofa. "I've got a question."

He dropped down next to her. "Shoot."

"I've been worrying. Sister Michaeline gave me her book. At first, I thought she had guessed I was pregnant and wanted to help me thrash that out. But maybe she knew I was wondering if I have enough talent for music or whether I should do something like history or journalism. Do I have what it takes to sing, you know, as a professional?"

"Sister Michaeline talked my ear off about you. She said she'd never seen anyone with your musical gift. It's not perfect pitch, but that doesn't matter. That's a technical thing. It's the way you grasp music. You hear a passage, the whole thing is yours. The words and the music, the tempo, the tone. What's behind it, what's under it. You get it on the first bounce."

"So you think maybe I could work at it and maybe—"

He stood up and folded his arms. "You'll have to work your fanny off. Like the rest of us. But I can't say it any clearer, kid. Whatever 'it' is, you've got it."

She squinted her eyes and frowned. It was OK to cry in front of Lucius. He handed her a handkerchief and she smiled. "My Grandma Mueller would have said 'work your keister off.'"

"And my Grandpa Claremont would have said 'break your skinny ass.' I can't tell you what my Grandpa Johnson would have said."

"Was it buns? Or butt?"

"You really think I wouldn't tell you that?"

"Was it rear end or fantail?"

"Nope. I'm not going to tell you."

"That's OK. You'll slip up and say it someday. But seriously," she said, shifting the sofa pillows, "why do you think Sister Michaeline gave me her Particular Examen book? It's almost like a diary."

Lucius paced in front of the sofa. "The book did come along when you needed it. But it's more complicated than that."

"Don't go all mumbo-jumbo on me. What are you talking about?"

He sat on the floor, stretching his legs the length of the sofa. "Have you wondered how she could've hung on to it all these years? You know the nuns don't have personal possessions. How much of that book would have been left if Sister Augustine or one of the superiors had gotten hold of it?"

"Lucius. Are you saying she didn't have it anymore? Did you lie to me?"

"Can't say I rushed forward with every detail. Sister Michaeline hadn't seen that diary since she was received into the order. She left it on my coffee table the day she went back to the convent. I was so busy saying goodbye to her, I didn't even notice at first. I always wondered whether she left it on the table because she was supposed to turn it in when she got back or if she was supposed to destroy it. I knew she didn't want the nuns to read it. I decided that she wanted me to."

"Don't tell me you didn't read it right then and there." She kicked off one shoe, then the other, and folded her legs under her, upright, ready for a story.

Lucius pulled a chair over. They sat face to face until she couldn't stand the silence.

"Come on, level with me. Remember the time I asked you if you knew the nuns kept the Particular Examen? You devil, I remember exactly what you said. You said, 'Nope. Can't say as I did.' I remember because that's how my grandfather used to talk."

"Which grandfather?"

"We're not joking now." She dug her fingernails into the sofa cushion. Her eyes prickled and her voice sharpened. She didn't know what to feel. "I mean, I didn't really believe that you never read it. That made no sense."

"I'm sorry," he said. He sucked his breath in hard and sighed.

"I guess this shouldn't surprise me," she said. "It's not that big a deal. What I want to know is why she asked you to give the book to me. She must have told you something. That's what I want to know."

Lucius rested his hand on her foot. "I'll tell you what happened. Pretend you're me. Sister Michaeline's talking and talking about this kid who's really good, who's thinking she might want to make a life in music. And then, just like that, Sister Michaeline's dead. I feel a responsibility to her. I want to do what I can to carry on what she's doing. So how'm I going to set that up? What would you have thought if I'd just up and approached you? What would your folks and the rest of society have done? Sister kind of introduced us. She kind of vouched for me in her book. How else were you going to check me out?"

"Wait, wait, wait a minute. You're not saying that it was your idea to give me her diary? You told me Sister Michaeline wanted me to have it."

Lucius pulled his legs up and rested his chin on his knees. "That was a fib. Sort of like 'Nope. Can't say as I did.' I couldn't figure out any other way to get to know you."

She was up now, marching across the length and breadth of Lucius' apartment. "That was no fib. That was a whopper. Don't you see that changes everything for me?"

He stood up and swiveled to follow her motion. "Listen to me, Sister, when you calm down, you might see that it doesn't have to."

"Don't you call me 'Sister.' Find some other nickname for me. Cook something up and see if I agree to it."

"So we're still talking."

"You bet, we're still talking." They stood facing each other, still. "Why didn't you just play it straight with me?"

"Too dicey. What if you'd just walked away?"

Part of her expected she would erupt in a Mount Vesuvius of outrage, a molten flow of accusations and recriminations that would incinerate the intricate lattice of bridges that she and Lucius had built between them. That would be how she would have expected to react. But anger did not rise. Nor did grief, though the thought that she had somehow lost Sister Micheline all over again came and went as a disembodied idea, flimsy, also without feeling. She was surprised that, aside from astonishment, what she mostly felt was curiosity and a certain amount of sorrow that, given the circumstances, a black man, realistically, could not have approached a white woman directly. These feelings had a life of their own. They weren't coming down via command central from some belief system about how she should behave. They were surprising her as they emerged.

"I guess you're right. I hadn't been thinking like that," she said. "So tell me about it now. I want to hear the whole story."

"Let's go back to the table," Lucius said. "Shall I make some more coffee or would you like a glass of wine?"

"In honor of Sarah," she sang, "Let's sip our tea."

"I've got a kettle I can use in the dining room. I'll be right back."

Lucius brought a crystal plate of chocolates along with the tea tray.

"These are Whitman Sampler's," Mary Kaye said, "but where's the map? It's like you know I don't need the map."

"I thought you'd get a kick out of that."

She plopped a chocolate into her mouth and sat back to listen.

"The biggest part of it was me being selfish. I clung to her book all these years. Read it over and over to stay afloat. I'd go back to my favorite passages when I needed anchoring. It was touch and go, until, miraculously, she got in touch with me when Benny was in the newspaper. There she was again, back in my life. I saw her every week. We talked like the old days. Then, out of nowhere, she was gone again. I was wiped out and belly up. You were the only person I could think of who could share her with me. I lost my world when she died. You can't bring her back. But you sure as hell bring her world back to me."

"Why didn't you tell me before?"

"I wanted you to react to her, not to me. I've held this stuff so close—gone round and round in my head, wanting somebody who knew her and loved her to react to what she said. I felt like if you had your own reactions to her, I wouldn't be talking to myself." Mary Kaye nodded as he spoke, in time with the cadence of his voice.

She stopped nodding and looked at him wide-eyed. "Ironic, isn't it? Up until very recently, I would have been devastated by the notion that it wasn't Sister's idea to give me her diary. But now it's different. I see through your eyes how she saw me. That doesn't take away from what I meant to her. If anything it confirms it."

"It's a relief to hear you say that. I didn't want to deceive you. But I didn't know what else to do. I feel better knowing that you know the truth. For yourself, of course, so you know what happened. But also so we can work together. Next time we'll meet at the Jazz Emporium. I want you to get used to singing there. Completely different acoustics. I'm going to send you home with 'Blackbird,' 'Take That Away,' and 'All of Me.' Let's see what else we can find.

"Oh, don't you know, I keep forgetting to tell you. Stan's guy went over Sister Michaeline's car and he thinks the crash was caused by mechanical failure. It looks like the power steering fluid sprang a huge leak. The steering wheel would have suddenly frozen in place. On the expressway—at that speed, with all those curves—she never had a chance."

"But does that mean it was definitely an accident? Couldn't somebody have tampered with it?"

18

THE FIRECRACKERS SCARED the horses and made them run faster, especially Lady, who was said to have been sired by the Lone Ranger's stallion. Mary Kaye had always known that there were dozens of white Arabian "Silvers" on the set when they were filming the show, but that didn't tarnish Lady's parentage. She and Dad always rode Lady and Diamond on the Fourth of July. They usually rode them so hard that the horses' coats foamed. That summer it would be dangerous for the baby. But then marriage, putting the baby up for adoption, abortion, all required actively deciding to do something she did not want to do. It might be easier if something just happened.

Lucius was right. Reymundo hadn't called. She had been such a fool to throw herself at him. It was one thing to loosen up, to give herself room to try new things, to set aside the rule book, to improvise, and quite another to do something that was just plain stupid.

Wearing tan jodhpurs and a white blouse with three-quarter sleeves and ruffles down the front, she sat astride Lady on high ground in the paddock. Taking the reins, she surveyed the O'Donnell Fourth of July picnic. The girls were playing croquet in the goat pasture while Nanny and Billie, temporarily staked to a crabapple tree near the horseshoe drive, baah-ed protest against their exclusion. Jack had abandoned the go-cart for the moment and was busy setting up the bar under the big oak tree behind the house. Mary Kaye hoped he would remember the gin and tonic that their father had said she could drink now that she had graduated. Another firecracker went off. Lady reared and neighed and stomped her hooves.

The lawn was nearly as green and plush as Dad demanded. She and Jack had been watering the grass nightly and digging up the crabgrass. But, here and there, she had spared some clover. If there was time after slot machines in the garage with Jack, badminton with the girls, and cranking ice cream with Mom, she would look for a four-leaf clover.

Jack set off a giant ear-splitting Roman candle. Mary Kaye struggled to hold on to the reins as Lady reared high again and again, backed against the stable gate, snorted, and hoofed the earth. She hung on tightly as Lady tore out of the paddock, broke into a canter, then a gallop. Ahead, she saw Diamond pounding over the sun-baked pasture, Dad bouncing in the saddle, careening from side to side. Dad had lost his stirrups. His reins and hands were wrapped around the horn of the western saddle. He was fighting to stay on the horse.

Meggie had run between the pond and the pasture, yelling, "Stop, Jack. You're going to get Dad killed."

Mary Kaye felt a familiar combination of alarm and impotence. If Diamond managed to brush her father off against the side of a tree, Dad might crack his skull against a tree root or the hard earth. But if she rode in to intervene, the horses might start to fight with each other. She had been through it before, Lady rearing back, her legs high in the air, using her hooves like claws, dropping her full weight wherever she could land a blow on the other horse. Diamond had his own, less elegant tactics to outmaneuver Lady. While her front hooves were in the air, he could move his rhinoceros-like middle and push and press her rump against a tree.

Mary Kaye gave Lady her head and galloped through the Queen Anne's lace toward the walnut grove. There was Diamond, rearing and bucking, scraping against one tree after another. She prayed to Saint Jude. She wished she could promise God that if He got Dad out of this spot alive, she would keep the baby. But she could not.

Dad hit the ground head first, a good yard away from any tree. He flopped over and lay still until Mary Kaye had dismounted and stood over him. He opened his eyes. She knelt and took his hand but he pulled his knees up, feet flat on the ground.

"I'm going in, doll," he said. "This old horse needs a drink."

She extended her arm but he didn't take it.

"I'm all right, I'm all right. Don't go telling your mother. She'll make a federal case out of it."

Mary Kaye stepped back. She had been thrown off by Lady any number of times and she knew the shame of it.

"I'll keep an eye on you. First sign your pupils are dilating, we're off to the emergency room. Deal, Dad?"

"Deal. Now get back on your horse."

"You sure? I'd feel better sitting here with you and Diamond." Not ten feet away, Diamond was munching prairie grass, the bit in his mouth clinking against his teeth. That's why Jack loved Diamond. The horse could buck you off and stomp on you, but he never left you. Mary Kaye thought that was not necessarily an asset. She would have preferred that the horse run back to the paddock. Somebody might have come to help.

"They see Lady charging back without you in the saddle, they'll all know something's up."

"OK, Dad," she said, her foot in the stirrup, ready to mount. She waved to Judge Engelmann, who was working the vegetable garden behind his house.

It was a relief to see Dad mount Diamond and canter away, looking generally intact. Maybe she should go back to the stable before Dad unsaddled Diamond. If she were determined to have an accident, she could ride Diamond until he brushed her off against a tree. But what if she had to go to the emergency room? There would be no way to hide her condition from Mom and Dad then.

Trotting back to the stable, she eyed the sea of hot pink sunflowers with dark orange pin cushion centers, shining like jewels in the late afternoon light. Pop Mueller had cleared the pasture of weeds the year he lost his pointer finger in a lawn mower, but prairie grasses had sprung up. Someday, if she ever got married, she would want prairie flowers at the wedding, but not these Chinese red delicate flowers on tough stalks, knee-high plants topped with gnarled knobs. They looked as disapproving as Grandma O'Donnell.

Through the trees she saw flashes of black and chrome, a black car parked in the west end of the horseshoe drive, too long to be anything but a limousine. It had to be one of the Marcianos.

She'd heard that Angelo Marciano had once sent his restaurant manager's wife a hand in a Christmas tin. "He'll be home by Christmas," the card read, "one way or the other." She knew the story was true, because Tony had told her that the manager had been caught with his hand in the cookie jar. She rode Lady from the pasture into the paddock and saw a black sedan parked next to the limo. Just what she needed. It was definitely Angelo Marciano and his men.

19

"YOU'RE OUT OF your mind, Angelo. She would have told us." The scorn in her mother's voice cut through the thick air. "I don't know why we're having Fourth of July in the yard for anybody and their uncle to drop in. It's hot as hell out here." Dressed in white capris, a low-cut sleeveless blouse in a leopard print, a short strand of pearls, and brown leather sandals with pearls on the straps, she was plunking down the last of nine china plates. Potato salad in a Waterford bowl, three Wedgewood trays of raw Porterhouse steaks, ketchup and mustard in cut glass bowls, Caesar salad in the silver bowl, mounds of berries and watermelon slices on a silver platter. Dad insisted it wasn't the Fourth unless they had a cookout. Mom insisted they do it with class.

"Ask her yourself, Aggie. She's right behind you." Marciano flicked ashes into the impatiens that ringed the oak tree and tossed his cigar into the grass. He coughed and spit at the base of the tree. The sleeves on his red and yellow Hawaiian shirt were too short.

Mary Kaye had seen Tony's father at his kitchen table in a T-shirt, balancing a baby on one knee and a glass of Chianti on the other. The Hawaiian shirt was an improvement. He had never addressed her, unless she counted pinching her fanny or whistling as she walked past. She could see the huge, round, golden face on his watch, which showed not only the time, but also the days of the week and months in the year. He kept track of everything.

His hands were enormous, wide palms and stubby fingers almost webbed together like a baseball mitt. She wondered why he didn't wear a wedding band and how he managed the weight of his two pinkie rings, one emerald, one sapphire, each surrounded by diamonds, impressively sized in their own right.

Dad arrived from the kitchen, dapper in white pants, an emerald green linen shirt with the sleeves rolled up, and white boat shoes, Manhattan in hand. "For God's sake, Aggie, would you sit down and stop yelling. Have a seat, Angelo. Jack, over here, get Mr. Marciano a Manhattan. Looks like you've had enough for now, Aggie. Now Angelo, what can I do you for?"

Marciano pulled a lawn chair over to the picnic table, lifted his Panama hat, ruffled the banana leaves, and dropped the hat over Dad's dinner plate. "I'll have a shot of Chivas Regal."

"Yes, sir," Jack said. "I'll be back in a jiffy."

Aggie sighed loudly and sputtered, "Mary Kaye, Angelo here seems to think you're expecting. How about you straighten him out for us, sweetie."

Mary Kaye took her time situating her riding helmet on the picnic bench and laying the riding crop alongside it. She carefully tucked the black cord underneath.

"How about you relax, Aggie. Let the man talk. He's come over on the Fourth of July, he's a guest in our house, let's hear what he's got to say."

Two very large men got out of the black sedan and stationed themselves in front of the limousine, arms folded across their barrel chests.

"Your daughter seems to think she's too good for my son. I expect you'll talk some sense into her."

Jack approached, and Dad said, "Put that bottle right here, Jack. You and the girls go to the garage and play the slot machines."

Marciano downed one shot of Chivas Regal, then another. "Unless, of course, she's been sleeping around and there's some question as to exactly who is the father."

Aggie gasped, picked up her copy of Mary McCarthy's *The Group*, and fanned herself. "Go with the kids, Bernie," she said, slapping the Saint Bernard on the rump.

Bernie raced around the table, huffed and puffed, and stopped at Marciano's feet. Slobber drooled on Marciano's shoes.

Dad grinned. "We got a real working family here. See? Bernie's already busy shining shoes."

"Well, that's what we are now, Frank. We're family. Right here around your table are three of the four grandparents of the baby this little lady is carrying. Next time, we'll have Marie and Tony join us."

Mary Kaye felt his message coming in waves, the way Lake Michigan looks when you're standing on sand and the colors go from tan, to green, to aqua, and then from blue, to violet, to black.

Marciano looked intently back and forth between her mother and father. "There's a lot we could do for your business, Frank. Now that we're family. You can't refuse family. You know that. Mary Kaye and Tony are just kids. We're the sensible folks. We got to take this in hand and do right by our grandchild. You know that's what God asks of us, Aggie. We're not going to stand by while they give our grandson to some riffraff, probably not even Catholic, total stranger. He's got to grow up with his own family." He picked up his Panama and dropped it back on his head.

Dad raised his empty glass. "Look here, Angelo, I'm not entirely up to speed, but I'll tell you without a doubt, nobody's giving away my grandbaby, not so long as I'm head of this family. You have my word on that."

Marciano clinked his glass against Dad's. "I knew I could count on you, Frank. You're a reasonable man." He waved to his driver. He did not say a word to Mary Kaye, nor look at her. Before he got into the back seat of the limo he turned and waved as if he were JFK, standing at the top of the steps on Air Force One on his way back to the White House.

She closed her eyes as the limo and sedan screeched out of the horseshoe drive.

20

DAD WAITED TO explode until Marciano was off the property. "You shit-for-brains, dumb-ass broad, don't you ever put me in a spot like that again! I didn't come all the way from Storm Lake, Iowa to sit on my own lawn and listen to a two-bit Al Capone make a fool out of me. What've you got to say for yourself?"

Mary Kaye shrank like a gull sinking in Lake Michigan sand, beached in high winds.

"You got nothing to say?"

"I'm thinking, Dad. Give me a chance to think."

"You're thinking, are you now? It's a little late for that. You want something to think about? I'll give you something to think about."

He stood. His face reddened. His eyes flared. He seized two corners of the tablecloth and threw it in the air the way you shake out a blanket when you make the bed. Crockery and cutlery and the wedding crystal rained on the lawn. The big Waterford bowl hit the oak tree on the way down, dumping potato salad on the ground. Caesar salad slipped in clumps from the picnic bench and the ducks ran in to pirate the lettuce. A squirrel scampered over the potato salad and stopped at Dad's shoes, which were dripping ketchup.

Blueberries, raspberries, and strawberries were everywhere in the grass, salted with chunks and slivers of crystal. Bernie wolfed down some steak and dragged a Porterhouse toward the woods.

Mary Kaye ran after him. "Oh, no, he's bleeding."

She followed him into the woods and knelt to check his mouth. Even in the dimness, she could see that what she had thought was blood was actually ketchup. She pulled her riding boots off and sat until she stopped heaving and trembling. She wished she could lie down on the cool forest floor and cry and sleep until whatever was happening had happened. But instead, she stood and made her way back toward the lawn.

Her parents sat facing each other, the Chivas Regal between them.

"Is Bernie all right?" Dad called as Mary Kaye walked toward them, hanging her head, staring at her bare toes, watching for shards of glass. The closer she got to Mom and Dad, the further away she felt.

By the time she reached the table, Dad had already shifted gears. He was laughing. "Sit down darling, no, over here next to me." He patted the picnic bench and waved her toward him. "We'll figure this out. You know I don't like surprises. Why don't we bring the goats over and let them clean up this whole mess? Hell, why not bring out the Fourth of July cake and let the goats take care of everything?"

"No, Frank. Half the crystal in the house is all over this lawn. You are not going to bring the goats over. The poor things will choke on it."

"Shows what you know. Goats'll eat anything, bless their hearts. I'll buy you new crystal. What kind do you want, Aggie? Just say so, you know I'll buy it for you." He paused and turned to Mary Kaye. "What I can't figure out is when was you gonna tell me and Mom about your condition. We don't know what's flying. How do you think that makes us look?" He poured a Chivas Regal for Mary Kaye.

"Mom, Dad, I didn't know what to do."

Dad stopped her right there. "What you do, goddamn it, is come to your parents. Who the hell do you think would wind up paying for a baby? Who does that dirty rotten Dago think he is, coming over here and telling me how it's going to be in my family? I'm the boss of my family. I'm the one who makes the decisions."

"I know, I know," Mary Kaye whimpered, her voice cracking, much weaker than she had expected.

"You're not thinking right," Mom said, reaching across the table and taking her hand. "All those A's in school don't amount to anything. A guy gets you in trouble and then proposes, you say 'yes,' for Christ's sake. You ought to know that." She dropped Mary Kaye's hand and pulled a package of Kools out of the pocket of her capris.

"I thought you quit, Aggie. Didn't I tell you there's nothing worse than a cigarette hanging out the side of a woman's mouth? It's not feminine."

"Won't you light it for me, Frank? I'm too upset." She turned. "Mary Kaye, you've got to get married. If you don't, you'll ruin your whole life. You've already disgraced your family."

Mary Kaye covered her face with her hands, bracing for the next salvo.

"No, no, no. Use your head, Aggie. Your daughter is right on this one. She is not going to marry Tony."

Mary Kaye tried to punch up her words to make them sound determined. "There's a lot I haven't figured out yet, but there is one thing I know for sure . . ." Her throat caught. She took a breath and tried again. "All I know . . ." Air rushed in and her chest heaved. Tears ran down her cheeks and she choked out what she could. "I'm not . . . going to . . . be able to"—This was as good a time as any to make a run for it—"hold a baby in my arms and see whose hair she got and whose nose . . ." She doubled over and held her middle, wracked with tears. She moaned. "What am I going to do? You guys have got to help me."

Had she really asked her parents to help her? More than anything else, this told her how much trouble she was in.

They sat quietly.

"Sure as hell hope it wouldn't be the Marciano nose," Aggie said. "The whole lot of them look like prizefighters."

"My point, exactly," Dad said.

"Well, we'll have to live with it. She's got to marry Tony."

"Get with the program, Aggie. No way are we gonna get mixed up with the Marcianos. It's out of the question. They've got no class."

For weeks, Mary Kaye had been trying to figure out by herself what to do. It was as if she had stationed herself in a lighthouse far out at the farthest end of the farthest harbor in Lake Michigan. It had been a treacherous expedition.

Now she certainly was not alone. She was hurt but unsurprised that her parents spoke only of themselves and the disgrace. But on the practical side, they were sometimes pretty good with ideas, and, once in a while, even followed through. She felt stupid and foolish and exhausted, but she was also feeling . . . relief. Her parents were with her. They did love her, more than she liked to admit.

"Say something, Mary Kaye," Dad said. "Come on, honey, give it a shot."

"Where does this leave me?" Her voice sounded hollow and far away. She cleared her throat, trying to warm up. "I can't get married. I can't have the baby." She choked up. "Maybe I should go back to the pasture and saddle up Diamond. He brushes me off on a tree and we'll all be happy."

Dad put his arm around her and pulled her tight. "You're not going to do nothing stupid, sweetie. None of us are, if we can help it. We got to sleep on this one."

"What about the kids? I don't want them to know I'm in trouble."

"No need to tell anybody unless you want to," Mom said.

Mary Kaye nodded. She was too tired to do anything but sleep.

21

JUDGE ENGELMANN'S HOUSE was taller than the O'Donnells', stucco and painted white, capped with a tower where he operated his ham radio. The windows had royal blue awnings, and, before he had taught Mary Kaye how to operate the radio and send signals in Morse Code, she had wondered whether the awnings were for show. Once she'd gone inside, she had realized that they protected his late wife's linen and silk upholstery from the sun. Nothing about Judge Engelmann was for show.

The judge was tall and skinny. The following day, as she climbed over the pasture fence and headed toward his house, Mary Kaye wondered whether the criminals who stood before him in court thought about—as she had with Sister Michaeline—what lay under the long robes.

It was long past time to confide in Judge Engelmann. He knew what to say and what not to say. He had taught her about radio silence. Sometimes, like right after the Japanese had attacked Pearl Harbor, you didn't broadcast, not simply because the enemy would hear the content of a message, but because they could trace the origin of your signals. Give away your location and you give them a chance to destroy you.

She surveyed the O'Donnell property from Judge Engelmann's side porch. The house seemed smaller, even slight. From this vantage, the horseshoe drives looked like paths for the tracks of a toy train set. She knocked at the door and tugged at her fire-engine red shift, one of two outfits in her closet that still fit over her middle. Judge Engelmann, of course, would see that she was showing. He didn't miss a thing.

The door opened. "You recovered from the festivities?" His salt-and-pepper mustache stayed in place over a deadpan mouth.

"Yeah, right," Mary Kaye said. "Bet you're surprised to see me."

Inside, the kitchen table was covered with newspapers. From Judge Engelmann she had learned that there was always another side to a story. He subscribed to the Chicago papers—the *Tribune, Sun-Times, Daily News,* and *American*—but he read out-of-town papers too, the *New York Times, Washington Post,* and *Los Angeles Times,* which he bought at a newsstand in the Loop. He took off his glasses, folded the *Tribune,* and pulled out a chair for her. "Coffee? Doughnuts? Glazed ones, the kind you like."

"I've got a legal question for you. Strictly hypothetical." She pulled the chair closer under the table and gave up trying to control the shift. "If a woman wants to put a baby up for adoption, is there any way anybody could stop her?" She looked around the kitchen. Judge Engelmann had left almost everything in place after his wife died, but a silent clock, which needed re-winding every eight days, had replaced Mrs. Engelmann's intrusive cuckoo clock.

Neither of them spoke for several moments.

"I'll skip the coffee," Mary Kaye finally said. "I've already got the jitters."

He walked over to the tap, ran a glass of cold water, and brought it to her. "If I'm not mistaken, that was Angelo Marciano's car in the driveway yesterday."

A sip of water caught in her throat. "It *was* Marciano's car, but how did you know that?"

"Hard to miss—the black Imperial limo, the entourage in the Buick. I know the license plate. He's a household name at the courthouse. He makes no attempt at camouflage."

"You've seen him at the courthouse?"

"Off and on. Mostly penny-ante stuff. He doesn't pay a parking ticket without a battalion of lawyers."

"Anything big?"

A sparrow landed on the outside window sill, thumped its head, and nestled against the glass.

"Yeah," Judge Engelmann said. "He got pulled into it when a guy escaped from Joliet, a guy they said was working with a fence."

She kept her eye on the sparrow. Taking refuge in her system. Trying to contain for the moment the startling thought: The escapee from Joliet, the guy working with a fence, could that be anyone else but Benny? She had to take in what the judge was telling her and piece together any Marciano-Benny-Sister Michaeline links later.

"Marciano's in a regular revolving door," the judge continued. "They call him in to testify, but nothing seems to stick. You can't put somebody in prison because you've got a feeling they're guilty or because you think they might be connected. I'm going to make a wild guess. Any chance he's connected to your hypothetical question?"

The sparrow had flitted away and come back to the window sill.

"For the sake of argument, let's say he is. What I want to know is, could the law stop him from getting in the way of an adoption?"

"You want the short answer?"

She nodded. She could feel her face reddening. She was fighting tears.

"Your question's not really a legal one."

"How can you say that?" Her voice was shrill. "They must have laws for this stuff. To protect somebody who has to put her baby up for adoption."

Judge Engelmann poured himself another mug of coffee and stacked two doughnuts on a saucer. With the tip of his finger he picked up a little crust of sugar glaze that had fallen on the table and popped it on his tongue. "Yes, of course, there are laws. But, when you're talking about Angelo Marciano, that's not what you're talking about. If I tell you something in the strictest confidence, can you promise me you'll keep it a secret?"

"Yes, of course, I will. I don't tell anybody anything we talk about."

"Yeah, I know that. But this has to be really, really confidential. When I saw that car tear out of the driveway yesterday, I said to myself, why on earth would Angelo Marciano be paying a visit to the O'Donnells? I thought it wouldn't be smart of me to say anything to you, but here you are now, sitting at the kitchen table looking as forlorn as I've ever seen. You're holding it together, Mary Kaye, you always do, and from what you've told me you've had quite a lot of practice. But you've got to be in over your head, kiddo, and I'm going to go out on a limb to help you."

He reached behind to the counter and dropped a box of Kleenex in front of her. Through her tears she saw a blur of lilies and greenery twisting and turning on the box. She mopped the tabletop with a tissue, dabbed her cheeks, and rested her face in her hands.

She was sobbing. "I don't know what I'm going to do."

"I don't either, but I'm going to tell you something that happened to me right before Easter. You do with it what you will. It's about somebody who's very important to you. I had not met her before, but I knew about her from you. You can't tell anybody because I haven't decided what I'm going to do. You know, sometimes you're better off in radio silence."

She could barely sit still. She was squirming in the red shift, taking shorter and shorter breaths, which made her feel light-headed and made the shift feel tighter and itchier. "Judge Engelmann, I swear, I'll never tell anybody whatever it is you tell me."

"OK." He patted her on the shoulder, took a deep breath, and handed her a wad of Kleenex. "You sure you're OK?"

"I can listen." She opened the Kleenex and spread it flat, lining the long side up along the edge of the table, rolling and unrolling the tissue, pulling herself together, as he spoke.

"In April, Sister Michaeline came to see me in my chambers. She knew I was the sentencing judge for the guy I was talking about before, the escapee from Joliet."

This was shocking news. So shocking that it took a few moments before she began to grasp what had just hit her. Sister Michaeline had regularly encouraged Mary Kaye to deepen her relationship with Judge Engelmann. And, when Mary Kaye had doubts about Tony, she had urged her to stay with him and to "get a taste of what grown-ups do." But she had never mentioned that she knew, much less had any tie to Marciano or to Judge Engelmann. Since her death, of course, Mary Kaye had been looking less and less to Sister Michaeline for guidance and more and more experimenting with her own take on things. But this revelation was still a powerful blow. It felt less like disillusionment than a kind of betrayal.

She nabbed another Kleenex and twirled it, one end to the other, into a tiny, twisted rope. "I'm reading Sister Micheline's book. It's sort of like a diary. This guy's father gave it to me after she died. His name is Lucius and he's Benny Claremont's father. I've gotten to know him pretty well."

Judge Engelmann raised his eyebrows. He pulled a doughnut in half, and bit off one end. "You don't say! You always told me Sister Michaeline encouraged you to confide in me. Then she turns up asking something from me. Now the father of the escapee gives you her diary. Somehow that does not feel like a coincidence."

"Are you saying Sister took me under her wing just to get near you? Do you think she pushed my relationship with Tony just so she could find out about the Marcianos? Saying this out loud makes me feel sick."

"I'm not surprised you're stunned. But if that was part of what she was thinking, I doubt it was her only reason, much less her primary reason. People are always looking for a single motive. In my experience, people rarely do things for just one reason."

"I guess I'll have to deal with reality, but this is going to take some time to get used to. Lucius says Sister Michaeline delighted in nurturing my talent."

"Would that be any less true," the judge asked, "if she used you for her own purposes as well?"

"The way I looked up to her. She was my model for just about everything."

They sat in silence for what felt like a long time. Her thoughts jumped from one thing to another and landed where Mrs. Engelmann's cuckoo clock used to sit.

Finally, she said, "So what, exactly, did Sister Michaeline tell you?"

"You OK? You ready for this?"

"Yep. Shoot."

"Sister Michaeline told me this kid was taking music lessons with her in the nuns' prison ministry and asked me to go to bat for him. She said Marciano had drawn him into his crime ring and that the kid was willing to testify in exchange for protection."

Judge Engelmann leaned back and rocked on the legs of his chair. She wondered how he could balance without hanging on to the edge of the table. "What struck me was how upset she was. I've seen desperate people in my day, but she took the cake. She was stumbling over words, scared stiff, hysterical. She was so angry she was shaking."

"Well, Sister Michaeline was more than Benny Claremont's music teacher."

"What makes you think that?"

"Lucius Claremont and Sister go way back. To before the war, when they were in a jazz band together. I guess she didn't mention that."

"No-sir-ee-bob, my friend, she did not. Well, well, well. How about that. That's the last thing that would have occurred to me. Lutherans know about nuns too."

Softening, Mary Kaye said, "So you're Lutheran. I guess I was scared to ask." She nibbled on the end of the doughnut, glad to know what kind of Protestant he was.

"Well, what do you know?" he said. "This news puts things in a different light."

She could feel the color coming back to her cheeks and the flush under her eyes. "You don't think Marciano was mixed up with Sister Michaeline's death?" She tossed the doughnut end from hand to hand. "Or, do you?"

The judge went to the refrigerator, looked inside, and closed the door. He glanced at the clock. "It's too early for lunch, I suppose." He went back to his chair. "From what I hear downtown, they think her death was an accident. But who knows?"

"Lucius said the steering fluid sprung a massive leak." She walked over to the sink and refilled her glass. "But he also told me that she was on her way home from seeing Benny when she died. Maybe seeing him was too much. In my book, either one or both of those things would be a pretty good reason why she might've crashed the car."

The judge nodded. "Could be. As far as the steering fluid goes, I suppose Sister Michaeline might have gone to see Marciano, like she came to see me. She was definitely on a mission. He might have taken action. But this is all speculation.

"I want to go back to what I was saying before. I told you my story about Sister Michaeline to show you what kind of man Marciano is. If you're thinking he's not the man you'd want for your father-in-law—and even if you didn't get married—your baby's grandfather, I'd say that's good thinking."

She rested her hands on the table and listened intently as the judge spoke.

"When you think about raising a child, everybody knows the importance of a good mother. I think nowadays the need for a good father is under-rated. It's almost as though men went from having one job—fighting the war—to having a different job—being the breadwinner. A father needs to be much more. Good fathers instill in their children the confidence to become their best selves. Look how your father does that for you, Mary Kaye. Fathers can also be a strong moral compass, a guide on how to treat other people, an inspiration of fortitude and strength."

"I should think more about fathers," she said. "You know me, I'm used to collecting evidence and organizing it logically. If this, then that. The conclusion is inevitable. I've drawn charts showing every possible implication of all the outcomes I can think of. But the charts don't lead anywhere because so many other people are involved and they are all wild cards—Marciano, Tony, my parents, adoptive parents. Not to mention the baby. Could I bear it if someday my child tracked me down and asked me why I gave him or her away?"

The judge fiddled with his glasses. "The sixty-four-thousand-dollar question. How do you give somebody what they need and still take proper care of yourself?"

She blew air from her mouth as if she were blowing up a balloon. "I met Benny in prison. Lucius took me to visit."

"Really? I'm surprised you didn't come to me."

"I've been too wrapped up in my own stuff, reading the diary, wondering if there's a message in it for me." She was quiet for a moment. "Sometimes people don't have it in them to give a child a fighting chance."

"Of course you're thinking that," the judge said. "It's written all over you. Are your parents behind you?"

"My dad will be."

"Take your time. You know you can be impulsive."

"When I know what I have to do, but I don't want to do it, I do it fast. Otherwise, I lose my nerve. I get scared I'll do nothing."

Judge Engelmann chuckled. "Not much chance of that."

January 11, 1948. Feast of the Holy Family: the Virgin Mary, Blessed Joseph, and Jesus.

I know what I'm supposed to feel. I can't make myself feel it. I don't miss Benny. The last thing I want to see is him barreling wild-eyed, screeching through the apartment, down the railroad corridor, ducking, room to room, clearing tight spots like a linebacker, until he cuts the corner to the dining room too close and slams his shoulder into the wall. Bouncing off, still running, clipping the edge of the dining room table, balancing himself, grabbing fringe on the lace tablecloth Grandma S. gave Michael and me for the wedding, taking the whole shebang down to the wood floor with him, even the crystal fruit bowl filled with Michael's funeral cards.

On a rare day when I had some pep, I used to stand at the end of the hallway and admire his moves, the speed, the coordination, the agility. Where did he get his spunk? Was he really my child, that dynamo who looked like he was switched in the womb with Sugar Ray Robinson? By the time I had picked up the holy cards, stacked them in the bowl where they belonged, and centered the bowl on the tablecloth under the chandelier, the wild man's path of destruction had taken him to the piano room. He slipped on the rag-rug and came to rest under the piano stool. I stood in the doorway, treasuring a tiny moment of silence, as he got to work pumping the piano pedals, pulling up and down as if he were milking a cow, forcing sound out of anything in reach.

Some days, I resolved to wait for my nap until he tired himself out, but more often I dropped off during the morning rampage and awoke to the sound of him playing "drums." I blame Lucius. He took Benny to the Jazz Emporium where the kid gathered fresh inspiration for turning my keepsakes into percussion instruments. At two, he was already too much for me. What kind of a terror will he be at nearly four? Which is part of why I do not want to go "home" in June to my Chicago family. I have not told Sister A. and Mother Isidore about Benny.

January 17, 1948. Saint Antony, after losing his parents, gave away all his possessions and went to live alone in the desert.

Sister A. is on to me. She knows I don't know one end from the other. She's got me delivering laundry, pushing a cart through the tunnels that run for blocks under the convent buildings, from the Motherhouse south to the sanitarium, from the Motherhouse west to the aspirancy, and then up the hill to St. Mary's, which turns out to be an insane asylum.

I'm too tall to stand up straight in the tunnels, but stooping is the least of it. I'm used to bowing. The darkness is terrifying. They've rigged up an electric cable that runs the lengths of both tunnels. Clipped to the walls every couple of yards or so, strung over iron nails, like the kind they use for railroad ties, hangs a single, naked light bulb. The easiest part of laundry duty is checking for light bulbs that are burned out.

I push the cart as fast as I can without veering into the walls. It's tricky because the tunnels are so narrow that the wheels of the laundry cart barely fit on the path and on either side is a ledge, not a big drop-off, but enough that, if the cart falls off the track and I can't right it without scraping the walls, my skirt gets stained with red-brown earth. It is a pill brushing the dirt off. It slows me down and I worry whether I'll be back in time for Vespers. When I arrive at a bulb that is burning, I stop and check the little round pocket watch that Grandma S. gave me to pin under my cape when I joined the convent. Easy stuff. It's the long stretches in pitch black dark that are spooky.

There are twists and turns in the tunnels that I learned to respect when I ran head-on into the wall where a light was out. I never imagined it was so cold or damp under the ground, but in order to get back on track I had to feel the sides of the walls. I'm used to dirt from planting tomatoes, but this was earth, clammy and firm, like a frozen Snicker bar. I try not to smear my hands on everybody's clean underwear. Except for collars and wimples, all that shows on nuns' outsides is black, but underneath everything is white.

Dropping off laundry for the aspirants is a gas. They are high school kids who follow the rule like everybody else, but they look as though half of their teenage energy goes into containing animal exuberance. Apparently, they get to bring their own linens because their towels are all different colors, even purple and orange. They are, after all, just kids. Then it's back to the dark in the tunnel and the worst part of all, the trip to the asylum. The paths from the Motherhouse laundry to the sanitarium and the aspirancy are well-worn by use in winter, but very few of us go to the insane asylum. It's the longest stretch and the whole way the cart rattles. Somewhere along the line, they must have redone the parts close to the Motherhouse, but this is the original cobblestone and it's rough. So few light bulbs hang from the cable that for endless stretches I push through darkness. At some point, far from the Motherhouse, the tunnel turns upward and I rattle and push the cart uphill in the dark.

The first time I got to the end of the tunnel, I opened the door to a shock. The entrance to the asylum from the tunnel was like a cave, nearly as dark as the tunnel itself. The corridors were lit dimly. Behind bars that reached from the floor to the ceiling stood a row of earthen cells, each with a solitary inmate. In front of me, in the first cell, a woman in raggedy black clothes sat on the concrete floor, leaning against a stone wall, her right leg in an ankle-iron, chained to a stake in the cement. She was grimy. Her hair was a scraggly tangle of black and white. She grinned and I saw that she had no teeth. She raised her arms toward me and howled, as if she wanted me to pick her up.

God forgive me, I did not want to see her. I have not looked at her again. All the way to the laundry I try to hold my breath.

February 3, 1948. Saint Blaise, bishop and martyr, whose flesh was torn from the bone with iron combs before he was thrown into a dungeon and beheaded. Today our throats are blessed with candles.

Sister A. says I must decide about going "home." She doesn't know that I came to the convent to put an end to decisions. I decided to move to Chicago. (My father cut me off.) I decided to learn jazz. (One thing no one can take from me.) I decided to marry Michael. (Will I ever get over the loss?) I decided not to take Gabriel to Dubuque when mother asked me. (He got scarlet fever and died.) I decided to let Lucius comfort me. (I couldn't live with the sight of Benny.) I decided Lucius could raise Benny alone. (Do I really want to know how that's going?) I'm as bad as Benny, stamping his feet, "No, Mommy, no!" I refuse to make a decision. I can't bear to make another mistake.

February 9, 1948. Saint Apollonia, virgin and martyr, threw herself on the executioner's pyre, which was not suicide because she acted on a special mandate from God.

A nightmare. I hear my mother's voice calling, "Maureen, where are you?" Benny is crying. He is hungry. I take the steel top off a trash can and look inside. The bottom gleams, smooth as ice. Suddenly, it starts to move. Maggots, thousands of them crawl over each other, hungry. The sky goes black with locusts. They sweep the field where books had been growing on the cornstalks. They leave only the book covers. Everything inside has been eaten.

March 19, 1948. Feast of Saint Joseph, husband of Mary, the mother of Jesus.

It was wrong to leave Lucius and Benny, but the greater wrong is how I dwell on it. In confession, again, Father Meier told me to keep my eye on the ball. I am here and must put the past behind me.

I didn't mind doing laundry as a girl, scraping clothes on the washboard, coaxing them through the ringer, pinning underwear on the line outside in the open air for the neighbors' scrutiny. I didn't mind doing Gabriel's diapers at my own place. But in Lucius's apartment everything closed in on me. I had to duck under and around a thicket of Benny's diapers, hung every which way between living room lamps and from chair to chair in the dining room. T-shirts, rompers, receiving blankets hung everywhere in varying degrees of dampness. No basement or backyard clothes line. The bathroom should have been the natural place for smelly, wet things, but it was my only refuge. I hid there, put my hands over my ears as long as I could stand the bawling. I pretended it was the baby next door, a nuisance, not an obligation.

March 24, 1948. Saint Gabriel, archangel and my boy's patron saint, announced to Mary that she would become a mother.

Sister A. reminded me that I had not sent a letter about going home before reception. She said the others had and asked why I was dragging my feet.

Obedience is supposed to be the hardest vow, but I do not miss making decisions. Walking down a corridor, I do not have to choose what to look at. Custody of the eyes dictates that I look only at the floor in front of me. Custom provides that I take a small helping of everything at table. The rule decides that I eat everything in my bowl. When the bell rings for the Angelus, I stop whatever I'm doing and kneel down to pray, the angel of the Lord declared unto Mary, and she conceived by the Holy Ghost. If I go "home," wherever that is—I have come to count on the convent as home—it will dredge up everything I'm trying to forget. I'll have to decide whether to leave all over again.

I did not want to raise Benny. Lucius reminded me that his grandfather performed medical arts, but I could not bring myself to do that. I gave Gabriel's things to Benny, blocks and teething rings, the booties and sweaters I had crocheted for Gabriel, the blue sailor suit with the extra pair of rompers my mother bought him at Sears. I sang him Gabriel's lullabies, "Somewhere Over the Rainbow" and "Swing Low, Sweet Chariot." I thought I could raise Benny if I did everything like I did with Gabriel.

Benny and Gabriel wriggled and clung and smelled the same, made the same different cries and noises so you could tell if they were wet or hungry, hurting or lonely.

Benny and I even had a special routine I never had with Gabriel. We read nursery rhymes together every night before I tucked Benny in. Before long, Benny knew most of them by heart. He would point to the picture in the book and "read" to me. Those were our happiest times.

In the night, when I cradled him in my arms in the rocking chair and sang him back to sleep in the baby bed, my voice was strong and steady. Troubles melted like lemon drops. Bluebirds made it over the rainbow. I stopped being a mother who had not saved her son. Scarlet fever had not taken him. He was alive. I was whole again.

But in daylight with Benny, I could not hang on to the feeling that everything was all right.

The light color on the palms of his hands indicted me. He was not Gabriel. Gabriel was dead.

March 25, 1948. The Annunciation of the Blessed Virgin Mary, the day on which the Word became flesh in Mary's womb.

What the dickens got into me last night? Benny's color never bothered me. Next to me, he was milk chocolate silk pie, instead of raw plucked turkey. I did not want to be reminded of Gabriel's white palms, which got whiter and whiter against the scarlet fever. Whiter every hour as he got closer to death. Benny was an easy baby. A little feistier than Gabriel, but no more work.

Maybe I've snapped out of it. Maybe I'll be strong enough to visit Lucius. If he's not out on tour. For crying out loud, Benny is not the problem. The problem is I haven't let the wound heal. I tried to get over losing Gabriel, but every time I worked myself up to give away the cradle, I'd bundle it up for Catholic Charities and the sobbing would start again. I'd wrestle the cradle into the car, only to drag it back to the house and start all over. Now, for all I know, Lucius may have put Benny up for adoption.

I used to get letters from him every Sunday, but they stopped. I don't know whether he stopped writing because I couldn't write him back or whether Sister A. hasn't wanted me to have his letters. She reads our letters, coming and going, blacks out the unsuitable parts, throws away upsetting pages. We send out only one letter a week. You would think I wouldn't care anymore what my mother thought, but even now, I can't stand to worry her, so every week the letter goes to mother. I don't know what she knows. She and Bill used to talk but I don't think he would tell her how embedded I got in the colored world and the Jazz Emporium. I don't know what to do. Could I stay with Lucius without telling Sister A. the whole story about Benny?

I want to stay here. I am barred from talking about the past. I am not allowed to touch anybody. Not even to tug on anybody's cape. I am forbidden to express a personal wish or betray a personal preference. The habit and the rule give me sharp boundaries. Our clear mandate is to love with abandon, to be connected at the deepest level of ourselves to all of humanity, but not to anyone in particular. This is what I need now, to care deeply about everyone I meet, to love them with all my heart, but to keep my distance.

No one here, no one anywhere, will think to ask of me, "Do you have children?" "How did your husband die?" "Do you think you will remarry?" No one will again say, "It won't be long. You will be reunited with them in Heaven." "God gives us sorrow. He has His own reasons." "God's ways are not our ways." "Michael wouldn't want you to cry." "God does not give us a burden that is too heavy."

Never again do I want to feel what I felt for Michael, then for Gabriel. I'll do anything for you. I will not ask whether it's good for me. If it's good for you, I will do it for you.

April 30, 1948. Saint Catherine of Siena. The youngest of twenty-five children, she took a vow of virginity at age seven and endured her parents' disappointed reproach.

I'm a jumble. Mother Isidore told Sister A. to tell me that, if I want to, I may stay at the convent instead of going home like the other postulants for a visit before reception. But that she would prefer that I face what is bothering me. She said the convent is a place for solving problems, not to escape. That I could take two weeks or as long as I need, but it might do me good to see my jazz family. Did she really say "my jazz family"? Were those her words? Sister A. said, "That's what she said, Maureen. Those were her exact words."

May 4, 1948. Saint Monica, widow, was the mother of Saint Augustine, who caused her untold worry.

We are getting ready for Clothing Day. We filed down to the seamstress station to pick up stacks of new clothes, which we will wear, and mend, and wear until they are worn out and replaced by identical pieces of clothing for the rest of our lives. Maybe that's why we call it the habit. I was surprised by the heaviness of the piles, a reminder that postulants' clothes are more like street clothes than the full nun's habit, which nearly touches the floor and has the full length scapular, like a sandwich board, front and back, to hide our curves.

May 12, 1948. Saint Domitilla, virgin, banished to an island where she suffered a slow death.

My pride again. Mother Isidore will not let me take the name Sister Hildegarde when I become a novice. Saint Hildegarde was a mystic and she was headstrong. She was a woman of the twelfth century but she managed brilliantly in philosophy, medicine, and music. Virginia Woolf would have loved her allegorical homilies, hymns and canticles, her anthems and her cantata. Hildegarde would have loved *To the Lighthouse*, especially "Time Passes" and how a trespasser, losing his way could have told by, perhaps, a scrap of china in the hemlock, maybe, that there, once, someone had lived. When I die, will there be a scrap of china?

All Mother Isidore wrote in her strong hand was "You shall be called Sister Michaeline." I know it's wrong to feel insulted, but why did she tell us to suggest new names for ourselves and then cast them aside? I feel tricked, teased, foolish. This is the first decision we have been called upon to make since we got here, if you call coming up with three names and ranking them a decision. Sister Hildegarde, Sister Cecilia, for the patroness of music, Sister Cecile Marie. Mother Isidore ignored my picks. No comment, no explanation. Is she is trying to teach me humility? She did not accuse me of reaching too high. She did not chide me for ambition. It was she who told me that I must study music, choir, and composition. It was she who said I should take my talent seriously.

Michaeline sounds too much like Michael. If Mother Isidore insists, why not Michaela or Michelle? A dozen times a day I'll hear the long "i" and turn to look for him. No, that's me, not Michael. Michael is dead. He's not coming back. Why does Mother Isidore put me through this, as if she wants me to carry Michael like a relic?

Mother Isidore is mad for relics. Every altar in chapel has its own reliquary—church law provides for that—but do a bunch of poor Franciscans need an entire Relic Chapel? The one she built off the choir is a tiny, airless room without a window. Floor to ceiling, walls are covered with glass cabinets containing little monstrances, miniatures of the big one that holds the Host in the Chapel of Perpetual Adoration. Each monstrance is a sunburst of finely filigreed gold around a crystal. Each holds a relic. Some are only an inch or two tall, but the bigger ones hold a splinter of the true Cross, a thread from the Virgin Mary's veil, a strand of Saint Francis's cincture. Each relic is marked, first class for flesh or blood from a saint's body, second class for something used by a saint in life, third class for something that has been touched to a relic. Mother Isidore has them arranged in alphabetical order. Saint Abachum, Saint Agapitus, Saint Agricola. OK, Saint Anne was Mary's mother, but who on earth are the rest of these folks? Who collects their stuff and keeps it for hundreds of years? Who would make it their business to rub snippets of red cloth against their bodies after they are dead?

I wailed and wept and nearly died of grief. I cried for Michael. I cried for Gabriel. If there is something to hang on to it is the continuing consolation that nothing anymore can hurt them. For Michael, no more exploding into smithereens or drowning in the deep sea, whichever it was. For Gabriel, no more cooking to death in his own sweat. Their relics are properly buried.

Is it wrong to forget them for a while, to clear a space inside for life without them? To want to smother the voice that cries, I'll do anything for you, I'll be a better wife, I'll be a better mommy, don't leave, come back, stay with me forever. Please, God, forgive me. I have that kind of love for You, but not for Benny.

May 14, 1948. Saint Boniface did penance after conversion by finding the remains of martyrs and giving them Christian burial. He was mangled with iron hooks as he swallowed molten lead.

I don't know what gets into me sometimes. It's a good thing nobody else will see my rant on the Relic Chapel. I think of relics very much like I think of the stories of the lives of the saints. Both have been passed down through the generations. One might quibble with the provenance of one or the other, but the relics are physical links in the chain of the family of Christians.

The more I think about what I wrote, the more it feels like I am still reacting to the sudden, total loss of Michael. Days after our wedding, he went off to war. Not only did I never see him again, but I don't have so much as a lock of hair to remember him by. No wonder I so want to hold his books.

May 15, 1948. Saint John Baptist de la Salle, confessor, proclaimed by Pope Pius XII the patron saint of all teachers of youth.

I'm glad I decided to come "home" to see Lucius and Benny. The first thing I did today was take Benny to Lincoln Park Zoo. Wearing street clothes felt funny, but I was determined to look the part. Benny will be four in September, but he seems older. I needn't have bothered with a stroller. He commandeered it like a kamikaze pilot, zooming past Abraham Lincoln, whizzing past Benjamin Franklin, bang-bang-banging past the barn where the Shetland ponies sleep. He crashed it in the weeds near the lagoon, threw himself down and dropped his head over the edge of the pier. "Shsh," he said. "Shsh, Mommy." I squatted next to him and looked into the clear water. A school of goldfish swam in circles. He reached over as if he were going to splash them. Instead, he waved his hand over the surface of the water and giggled, "Nice fishie." In a flash he was up and running. "Squirrel, Mommy!" He charged into a gray one standing on the path in front of him. I went to retrieve the stroller. He found a pug off its leash and followed it to its owner.

"This little ball of fire seems to have lost his mother. I'm going to look for a cop."

I had my wits about me. "Not to worry. He's with me."

"I'm so sorry. I didn't see your stroller."

He fell asleep on the bus back to Lucius's place. As I turned the key, Benny pushed through the door and made a beeline for the dining room table. A giant puzzle was underway. "Argonne Forest," it read in the bottom corner.

"A long time ago, your daddy was there in a war," I said. "I guess you know that."

He picked up a piece of green foliage and tried to snap it into the edge of the spreading forest. My mind was mush from racing after him at the zoo, yet he was concentrating and showing off as if his life depended on it. Was he trying to please me? To get me to stick around? Maybe. But a calm came over me. For the first time, I had the thought that he was going to grow up and make his way in this world, whether I was a part of it or not. Lucius and he were doing a fine job. It was up to me to let myself off the hook. If only he would stop calling me "Mommy."

May 17, 1948. Saint Paschal Baylon, confessor, a Franciscan who, as he lay dead on his funeral bier, opened and closed his eyes twice when the consecrated Host was elevated at Mass.

I didn't want to go, but Lucius's cousins had come up from Louisiana. Shirt-tail relations. I figured if he hadn't seen the Johnsons since before the war, why should I drop everything to meet them. I have only a few days in Chicago to decide whether I am going back to be received into the order.

Lucius went to the trouble of reserving a spot in Lincoln Park, which made it worse for me. I couldn't shake the dislocation I felt when that well-meaning woman who found Benny nearly called the police. She would never have guessed he belonged to me.

The Johnsons are darker than Lucius and Benny. I don't mind their color. I'm so used to Lucius that I hardly see color except when they are very dark. What I minded was sitting at a picnic table full of people who could become my relatives and not being able to understand a word. Even Lucius was talking some other language. I picked up words here and there, but mostly it was too loud and too fast, like they were hurling insults at each other, except that it obviously wasn't insults because they were laughing so hard they were crying.

I tried to go along for the ride, but it was too much work. Deep blue sky, warm breeze, perfect picnic weather, but I sat there as glum as can be. I gave up trying to break in.

The Johnsons are good people. They are not the problem. The problem is that I didn't recognize Lucius. Not just his accent, but the words he used, the way he was mocking back and forth with different people at a speed I couldn't keep up with. What happened to the bass player I count on for a steady beat? What happened to the elocution lessons? When Lucius is with me, he talks and acts mostly like me. When any of the Johnsons spoke to me individually, we did just fine. Everybody, including Lucius, was so different in a group of their own people. Everybody in the group except me.

I can't marry him. I'd always feel like an outsider. I'd wind up being angry and resenting him and Benny.

Lucius noticed that I barely said anything at the picnic. He said he was glad that I had gone along with him. But he will never understand how alone I felt today. He is perfectly at home flowing back and forth between the black-and-white worlds. I admire him for that. For Benny's sake, I wish I could do that too. I felt something like this when Michael and I went to an Irish family reunion. With the Irish it was an aversion to the blarney and the boisterousness. Knowing that you could not trust a word that anybody said. But at least I could understand what they were saying.

The convent is the first place where I have felt that kinship is a safe place. It is the first place where I don't have to make an effort not to have mean, critical thoughts about other people.

May 26, 1948. Saint Philip Neri, confessor, so consumed with divine love during the Octave of Pentecost that the beating of his heart broke two of his ribs.

In two days I return to the convent. Tonight Lucius took me to the Palmer House and proposed to me again, black postulant outfit, veil, and all. He had got the piano player's mother to babysit Benny. He had pinned an orchid on my black postulant cape. I have been "home" for nearly two weeks and I have never seen him so happy. I didn't respond to his proposal, but he didn't push me. He folded my hands in his, rested them on the table, and bowed his head.

There is a flaw in me. He is a fine man. I admire his tenacity and steadiness. He is even-tempered, ready to try anything, quick to bounce back. He complained that the Army wouldn't take him in the war, but not that mustard gas in the last war had ruined his lungs in the first place. He stepped in for me and Gabriel after Michael died. I would do anything for him except the thing he wants, for us to make a family with Benny.

Is it his color? I don't think so. I love the soft caramel shade of his skin, warm and easy on the eye. His age? He's twenty years older than me, but he's the most adaptable, open-minded person I have ever known.

In the convent I've been able to go days without thinking of Michael. It has taken such effort to get to that place. Then, tonight after the Palmer House, we were back at the Jazz Emporium where Lucius was playing. A single song washed away all the walls I had raised. I closed my eyes. Michael was there. His long arms embraced the breadth of the piano, his fingers delicate, then insistent, devil-may-care, then deliberate. He had his way with the keys, slid up and down the arpeggios, punctuated with the pedals, lifted me up, set me down. At every turn he surprised me with the newness of his sound.

The boys were playing one of their standards, "Bye Bye, Blackbird." When they got to the part where the song takes you to somebody waiting for you, I opened my eyes. I watched Lucius mouth the words in the way that he always does, keeping perfectly dependable time to the perfectly predictable beat.

I closed my eyes in time to see Michael turn his head to me and wink. He flashed his eyelashes, hamming it up in a kiddish, exaggerated, Groucho Marx moment. I looked at Lucius again. He was smiling. He didn't know what I know. I have to go back to the convent. He was playing "Bye Bye Blackbird," but he didn't know that he was singing the song to me.

22

IT WAS SATURDAY, July 13. Dad let Mary Kaye pick a car for the drive. She ruled out Mom's convertible and the 1959 Eldorado with the signature fins. She didn't want to make a spectacle. That meant they had to take the 1962 Eldorado, which always made her think of a hearse. She packed two of the three jumbo boxes of Kotex she had bought at Walgreen's in the trunk, along with a new napkin belt, in case the old one got soiled.

She had packed and re-packed her purse. Usually she carried an extra single seamless nylon, but a run in her stocking no longer counted as an emergency. Also gone were the compact Aunt Nancy had given her for Confirmation; the handkerchief embroidered with a shamrock, which Grandma O'Donnell had brought back from County Cork; and the two mother-of-pearl barrettes Tony liked. The Miraculous Medal, Lourdes water, and copy of *A Room of One's Own* stayed.

Nothing in her closet fit except a black-and-loden-green jumper, another Grandma O'Donnell gift. She would deep-six it at the end of the day. She wasn't wearing a slip, on the general principle that it never made sense to buy underwear for a single occasion. She covered up with the jacket she had worn playing Mr. Webb—or had it been Mr. Gibbs?—in the high school production of *Our Town*. Had it not been the third straight day of a heat wave, she would have added Jack's Dracula cape. Since her feet, if nothing else, should be comfortable, she put on bobby socks and Keds.

She had asked Jack to broach the subject of the procedure with their father. What a relief when he said that Dad had reacted immediately: "Hell, yes. I was wondering when she'd come to her senses. I'll get my ducks in a row. Tell her I'm shooting for Saturday."

"Is that all he said?" she had asked her brother.

"That's all you want to know."

In the Eldorado, Dad and Mary Kaye headed to the industrial outskirts of Milwaukee. He had been told to drop her off on National

Avenue. They needed her to walk the last few blocks alone. Under no circumstances was Dad to come to the house.

On the drive, Dad laid it on her. "They don't get everything, you can die." "You can get scar tissue and never be able to have kids." "It's supposed to be like a heavy you-know-what-I-mean, but you got to be careful. You don't want to bleed to death." And: "Watch that anesthesia. Sometimes that's what kills the gals."

So much for nonchalance. "I thought you were for this." Her voice was already cracking. It was already hard to breathe.

Dad glanced at her. "You'll be fine, baby doll. Maybe pretend you're getting a tooth pulled."

"What about that other stuff. The scar tissue? The bleeding? You make it sound horrible."

"You've got to face it. I seen it get pretty gruesome."

"What do you mean, 'you've seen it'? Are you saying you've actually seen someone get an abortion?" Snapshots of her mother, her grandmothers, her aunts, her cousins sped through her head.

"Oh, come on. You know I don't mean that." He rapped his knuckles on the steering wheel.

"Now listen to me, Mary Kaye, you're going to tell Tony that you had a miscarriage. Simple as that. It was dumb luck and the whole family's broken up about it, but sometimes nature takes its course. There's nothing nobody could have done. One of those terrible things that just happens. You're going to say the same thing to every single person who knows you're pregnant. You hear?"

She was nodding, but she was not entirely convinced. "Do you think Tony's father will go for that?"

"If he doesn't, I'll take care of it."

"What about Mom and the girls?"

"Same story. Don't you worry about a thing."

"Dad, if you're trying to calm me down, it's not working. I feel sick. I'm going to maybe throw up."

Dad reached into the back seat for a blanket. The car swerved into the next lane. Mary Kaye grabbed the steering wheel. "Maybe you're not Mr. Cool yourself."

She tugged the blanket over her lap. The weight of it felt reassuring.

He patted her knee. "It's good you know what you're getting into, sweetie."

"If I'd known what I was getting into," she said, "I wouldn't have gotten into it."

"No kidding. You see why I waited to tell you?"

23

THE MAN WHO was to take care of her had been a doctor once, in Germany. He had not been able to get a license to practice in the US. She wondered if he was Jewish. Or, God forbid, a Nazi.

What bothered her more, though, were the brightly painted plaster gnomes standing on the front lawn. There must have been a dozen, each a foot or so high, with different hats and boots and beards. What kind of person would collect weird little men, let alone show them off? As she walked the path around the house, she spied even more hiding in the bushes.

The woman who answered the doorbell at the back entrance reminded her of Ingrid Bergman. She was wearing a white snood. She disappeared into the house while Mary Kaye took in the smell of chocolate baking. When it was over, would she be invited into the kitchen for a brownie, or a slice of chocolate cake?

The woman in the snood returned and asked for the money. Mary Kaye opened the envelope from her father and counted out eight crisp bills, all hundreds. Dad always said that for something important you ask the teller for new bills. She followed the woman in the snood up a narrow staircase, lit by a hanging lamp. One of the light bulbs was burned out. She thought she smelled blood. Maybe that was why they baked chocolate, to cover up the stink.

At the top of the stairs was a hallway with three doors. The first was open. The room had no windows. Opposite the door, above a sofa, hung a print of a still life, fruits and vegetables that made her think of Peter Rabbit's garden. Two wing-back chairs, their upholstery faded, faced away from her. Thank God, one of the chairs was empty because the sofa sagged like a swayback horse. The girl sitting in the other chair had bleached hair that had grown out at the roots. In the middle of the blond wood floor lay a dark, round rag-rug. It was too small for the space and not properly tacked down.

The frisé on the armchair felt scratchier than it looked and she wondered whether she should reconsider the sofa. The woman in the snood came in and waved to the other girl, who sprang forward, catching her heel on the rug. She nearly went flying. Mary Kaye watched her recover, then turned to stare at the wall.

The woman in the snood returned and led Mary Kaye to the third room. Again, no windows. At the room's center stood a gray formica kitchen table trimmed with aluminum. At one end of the table was a pillow. At the other were stirrups. Mary Kaye could hear sounds coming through the wall, but she could not make them out. There were shelves with knives and scissors and other metal instruments she had never seen before. There were brown bottles in different sizes with labels on them. In the corner there was a two-foot-tall canister with rubber tubing rolled and stored on a hook, and a rubber mask hanging on its side. There was a double sink and a small kitchen stove with empty cast-iron pots on its burners. The woman in the snood filled two pots with water and lit the burners.

Mary Kaye had no idea what was going to be done to her, beyond the man "fixing things." She had got this far without the flask of Jim Beam that Dad had poured in the car, but there was no point in being a hero. She took a good swig, then another.

"Take your clothes off," the woman in the snood said.

She looked around for a closet or a hook.

"Anywhere will do," the woman said. "Most of the gals pile their stuff in the corner. I'll give you a towel to wrap yourself in."

Mary Kaye undressed quickly and took the towel handed to her.

They seemed to have a system, which was encouraging. "Thank you. What shall I call you?"

"No names here. I don't know even *your* first name. Doctor likes to keep it that way."

"Could I have a fresh pillowcase?"

"Put these over the pillow." The woman handed her some paper towels, and led her to the table. It was cold.

The man came in without knocking, holding his forearms in the air and shaking his hands. He was short and almost bald. He wore gold wire-rimmed glasses and had a belly that hung over his pants. Maybe he was not a Nazi. Maybe he was like one of the immigrant workers at her father's shop, the kind of man Dad called "salt of the earth."

"Lie on your zaiht. I give you ze shot." The man smelled like iodine.

"I'm cold. I need a blanket."

"Ziss iss nerfs. Efrybody gets nerfous. Nurse, bring ze tablecloss."
He took a paper tablecloth from the woman in the snood and shook
it out over Mary Kaye. She wriggled down so it would cover her. The
man gave her a sharp look. "You made it hard. You vaited long."

His accent was hard to understand. She was listening to every
consonant. "What exactly are you going to do?"

"Zere are diffrent vays. Too late for scraping ze easy vay. Now I do
forceps. Or injection. Salt."

Her chest tightened.

The thought of injecting salt into the baby made her cry. Maybe
he meant salt water. Maybe he meant into the water where the baby
swam. It sounded like it would burn. She had not imagined that he
would make the baby hurt. "What about the baby? Have you got a
shot for the baby?"

"Salt takes a vile. First, you vait until nossing insite you iss
moving. Zat takes an hour or so. Zen, you go home and vait. Can
take a day or so, before it comes out. Forceps is different. You reach
in. You pull out. Zat's ze vay I like it."

She pictured the baby floating in poison. How could she lie
waiting while the baby swallowed salt water and died? That was
horrifying. On the other hand, the doctor had shelves full of shiny,
sharp instruments, which he worked with all the time. That was the
way to go. Better to get it over with, precisely and efficiently: better
for her, better for him, better for the baby.

"Do it the way you like it," she said. When she said "like," she
heard the hard "k." She imagined the sound of forceps, of bones
cracking and limbs crunching, of a skull being crushed. She hadn't
meant to wait so long. This was the hardest decision she had ever
made. She hoped it turned out to be the hardest decision she would
ever make.

The doctor picked up her right arm, then her left. He found a
vein.

"What's the shot?" she asked. She tried to raise her head to look,
but it was already too heavy to lift. She felt heavy all over, except for
her stomach, which felt wildly untethered.

"Sodium pentothal," he said. "I vill giff you gas from ze mask."

"How long . . . ?"

24

WHEN SHE WOKE up, the doctor was gone. She was lying in blood. The woman in the snood stood over her, pinching Mary Kaye's cheeks.

"You're going to have some bleeding and cramps, like a really heavy period. I want you to rest. Sleep as much as you can. You lost blood. The doctor says you should eat lots of beef." The woman pinched her cheeks again. "Come on, don't look so pale."

She tried to sit up, but she was weak.

"I'll be back in a little while," the woman said, throwing another tablecloth over her, propping her up on a stack of pillows. "Cool it. You're almost done."

Every time she opened her eyes, she tried to fix her thoughts. The fruits and vegetables in the other room. Hadn't one of Peter Rabbit's friends wound up in a pie? She had to get out of this place. The wash basin on the cupboard had suds foaming on top. Was anything sterilized? Another thing she should have asked about. She closed her eyes and opened them again. It seemed like a very long time had passed, but she couldn't be sure. There was no window. There was no clock.

She wanted to go home. She planted her arms firmly on the table and swiveled her legs over the side. Her toes reached the floor and she tried to stand, but her knees buckled. She cried out and doubled over in pain.

The woman in the snood appeared in the doorway. "Want a shot to wake up?"

She did not want another shot. She did not even want to wake up. She pulled the tablecloth around her shoulders and pulled it down to cover her front. There was a thick towel between her legs, which made it hard to walk. It had clearly started out white, but was now saturated and dripping with blood. The woman pulled Mary Kaye's arm over her shoulder. They slid together along the wood floor, stopping from time to time to rest.

Around the corner, on the floor of a room she hadn't previously noticed, her clothes lay in a heap. Someone must have moved them. She sat on a wooden bench. The towel squished blood. She spotted a stack of hand towels on a table nearby, and rolled a fresh one between her legs. She tossed the old one at a trash can. It missed. She wiped the bottoms of her feet with another towel and pulled on her socks and Keds. She put on the jumper and her blouse, but threw the jacket into the trash.

The woman in the snood came in and helped her down the back stairs, out the way she had come in. There was no chocolate smell. "Good luck to you," said the woman. She closed the door behind her.

The gnomes in the garden were lit up in the dusk. She put one foot in front of the other, stopping to lean on trees. If only Dad would not lose patience. If only he could have picked her up.

When Mary Kaye saw him running toward her, she stopped. He hugged her and kissed her cheeks. He sat her down under a street light and told her to stay put. He would get the car. When she saw the tears in his eyes, she started to cry too.

"I forgot my purse," she wailed. "How could I do something so stupid?"

25

IN THE ELDORADO, pain reared and bolted like a runaway horse. She could not control her breathing, any more than she could control Lady when the horse took the bit between her teeth and tore up and down the pasture. This pain did not answer to anything.

Dad pulled the car off the road into the woods. He took the Kotex from the trunk, mopped up the blood from the seat, and tore the floor mats from the front seat. "Come on, get up. I got to get these under you."

Mary Kaye did not move.

He gripped her shoulders and held her face. "Listen. Listen. Open your eyes. Look at me!" he cried, slapping one cheek, then the other. "Watch me breathe. That's it. Deep breath in, now blow, blow, blow, keep blowing. I picked this up in the Navy." He shook her shoulders. "Breathe with me. In . . . now, long breath out, longer, longer, keep blowing."

He wrapped her in the car blanket. She pulled the edge of it up to her face, the way she did with her blanket at home. The edge of the car blanket had little round holes, burnt out where sparks from the Fourth of July fireworks had landed when she was five years old. Little balls of fire had hurtled toward her and snuffed themselves out, leaving black cookie-cutter circles. She slipped her pointer and her middle finger through the holes. She breathed slowly. Like Dad said.

"I'm sorry. I'm sorry. I got blood all over the car." She started to lose it again.

Dad slammed the car door and yelled, "Will you quit the sorry stuff? I'll buy a new car. I'll tell everybody we shot a deer and I was fool enough to put it in the back seat because I didn't take the time to strap it to the roof of the car because it's not hunting season and I didn't have a license. We'll tell them you had a miscarriage and we went to a hospital and you wanted to come home. We'll tell them something, anything. Leave that to me. I can always come up with a story."

They drove in silence for a few minutes.

"We could go to the emergency room here, but it's better if I get you closer to home, where I got connections. I don't want no questions. I don't want my buddies in trouble. I don't want nobody calling the cops."

She didn't ask any questions. She didn't want to know how Dad knew so much about abortions, or who his buddies were, or how he made the arrangements. She knew he had told Mom that Mary Kaye was tagging along on business to Milwaukee. Mom would tell the girls that story. She knew that she and Dad had gone somewhere near Milwaukee, but she didn't want to know the name of the town. Having a vague memory that it had happened in Wisconsin was bad enough without pointing to a specific dot on the map.

Dad took her to a hospital where he had connections. All she remembered from the ER was the noise—like the dimly heard back and forth of Mom and Dad bickering in the car on a hot summer evening—and a nightmare, in which she sat in an enormous, white room with a giant wasp on the ceiling. The wasp had come at her; a little boy had run to her and put his arms on her legs, to be picked up. When she hadn't responded, he'd started thumping on her thighs. She had looked at the wasp and thumped her belly. She had thumped and thumped but there was nobody to answer inside.

After the surgery, a doctor sat beside her. She eyed him groggily, "Can I go home?"

"We're going to keep an eye on your temperature and your blood pressure. We've got you on penicillin and morphine. You lost a lot of blood. It's like somebody took a knife inside you and tore everything up."

"Am I going to be OK?" She had never heard her voice so weak and so empty. Or so low.

"That's the job now. We'll get you healed up."

"You're not saying I won't be able to have a baby."

"Maybe, maybe not. We'll have to see about scar tissue. Let's put it this way, for now: You're a very lucky girl."

The week she was in the hospital nobody in the family asked her questions. Jack, who came every day, did not. Nor did Tony, who called to wish her a speedy recovery. Radio silence, as Judge Engelmann would say. It was the only part of the whole fiasco that didn't make her unhappy.

She cried all the time. She ate almost nothing. Her parents came to visit and made a show of getting a television brought to her room.

"I cried and cried for weeks after all of you kids were born," Mom said. "But you bounce back." She passed a hand over the TV. "This way you can get the news, Cronkite's at six on Channel 2. Oh, I know, you like Huntley and Brinkley."

If there was any comfort, it was the hospital routine. Every few hours a nurse came in to take her temperature and knead her belly. "Does this hurt? How about this?" The warmth of the nurse's hand was calming. She wanted to lie, to go home, but she had promised herself: no more secrets. So when the nurse asked, she answered, "Everything hurts."

Her room was in the back of the hospital. Outside the window was a large patch of prairie grass. As the week dragged on, she took to standing at the window in the afternoons, trying to identify wildflowers, the ones that Tony had taught her by name. One day she spent a long time watching a stand of prairie blazingstar, nearly as tall as herself. The purple flowers looked like the brushes Mom used to clean baby bottles. Against the window, fastened to one of the plants, was an enormous butterfly, its wings like a church window, stained glass splintered in triangles of auburn and olive green, black, and gold. Late in the day, she returned to the window. They were still there, the blazingstar and the butterfly. They belonged together. They were attached.

As she watched the butterfly cling to the blazingstar, a new kind of tears started, shaky at first, then stronger. Heaving and sobbing started in her throat and chest and rolled into her guts and down from there. Every so often the butterfly made a sharp open-and-shut move, negotiating its wings. She hugged her belly. The pain subsided and she noticed a peculiar sensation in its place. Over the past weeks, she had grown used to following every flutter and hubbub inside. Now there was no movement. Everything was still.

Finally, Jack came to take her home. It was a workday. Dad was at the office and Mom was shopping, but that was just as well. With Jack she didn't have to talk. At a stoplight she watched a flock of crows sweep up from an open field, wings spread, feathers fluffed, flying every which way and cawing. It sounded like chaos until groups of them settled in the leafy tree branches, bobbing their heads, stretching upward, looking at the clouds, as if to divine what would come next.

She spent another week at home in bed and then a month hanging around the house. The desolation would have to lift at some point. It was a strange feeling, very different from the wounded pride that had dogged her after the affair with Reymundo. It was not the sense that she had made a mistake; it was not shame; certainly, it was not regret. She considered starting a diary then, but didn't. It was hard to imagine she would ever forget the events that had led up to the abortion or how inevitable her decision had come to feel.

At loose ends, she made a trip to the Loop and bought new sheet music: "Black Coffee," "Embraceable You," and "Love is Here to Stay." The piano accompaniment for "Bye Bye Blackbird" came easily, but she choked when she tried to sing. She decided that she would never again get past the line about somebody waiting for a loved one and buried all of the old sheet music in the piano stool. It was not the time yet for "I Can't Give You Anything but Love," or "They Can't Take That Away from Me."

Another day she drove to the Chalet Nursery, intent on buying a window box of golden chrysanthemums for the stable. Not a single flower caught her eye. She left empty-handed.

She was sure that she would go to college, but not about what she wanted to study, or where to go, or when to apply. She picked up John F. Kennedy's *Profiles in Courage,* but it left her cold. She did sign on, however, when the nun who had taken over the parish choir asked her to start preparing a solo for the Christmas production of Handel's *Messiah.* There were high notes in "I Know That My Redeemer Liveth," but she hoped she would be ready in a few months.

She had closed so many paths for herself at once. The new postulants had started at the Motherhouse. Her high school classmates had left for college. The women in the waiting room at the gynecologist's office, where she was still going for checkups, were getting bigger and bigger, closer to delivery.

At her last checkup, the day before Halloween, the doctor said, "You seem down. I can give you a little pill, what we call a pick-me-up."

"Sometimes I'm down. But the rest of the time I'm a nervous wreck. What would pick me up is some good news."

"Scoot down now . . . that's good. You'll feel a little . . . what you want to know is whether you'll be able to have kids, yes? Does that hurt?"

"I don't know if you'd call it 'hurt.' It's more like an ache."

"The big question is scar tissue," the doctor continued. "We won't know for a while whether you can get pregnant. We won't *really* know until you actually get pregnant. Even then we won't really, really know until you deliver a baby."

"I pictured this all differently. That when the time was right, I could have a baby. But what if I can't, and nothing I ever do is as important as being a mother? What if next to that everything feels small?"

26

ALL THE WAY up to Fond du Lac County, they sang the songs that Sister Michaeline had taught them. It seemed the thing to do en route to Sister Michaeline's grave. Mary Kaye especially liked the song that invited a playmate to come outside and play. Lucius remembered his own version, which included "Swing from my apple tree" and ended "And we'll be folly friends forever more."

"It's *jolly* friends." She laughed. "How could you get that wrong? Sister didn't use gallows humor."

"Don't bet your boots on that. Your Sister Michaeline wasn't the Maureen I knew."

"No kidding. So I've been reading. When were you going to tell me about you and Sister Michaeline?"

He wiped the sweat on his face with his handkerchief and Mary Kaye wished she had asked to borrow one of Dad's cars, all of which were air conditioned. The Nash was gorgeous but, the further they drove west of Lake Michigan, the hotter and stickier it got.

"I figured I'd let you finish reading the diary. You can put two and two together. Why spoil it for you?"

She bit her tongue. Why get combative with Lucius just because she felt vulnerable. "You know, I didn't just lose the baby."

"When I didn't hear from you, I knew something was up. That's why I called."

Mary Kaye reached over and brushed Lucius's shoulder. She turned and looked at him as he spoke. "I told Maureen she didn't have to have the baby. I think it's wrong to take a life—I couldn't do it after the boxing ring. But I grew up with it. And I get it. Women would come to my grandfather's house. I knew what was going on. I told Maureen I could arrange it. She was afraid of the guilt, but there's no way to escape that—either way."

"You're right about the guilt." Mary Kaye's voice broke.

Lucius had a rare refinement, part discretion, part diplomacy. Sister had rebuked him early in the diary for "failure of nerve" because he hadn't killed anyone during World War I. But he certainly wasn't weak. Mary Kaye admired how he had managed to revere what he had learned in the boxing ring while serving honorably on the battlefield. He wouldn't take a life again, but he wouldn't have judged Maureen had she opted for an abortion and he wasn't judging Mary Kaye.

She slid her hand across the soft leather seat of the Nash. "What's a folly friend anyway?"

"A folly friend is somebody who gets you to do things you wind up regretting."

"Like?"

"Like me letting Maureen abandon Benny."

"That was in the book," she said. "Sort of. She didn't exactly make it sound bad like abandon. Anyway, how could you have stopped her?"

Lucius coughed. Twice. "For one thing, I could have gone to Sister Augustine and threatened to blow Maureen's cover. The archbishop wouldn't have taken kindly to the idea that a mother left her child to enter the convent."

"Did you talk to Sister A.? Did you actually know her?"

"You better believe it. We shook hands and talked some when I delivered the Whitman Samplers. I wrote to her a few times and she wrote back."

"You're kidding. Did Sister Michaeline know that?"

"Nope. Sister A. is a class act. We're going to see her today. You'll see for yourself."

"What do you mean we're going to see her? I thought we were going to visit Sister Michaeline's grave."

"We are. But first we're going to talk with Sister Augustine."

They had driven over the Wisconsin border, past the Motherhouse in Milwaukee, past Richfield, past West Bend, past the signs for the forest at Kettle Moraine. Lucius's mood perked up when he spoke of Sister A. Mary Kaye wasn't sure why he was so eager to see her or why she was beginning to get the jitters. "OK. But no more surprises."

The sign said, "Sisters of Saint Francis Home for the Aged." They turned off the highway into a narrow dirt road that ran through a good-sized apple orchard.

"These must be the apple trees Sister wrote about," Mary Kaye said. "There's a passage in her diary where she says she spent the happiest day in years here."

The apple trees were shorter than she had imagined, but she could see Maureen planting a foot on a low branch near the base of a tree and hoisting herself up, clinging to the tree as she climbed from branch to branch, balancing on one foot, then the other. It would have been cooler in later fall when the nuns picked a year's worth of apples to store in the Motherhouse basement. Maureen's breeze had played with her veil. On a beastly hot Indian summer afternoon Lucius and Mary Kaye were lucky to have a breeze.

Forking off Lucius's side of the road was a footpath marked "Saint Joseph Cemetery."

"That's where she is," he said. "Or, I guess I should say, that's where her body is."

Mary Kaye made the sign of the cross, more out of habit than anything. They rode past the footpath in silence, past a tall, stocky tree that, by the shape of its leaves, she took to be an oak.

Lucius parked the Nash in a small clearing in front of the rest home and nodded. "You see the short nun pushing the big wheel chair?"

"You mean the young one?"

"That's Sister Augustine. They're never as young as they look," he said. "What with a lifetime of no cigarettes, no alcohol, no sunbathing, early to bed, early to rise, it's anybody's guess."

"I know. I thought Sister Michaeline was closer to my age than Mom's. Not just her face, but the spring in her step."

"It's the hair. At least that's what Maureen always said."

The rest home looked like a miniature Motherhouse, the same dark brown bricks and dormered windows. But there were no bars. That, along with the surrounding orchards, gave the rest home a less austere look.

"I think you're right. That must be Sister Augustine," Mary Kaye said. "She's waving at us."

Small and slim, Sister A. was the picture of compact composure. She parked the wheelchair in a circle of nuns in wheelchairs. The old nuns were dressed in the order's habit, but their veils were softer and fit closer around the face. Their bibs had not been starched. One sister bounced a baby doll on her knee, reciting multiplication tables to her pupil. Another whimpered, "I'm so tired. I want to go to sleep." Another slept soundly, head drooped on her shoulder, drooling on her bib.

Sister Augustine waved Lucius and Mary Kaye toward chairs and a wicker table set for tea. "Come sit down. I'll be back with a tray for you. Maybe it's just as well that Sister Michaeline died in her prime. She was a ball of fire. I can't imagine her happy being wheeled around." She folded her arms under her scapular, tucked in her chin, and skimmed across the lawn and up the steps to the rest home.

"Lucky for Maureen, Sister A. was her postulant mistress," Lucius said. "They all wear the same clothes. They obey the same rule. But boy, oh boy, are these gals individuals. Georges was like Sister A. He was French, of course, smooth as silk, but put together inside like a Swiss Army knife."

Sister Augustine glided back to the table and dealt Mary Kaye and Lucius slices of apple pie and cups of strong tea.

"Sugar? Cream? How's your son doing, Lucius?"

"I take mine black. Well, you know he's in prison."

Mary Kaye reached forward with her cup. "I'll have sugar, please."

Sister A. settled herself at the table, hands under her scapular. "I know because you sent me the newspaper clipping. You know, I never told Sister Michaeline, she was Maureen then, about the letters you wrote me. She had the idea we didn't know about Benny."

"That was fine with me," Lucius said. "But what kept my blood boiling all these years, was why, after she left us in Chicago, when I kept coming up to the convent begging, why wouldn't you let me see her? The kid was a zombie. He couldn't sleep. He had nightmares every night. He kept wetting the bed. I'd take him over to Lincoln Park and he'd run around like a wild man, screaming, 'Mommy, Mommy.' He looked for her everywhere."

"Oh, Lucius, reading the newspaper story last year, that was a jolt." Sister Augustine seized a sharp breath, pulling her hands out from under her scapular, then quickly slipping them back in place. "But back when all this happened I thought I was doing the right thing. You wrote me, you kept writing me. It was an awful struggle. I finally decided my first responsibility was to Maureen. Anything she didn't do perfectly made her feel terribly guilty. Before she went to visit you she was so upset I was afraid for her sanity. When she came back I didn't want to put more pressure on her. I thought, for her own sake, she should do what she was capable of doing, not what she thought she was supposed to do."

Mary Kaye rested her fork against the slice of apple pie. As good as it had looked when Sister handed her the plate, she had not touched it. She tried the tea but decided to let it cool. Lucius had touched nothing.

"I wanted Sister Michaeline to stay with us or return to you freely, not under duress. What exactly happened when she was in Chicago? I didn't press her and she never said."

In the silence that ensued, Mary Kaye's attention darted around the rest home grounds. The old nun who had been teaching multiplication tables had fallen asleep, doll in her lap. The nun who had been drooling was awake, rocking in her wheel chair, crying, "Pie, pie. Give me some pie."

Mary Kaye stood, looking back and forth to Sister A. and Lucius. "May I give my pie to Sister over there?"

Sister A. leaned toward her. "Maybe this is more than you bargained for—"

"Maybe more than she wants to hear, but keep talking, Sister. Like I wrote in my letter, we all need this." Lucius's voice wavered. There were tears in his eyes.

Mary Kaye walked slowly over to the nun who wanted pie and knelt in the grass. She fed her, forkful by forkful. Strong winds started to blow through the orchard, rustling leaves and tussling with branches.

When she came back to the table, Lucius was speaking. "I came in and there was Benny, standing on a small stool at the dining room table, making like he was trying to put some pieces of the big puzzle together. The one of the Argonne Forest I had going there. I stood in the doorway watching, but I didn't make a peep. Maureen was kneeling on the floor next to Benny. I had to listen hard to pick up what she was saying."

Lucius struggled to hold it together. "Maureen stood and Benny stepped down off the stool and started tugging her leg. He nearly yanked her skirt off. He was fussing and boo-hoo-ing, and crying his eyes out. 'Stay, Mommy, stay.' She peeled him off and gave him a toss. He turned over on his back and started kicking the floor.

Maureen's voice came like machine gun fire. 'You've got a great Dad, Benny. You don't need me.'

"I couldn't move. I stayed in the doorway. I tried to listen to her words, but what I heard was rapid-fire music. 'Your dad clawed his way out of the Argonne Forest. There were rocks all over. You know how rocks are, Benny. A lot of guys couldn't climb over those rocks. But your Dad did. You and your dad will do great together. I'm just going to spoil things—don't kick like that, Benny, you're going to hurt me.'

"Benny, he kicked and screamed all the harder. He was out of his mind crying. I wanted to rescue him, but I felt like I was nailed to the floor. I had this weird feeling I wanted to see what she would do.

"She bent over and tried to hold his feet to make him stop kicking. He kicked her in the mouth. Must have been the heel on his little shoe caught her on the lip. She reached up to her mouth and from the doorway I could see she was bleeding. Suddenly, she exploded, 'Don't look at me like that. You make me hate you! Don't you know? You're better off without me!'"

Sister Augustine winced. She reached her hand across the table, nearly touching Lucius. Mary Kaye pulled her chair closer under the table and brushed his hand.

"I can still hear Maureen yelling. 'You're a big boy now. Stop acting like a baby.' She stood up and rested her foot on his behind. 'Stop crying or I'll give you something to cry about. Do you hear me? Benny, do you hear me?'

"I didn't want her to know I'd heard her, so I snuck back out on the landing, made a lot of noise coming in the front door."

Mary Kaye felt like throwing up. Which was worse, what Maureen did or what Lucius didn't do? He stood there and watched her brutalize their son, yet he didn't step in. She knew that line "Stop crying or I'll give you something to cry about." She knew from experience that Benny had run out of ways to let his parents know what he needed. And she was virtually certain what Lucius would say next.

"He was limp as a dish rag, the poor little fellow. He was so tuckered out I figured best let him sleep. I didn't see her again until last year when she found me at Cabrini-Green. She didn't see Benny until she started the prison ministry at Joliet."

Sister Augustine was leaning on one arm, her hand tightly gripping her mouth. "I think Maureen had hit her limit," she said after a long silence. "I don't think Benny was a real person to her. Her husband had died. She had lost her baby. She was looking for a way to stop the losses."

She paused and cleared her throat. "I think she felt the convent gave her the security that she'd never have to lose anybody again. I told her at the time that was the last reason why anybody should become a nun, but she couldn't hear me."

Lucius put his hands on the table and leaned toward Sister Augustine.

"I had no idea. She came back from Chicago and told me Benny was your son. She said he was dead. Something about how she said it, so matter-of-fact. I didn't entirely believe her, but I wanted to. She seemed liberated, as if a great weight had lifted off her. When I realized from your letters that Benny hadn't died, I prayed over it long and hard. But I thought maybe the best thing was to leave well enough alone."

Lucius shook his head vigorously. "I blame myself. When she first went in as a postulant, I didn't fight her. I knew she was running out of gas. I thought she'd have a little retreat, get herself back, then come home. But when she left the second time, I should have done something."

He rapped his fingertips on the table, rattling a tea cup. "I was so steamed up at first I couldn't see straight. She made it harder for him when she came back those two weeks, like he'd been hoping she'd come back, and when she did, he got his hopes up. The day she left, the starch went out of him for good. It was the second time she broke his heart that did him in—"

"Oh, Lucius, if anybody should have seen that coming it should have been me," Sister Augustine said. "I kept thinking she needed some peace of mind. I figured you could handle things no matter what she did. I never really thought about Benny."

Mary Kaye had been holding her breath. She wasn't sure how long, but she was getting dizzier and dizzier. Had anybody ever really thought about Benny?

"You all right?" Lucius asked her.

"I'm listening."

"Lucius, I still don't know what happened to Benny after Maureen left you," Sister said. "It's a long way to Joliet Prison."

"Not as long as you'd think, Sister. For years he was a ghost. Then, I remember getting so excited, it seemed like he was coming back to life. One day we were at Lincoln Park, he must have been six or seven, we were watching the monkeys. He ran up to a lady and grabbed her purse. I can still see him, running like a wide receiver. He went a hundred feet or so to his finish line, tossed the purse in the air, and ran it back to the lady. Before long, he started keeping the purses, picking locks, you read this stuff in the paper. I tried to talk to him but the peculiar thing was that it was all play to him. Not like a real conversation. He started answering me in rhymes. I can't remember when I got a straight answer out of him."

"I once saw a patient at the asylum we run in Milwaukee. Anything we said to her, she turned into rhymes."

It took all the restraint Mary Kaye could muster to stop herself from blurting out. So Lucius, why don't you try *talking* to him? Instead, she breathed deeply and said, "Lucius, it's been hard."

A mighty wind swept across the lawn and the sky blackened. Sister Augustine began to move briskly, stacking cups and saucers, plates and forks on the tray. "There's a storm coming," she said. "You two going to come in?"

"Thanks, Sister . . ." Lightning flared and crackled. Thunder crashed. Lucius had to repeat himself. "I think we best make a run for it."

"Let's get together soon to plan what we can do for Benny now," Sister Augustine said, using both hands to secure her veil.

Lucius and Mary Kaye said their good-byes in haste. As they dashed to the car, rain started to fall. Soon it was a fierce downpour and Mary Kaye saw that, even with headlights, Lucius struggled to see the dirt road. Already, branches were down.

"Why don't you stop where the road goes off to the cemetery," she said.

Lucius pulled over and she saw that he was weeping.

"I don't need to see the grave today," she said. "I want to remember Sister alive and free in the apple orchard."

"She'll always be here," he said, wiping his face with his handkerchief. "We can visit her anytime."

"Come on, slide over. It's your car but I'm going to come around and drive. At least for a while."

"OK, sugar."

She slipped out of the passenger seat and ran around to the driver's side.

Lucius slid over. "And I thought I was bringing you up here to help you out."

27

MARY KAYE SPENT much of the next week running through her new Ella Fitzgerald songs and the sheet music Lucius had given her. When she wasn't at the piano, she sat in her bedroom singing along with records. She loved the broad, deep warmth of Ella's sound, but as much as she envied her voice, there was no point in trying to imitate Ella. She heard in her own voice capacities that drew on what she had learned from Sister Michaeline when they had worked on Mozart arias: articulating clearly, hitting notes head-on, sustaining them steadily, tapering them tenuously. Jack had mocked her operatic ambition, but listening to Sarah Vaughan sing "All the Things You Are," she was glad for the training. She heard herself more in the style of Vaughan than Fitzgerald.

On Friday she drove to the Jazz Emporium, singing a cappella, going over "They Can't Take That Away from Me," moving away from Ella's smooth gloss. She sharpened phrases, spattered t's with percussion, added staccato. She knew what loss felt like. The line needed some seriously irritated bite.

The door to the Jazz Emporium was open. She could see that Lucius was alone and she could hear "Moanin'" blaring. At the sight of her, Lucius turned the sound down and said, "Nobody does the raising-Cain side of grief like Mingus. Next time I suggest visiting Maureen's grave, tell me 'thanks, buddy, but no thanks.'"

"You don't look like yourself today."

"I've been stewing and stewing about Benny," he said. "There's something I need to get off my chest."

"Have you got some plain hot water? It seems to help me stay calm."

"Yeah, sure. Sure as shooting, good thing he's in prison or I'd wring his neck."

"Hold on. I've got to sit down for this." She sat at one of the tables in the back near the bar, while Lucius paced the floor.

"More than likely there are lots of reasons why Maureen left me, but right up there is Benny. No way he could ever wipe the slate clean on that. But then, after all those years, she was back. I didn't see her that often but I was alive again. Alive and kicking." Lucius's voice rose to a shout. "Now I've lost her again, and it's his damn fault! I don't even have her Rouault. Had to sell that to pay his lawyers."

Mary Kaye waited a while before she spoke. "After Maureen left, what did you tell Benny?"

"What difference does it make? Some things can never be fixed."

"But I want to know what happened. And, anyway, you can't manage this alone. Just look at you. You're a basket case."

"OK. OK." Lucius stepped behind the bar and mixed a drink. "Can I get you something stronger than that water?"

"I'll have what you're having."

"Ever have a Manhattan?"

"Nope."

"Welcome to the big leagues."

She took a sip and slid onto the bar stool. "I'd like some extra cherries."

Lucius plopped four extra cherries into her tumbler and patted her cheek. He walked around and took his place on a bar stool. "Take it slow."

"I started out telling Benny that Maureen had gone to her mother's and was coming back, and when he stopped asking about her I didn't say anything more. I lived every day like it might be the day she'd be back. I'd go up to the Motherhouse on her birthday, bring her the Whitman Sampler."

Mary Kaye interrupted, "But what about Benny?"

"What about him?"

"Kids pick up on everything, even if they don't put it into words. What did he think about you driving to Milwaukee with the chocolates, his waiting around all day in the car?"

"I never told him where we were going."

"That's my point," she said with more force than she intended.

Lucius turned to face her. She had never seen him look so distressed.

"You've got to understand, I could barely stand the sight of Benny. I looked at him and all I saw was rebuke. The awful aloneness of missing Maureen, the mocking inadequacy I felt, that I wasn't enough for her, that she loved Michael more than she loved me. I'd drag my cotton-pickin' sorry ass out on the road, play with the boys, feel sort of like myself. But when I came home I'd see the emptiness in Benny's eyes. I'd go dead inside again.

"Nobody ever talks about grief. I didn't know what hit me. For months after she left, I'd go outside and the sun was too bright. Everything extra-sharply defined, colors overly intense, sounds louder, ultra-crisp around the edges. As if all of my senses had gone into high alert, determined not to miss some slim clue to something that just possibly might bring her back to me."

Lucius paused. Mary Kaye waited for him to resume, remembering Sister Michaeline's diary entry on the shapes and colors of grief, thinking that might be a well-worn passage for him.

"For years on the street I'd run up behind nuns wearing the Franciscan habit to get a look at their faces. But it was never her.

"I went through a phase where I was possessed by the idea that she had come to her senses, left the convent, taken a late train from Milwaukee, and was headed for Flo's, the all-night diner near our place where we used to meet after we'd had an argument. I'd sit there for hours talking with Flo, expecting Maureen any minute."

Mary Kaye gasped. "But what about Benny?"

"He was OK."

"If you mean physically, but . . ."

"I remember rounding the corner and seeing a light on at home and thinking, 'Benny's been up again. I wonder if he's still up or he just forgot to turn off the lamp when he went back to sleep,'" Lucius said.

Mary Kaye decided that what Lucius needed from her, for the time being, was simply to listen. She slipped off the bar stool and stood next to him. She slid one hand over his, then circled both hands around the empty glass and held it.

"Sometimes I'd come back and he'd be running around the apartment crying. I'd hold him for a little while and put him back to bed. I didn't think he should see me upset.

"Every night I'd sit at the piano and sing 'Cry Me a River.' Benny used to accompany me on his little toy instruments. He had a tom-tom, a triangle, and real natural rhythm. Pretty soon, he'd picked up the lyrics too. Some of them he mangled, but they made his own kind of sense. I would sing a line or two and he would try to drown me out by making up his own words: 'You told me love was you an' me an'.'"

Lucius raised himself up on the bar by the palms of his hands so that he sat a little taller on the stool. "Why am I telling you this? You asked about Benny."

"And you started telling me about the song you sang every night. I don't know 'Cry Me a River.' How does the rest of it go?"

Lucius walked the length of the Jazz Emporium. He sat at the piano and began the song with a doleful, wordless wail. He leaned forward as he sang each word, softly, precisely, tenderly, reverently.

Mary Kaye stood next to him, as if she were the page turner.

When he got to the title line, he bent his head down close to the piano keys, and wept. In between sobs, she put together that he was saying something about the song.

"What about 'Cry Me a River'?" she whispered.

Lucius sobbed harder.

When he found his voice it was a lamentation. "Benny. Benny. Where did you go?"

After a while, Mary Kaye took his hand and walked him over to the sofa. He lay down and she sat on the floor next to him, her knees under her chin, her face in her hands.

"One time, not long after Maureen left—Benny was maybe five years old—we were downtown on Michigan Avenue," Lucius said plaintively. We walked over the bridge and Benny ran over to the side. He came back and pulled me over as if his life depended on it. 'Daddy, Daddy,' he kept saying. 'Is that our river?' I said, without thinking, 'Of course, that's the Chicago River.' He said, 'No, I mean *our* river.' I was so wrapped up in myself that I didn't get it."

Lucius blinked, then closed his eyes tightly.

Mary Kaye reached an arm around him. Her hand nestled on his back, rising and falling as his chest heaved in and out and he tried to catch his breath in a torrent of tears.

"It's so simple. It should have been *our* river. I never thought of that," he sobbed. "Why didn't I think of that? It was about me, but it should have been about Benny too."

She handed him a cocktail napkin and he wiped his face. "Maybe it was too close to the bone."

"But he was trying to tell me."

Lucius pulled himself up from the sofa, slouched back to the bar, started to pour another drink, then slammed the bottle down. He crept back to the sofa and lay down on his side.

"You want to rest a while?" Mary Kaye asked tentatively.

"No, I want to call Sister Augustine, take her up on the offer to help. Maybe you two can tell Benny. . ." Lucius wept again, quiet whimpers giving way to wailing.

Mary Kaye sat on the floor next to the sofa, her legs extended, one hand on Lucius's boot.

"We'll figure this out," she said when he was quiet. "One idea I've got is I can get you together with Judge Engelmann and maybe we can start a jazz band at the prison—for Benny and some of the other guys, like Sister Michaeline's prison ministry, only jazz. You can get to know Benny. I'll help you. So will Sister Augustine. We'll stick with it—no matter what it takes."

"God love you, Mary Kaye. I need to hear that. You always point your face toward the future. Sister Michaeline used to say that."

"Remember that day at your place when you said that if I worked my fanny off, or was it keister, buns, butt, do you remember?"

Now Lucius was nearly smiling. "You're not going to trick me into telling you what my grandfather called it. Let's just stipulate you're going to work your skinny ass off."

"I'm going to college next year. I'll try to win a scholarship, but I'll need some cash."

"If you watch your pennies, you should be able to start a college fund with what you'll make singing at the Jazz Emporium."

"I'll need a day job, of course, maybe working in a bank or Marshall Field's on commission."

"What do you think you want to do for real?"

"Right now, it's between science writer at a newspaper or get another degree and become some kind of social worker or therapist who could help kids. Or maybe a history professor."

"Atta girl," he exclaimed. "Sister Michaeline would be behind you one way or the other. You'd be a good therapist."

Lucius stood and stretched his arms. "Later I'm going to call Sister A. We'll set up a time for you to visit Benny—for us to visit Benny—we'll take it one step at a time. I've got to start thinking there's a chance."

Mary Kaye stayed still, looking up at Lucius. Would he ever forgive himself for the time he had lost with Benny? What if, God forbid, Benny never came around? What if, in the end, she would never be able to have a baby. Would she be able to forgive herself?

When she was little she used to imagine that when she did something wrong, something she regretted, it made a black smudge on her soul. And that when she went to Confession a warm bath flowed over her, washing the stain away. She knew that for her, and for Lucius and Benny, it would be more complicated. But sitting on the floor of the Jazz Emporium in her stockingfeet, leaning against the sofa, gazing up at Lucius, she felt she could be forgiven if—at least in that moment—she thought she heard the sound of water, not the pounding of a waterfall or ocean waves, nothing so dramatic. More like the gentle slosh and swish of Benny's river.

She remembered as a fourth grader learning that in the 1800s the Chicago River was such a mess that they had to reverse its flow so that it fed into the Mississippi, instead of Lake Michigan. She had pictured everybody in the city turning out with buckets, and on the count of three scooping all the water out of the river, then on the count of ten, turning around and dumping it back in, this time going the opposite direction.

She loved that image. Chicago really did reverse the direction that its river flowed. But it took armies of engineers working decade after decade to build the locks and canals and channels to make it happen. She chuckled at the thought of Lucius among them, wielding a hammer; Benny, toolbox in hand, sweating beside him. Side by side with them, a young woman, having continued to hope, in her own kind of labor.

28

WITH JUDGE ENGELMANN'S help Mary Kaye and Lucius launched a jazz program for the inmates at Joliet. The Holy Ghost Women's Club raised enough money in memory of Sister Michaeline and Sister Jane Denise to equip the jazz band with a piano, trumpet, saxophone, clarinet, xylophone, and drums. So many inmates begged for a shot at percussion instruments that Sister Haraldo persuaded parishioners whose sons had outgrown that particular phase of combative self-expression to donate a dozen drum sets intended for enthusiastic soloists.

As it happened, the prison itself had a pool of older inmates eager to teach younger men how to play their instruments. Benny was skilled enough that he could have taught piano lessons, but he opted to take his spot as pianist in the jazz band and took formal lessons on the drums. Since Lucius led the band, father and son worked with each other every Thursday at the jam sessions.

Mary Kaye often rode along with Lucius to Joliet, where she gave voice lessons to a number of inmates, but, even more importantly, to check in with Benny. On a bright Indian summer day, nearly a year after they had visited Sister Augustine, Lucius and Mary Kaye drove out to Joliet to see Benny.

As the prison tower came into view, Mary Kaye remembered reading that the prison was a Panopticon, designed so that inmates, who lived in circular tiers around a watchman at the center, could never escape the awareness of being seen. The way Lucius spoke about Benny, she couldn't imagine that Benny had felt he was seen at home and she guessed that might make the twenty-four-hour-a-day surveillance all the more unsettling. Benny certainly went from one extreme to another. Lucius had been attentive to her, nurturing and solicitous as a good father. Which made it all the more striking to Mary Kaye how little personal interest he seemed to show in Benny.

They rode in silence into the parking lot.

"I'm a bundle of nerves. I can only imagine where you're at," Mary Kaye said. "But we're in this together."

The sign-in went smoothly. Two guards, neither of them familiar to Mary Kaye, escorted them to the small steel compartment with two doors, a table and three chairs, all quite familiar.

The door banged open, divulging Benny. Same orange jumpsuit, hands cuffed behind his back, shuffling shoes. Mary Kaye thought she saw his eyes twinkle.

As usual, one guard—this time an older black man—seated Benny, freed his hands, and stood about a foot behind him, facing Mary Kaye and Lucius. The other guard manned the door behind the visitors. Benny closed his eyes and nodded his head. He mouthed some words, which Mary Kaye guessed were a song because he tapped rhythmically on the table and shook his shackled feet against the gritty floor.

"I've been thinking about you," Mary Kaye said.

Benny bowed his head. "A dillar, a dollar, a ten o'clock scholar! What makes you come so soon? You used to come at ten o'clock, but now you come at noon."

"This performance must be for my benefit," Lucius said. "Mary Kaye tells me you speak to her in plain English, son. And you haven't been doing that rhyme thing in our jam sessions."

Benny bowed ceremoniously toward Lucius. "You shall have an apple, you shall have a plum, you shall have a rattle, when Papa comes home."

"I've been coming to visit you all year," Mary Kaye said, "but today I show up with your dad. Pulling a surprise on you like the ten o'clock scholar."

"Do we really have to do the damn rhyming thing, son—"

"Maybe it's time that you talked and your dad listened," Mary Kaye said. "You've told me why you sometimes speak in rhymes. Why not tell your dad?"

Benny closed his eyes and shook his head. Tapping the beat on the table with his fingertips, he sang, "Did you ever see such a sight in your life as three blind mice?"

He looked at Lucius tentatively and Lucius returned his gaze with a solid nod. A few moments later, Benny cleared his throat. "Just like that, huh? We'll be bosom buddies, yakkety-yakking our heads off.

You don't give two hoots what I think for twenty years. Now I'm supposed to turn it on like a faucet?"

"We've got to start somewhere, son. I'm all ears."

"Well, Daddio, two things we both already know. You're a whiz at decoding my rhymes. They've been a sure-fire way to get you to pay attention to me and really think about what I'm trying to tell you. And they sure as hell drive you batty.

"After a while, I guess I kept the rhymes going just to get a rise out of you. But it didn't start that way. Coming up I never knew who was going to be in the house. Were you going to be there? Was there going to be food for breakfast? You kept talking about the bass player keeping the beat, but in our house there was no order, no reason, no rhyme. It was all seat-of-the-pants. Some of the ladies would read to me. I loved their rhymes. Rhymes tell it like it is and some of them give you pretty good advice. This is going to sound funny, but one thing I don't mind about prison is that you pretty much know what's going to happen next."

Lucius looked at Benny intently. "Hell of a thing you just said about prison, but I get it. From one day to the next I never knew where I'd be out playing, and even when I knew I did a piss-poor job of talking with you about it."

"Well, when you weren't home, I figured you were out on tour."

Lucius squinted and rubbed his forehead. "I didn't see it back then but I know now that I missed what you were trying to tell me. Do you remember us singing 'Cry Me a River'? One time—I told Mary Kaye about this, but I've never talked about it with you—you were about five years old, we were standing on the bridge over the Chicago River downtown and you said 'Is this our river, Daddy?' I just didn't get it. Took years for it to hit me that you and I were both crying a river of tears over losing your mother."

"She just disappeared," Benny said. "You never talked about her."

Lucius stared at the table, silent.

"Bet you remember the Art Institute days," Benny snickered. "Have you told Mary Kaye about that? 'Hey, son, I'm taking you to the Art Institute!' I'm all jazzed—my daddy's taking me on a toot. First, we're staring our eyes out at a picture of a lady getting out of the bathtub. Next thing you're putting the move on some foxy chick, setting up your easel. 'This here's my son, Benny.' He's my stunt man, he's supposed to make you feel all at home. This nice man here's not up to nothing but painting your ass. You believe that you're as dumb as you look. Come on, honey, get ready for the joy ride!"

"Did your dad do his paintings of the women at the museum?" Mary Kaye asked.

Lucius shifted in his chair and gripped the table edge.

"My dad was king of the one-two punch. He and the ladies started out with me at the museum. Pretty soon, 'Oh, my! How time flies, little Benny's bedtime, we better get him home. He must be plum tuckered out.'

"Yep. That be my visit to the Art Institute. Watching some tootsie twist herself like she be dryin' with a towel. Posing for my dad's painting hour after hour, stiff as a statue. Then go home with us too late for supper." Benny's voice broke. He glanced at Lucius, then fixed his eyes on the table. "One chick, one morning, she stopped by my room. Waved goodbye.

"There was another gal, I call her Bambi. She give me a toothbrush and a dish for soap with a little picture of Bambi's face on it. She took me to the store and we bought fixin's for lunch. Black-eyed peas, stuff to make corn bread. She had me stir the pot, while she made the corn bread. I remember she tied a tea towel around my neck. She said if I was going to be a real cook, then I needed an apron. She stayed about a week, but I thought she was just going to stay. After that, I made it my business not to take gifts from any of them.

"Dad, you would say, 'Benny, don't be pig-headed. You're missin' out.' I would think, 'I sure as hell am. You don't know from shit.'"

Mary Kaye found herself trying to remember how many paintings in the style of Degas' bathers she had counted in Lucius's sunroom.

She turned to Lucius. "These women Benny's talking about must have been after Benny's mother left." When Lucius didn't react, Mary Kaye touched his hand.

Lucius snapped his head back with a start. His face reddened and tears welled up in his eyes. "Sitting here now I almost can't believe I've never talked with you about your mother. Me of all people. I lost my mother at practically the same age that you did. It was devastating for me. You would think I would have taken extra care with you, given what I went through."

"All you talked about," Benny said, "was how the nuns swooped in and saved you. I kept thinking, bully for you. I don't see any nuns swooping in to take care of me. Weird how you always had a thing for nuns. It made me sick how you fussed over Sister Michaeline—she sure wasn't one of the nuns who helped you as a kid.

"I kept telling myself you must love me, you just don't show it. You're not a mushy guy. Then this Sister Michaeline turns up. You're falling all over yourself fussing over her. What does that say about how you feel about me?"

There was a long silence. Mary Kaye came close to blurting out, "Lucius, for God's sake, tell him who his mother is," but she held her tongue, hoping that Lucius would get around to it himself.

Benny brushed away tears. "I couldn't make you happy, Dad. I tried everything I could think of. I knew you were miserable and it felt like it was my fault."

"Amazing you should put it that way," Mary Kaye said. "You know this nun you've been talking about, Sister Michaeline. Your dad gave me a book that she wrote. It's supposed to be a book for recording her sins, but it's really more like a diary. Well, Sister Michaeline says in this book that if a mother is happy her little one has a fighting chance. I'm sitting here thinking, with your mother gone and your father so miserable, did you have a fighting chance?"

Lucius pulled his shoulders up straight and spread his arms wide. "Mary Kaye, you know damn well where I was at—so wrapped up in grief that I couldn't see what Benny needed. Benny, I was afraid if I talked about your mother, I'd just make both of us feel worse. I had this cockamamie idea that I should soldier on and that because you weren't talking about your mother maybe you didn't have any memories of her."

"Didn't have any memories? Where'd you get a bird-brain idea like that? I don't have a lot of different memories, but I've got a few. And they are very vivid. I think about them almost every day.

"But when this Sister Michaeline started coming out to the prison, something big turned upside down for me. I saw the two of you together and you both just lit up. I decided that you weren't just plain miserable, you just weren't happy with me. She became the center of everything for you. You two clicked so fast that I started wondering whether she might be the woman who left you when I was little—that maybe she was my mom. I've been wanting to tell you and Mary Kaye something about that, but I was afraid because it seems like you already blame me for all of the sorrow in your life."

"Oh, Benny, I messed up. Big time. We should have been talking all these years. Let's start now and see how far we can get."

Benny's face flushed. He turned around to the guard behind him and said, "I got time, huh?"

The guard put a hand on his shoulder. "Not to worry, son."

"You're right, Benny. I always said it was your fault that your mother left. It's only recently I've come to understand what she meant when she said she was leaving because I was weak. Always afraid of making a mistake. Stingy with myself. Afraid to take a chance by sharing myself. Lately, I've been asking myself why am I so afraid of making a mistake? So much so that instead of getting to know you and share myself with you, I've been trying to avoid making a mistake with you, as if I might hurt you without meaning to."

"What you're saying makes me think of when you killed that guy in the boxing ring," Benny said. "It wasn't on purpose. But that didn't make him less dead. Maybe that makes it harder to talk about difficult things with me—for fear something might upset me, hurt me, put me down for the count, so to speak."

Lucius slumped in his chair. "You know, recently I've been noticing that I'm scared of my own strength. Hasn't made any sense to me. Maybe you're on to something. I've always acted as though I had to be careful with you. Better safe than sorry."

Lucius walked around to Benny, knelt down beside him and embraced him. Both men were in tears.

"Worst of all, I blamed you for driving your mother away." Lucius buried his head in Benny's arms. Benny leaned over his father, kissing him through his tears.

"I'm ashamed to say this because if I were a better man she would have stayed with both of us," Lucius continued. "She said she didn't stay with me because I was weak—not that I did wrong—but that I was stingy with myself. I didn't take any chances by sharing myself.

"If I had been a braver man there's so much I could have taught you, Benny, from little on. No wonder you clung to the rhymes that the floozies read you. And it wasn't just the floozies who read you rhymes. You and your mother read rhymes every night. You adored your mother and she adored you."

Lucius turned to Mary Kaye. "Do you think it would do Benny good to read the diary we were talking about before?"

"Yeah," she said, "if you and Benny read it together. Little by little. The two of you talk it through."

Benny drew a sharp breath. His hands trembled. "I've got something of my own I've been scared to tell you. While I still have the guts to do it, I've got to tell you what happened the last time I saw Sister Michaeline. The day she died. I tried to hint at it the first time you visited after she died, the first time you brought Mary Kaye."

"I remember that day," Mary Kaye said, "because your dad told me that Little Jack Horner lived at your house, so you could get reassurance by reciting that rhyme and crying out 'What a good boy am I!' That stuck with me."

Lucius brought his chair over to Benny's side of the table. "Go ahead, son. Tell us what's on your mind."

Benny straightened his shoulders and swept his hand across the table, like a card dealer making a fresh start.

"Last time I saw Sister Michaeline, last time I saw . . ." Benny choked on his words. "I think I may have had something to do with her death."

Mary Kaye reached across the table for Lucius and squeezed his wrist hard. She looked into his eyes, making every effort to hold him steady.

"Tell us what happened—as much as you can remember," she said, quickly.

"Remember? It's the last thing I hear every night before I go to sleep. First thing I hear every morning. I keep asking myself, why'd you say that to her? Why'd you stir up that hornet's nest? Why not just take the music lessons and be cool?"

"Tell us how it started," Mary Kaye said. "What you said."

"Sister was leaving, packing up her music and the little keyboard she let me use. Something about the way she wrapped up the keyboard." He was struggling to quell tears and Mary Kaye and Lucius had to lean in close to make out what he was trying to tell them. "That little . . . flannel . . . blanket. Got me going. I said, 'Georgie Porgie puddin' and pie, kissed the girls and said goodbye.' I was pissed. Could have been her leaving. Could have been her wrapping that keyboard. I was hopping mad. So I said to her, 'I had a mama once. I lost my mama. Before I was even four years old.'

Then I said, 'Bet you know this one . . .' She didn't make a peep, but I had her attention, so I kept going.'"

As Benny rhymed, his voice started slowly and softly, then accelerated, like a train loaded down with freight, moving tentatively at first, then picking up a head of steam, hell-bent on its destination.

"Diddle diddle dumpling, my son John,
Went to bed with his stockings on,
One shoe off and one shoe on
Diddle diddle dumpling my son John.

"Then I made the verses:

"Diddle diddle dumpling, my son Paul,
Went to bed with his ear muffs on,
One muff off and one muff on
Diddle diddle dumpling my son Paul

"and

"Diddle diddle dumpling, my son Nick,
Went to bed with his raincoat on,
One coat off and one coat on
Diddle diddle dumpling, my son Nick

"and

"Diddle diddle dumpling, my son Jim,
Went to bed with his t-shirt on.
One shirt off and one shirt on
Diddle diddle dumpling my son Jim

"and

"Diddle diddle, dumpling, my son Joe,
Went to bed with his Cubs' hat on,
One hat off and one hat on
Diddle diddle dumpling my son Joe,

"and back and forth until finally, I said to her, 'and *you* would answer me:

"'You're not John, or Paul, or Nick, or Jim, or Joe.
Your name is Benny!
And it's time to go to sleep, my son.'

"She shrank back as though I had slugged her. She looked down. Her face went all red. She didn't make a sound. Out of nowhere, she took a snort of air, like she was catching her breath. I looked down at her. 'When are you going to stop playing with me, Mom?'"

Mary Kaye gasped and folded her hands around her mouth. Lucius groaned.

"Then, like a bat out of hell—she was gone."

Benny slumped on the table, immobile, derailed.

Mary Kaye and Lucius sat motionless for a few minutes. Stunned.

"I'm afraid I killed her," Benny whispered.

"You're the reason she came back, and now you're the reason she's gone again?" Lucius sounded on the verge of anger. "How am I supposed to deal with that?"

Mary Kaye jumped in. "You really think you killed her? I can't imagine what it's been like carrying this burden all this time. I think it has to be more complicated than that."

Lucius dried his face with his handkerchief. "I guess I better not blame you. I've got to put some of this on my own shoulders. If either of your parents had had the common sense to tell you the simplest fact about yourself, we could have spared everybody a world of grief."

"So Sister Michaeline really was my mother," Benny said. "Sometimes I can't stand the thought that maybe I killed her. And sometimes I comfort myself with the thought that she left, her face all messed-up, a wreck, then she crashed the car. To be upset like that? There must have been something in her that cared about me a lot."

"Yes, son, she was your mother. And she sure as hell did care about you a lot. You're the reason she kept coming out here. Before she became a nun her name was Maureen Rieger and she left me to enter the convent. You should know that she only came back into my life because of you. When you read about you in the newspaper, she got in touch with me and started the prison ministry so she would have an excuse to spend time with you."

"She came back because of me? I want to read her diary," Benny said.

"You'll hit some passages when you'll feel that she got what she deserved," Mary Kaye piped up. "Do you want us to delete sections that might be hurtful?"

"Not on my life," Benny said. "Have you been listening to my dad? Forget about protecting me. Sister—my mom taught me a lot of things in the ministry. She used to say to me 'Not so fast!' If she heard me blame myself for the car crash, I could just hear her voice snap at me, 'Benny, not so fast. It wasn't you, Benny, that crashed the car,' she'd say. 'And maybe somebody messed with the car.'"

"You mean the steering fluid?" Now Lucius's voice sounded hopeful.

"They say it sprung a leak," Benny said. "Could have been spontaneous or maybe with a little help from the guys who keep messing with me in here. She was definitely upset. The car may have been hard to handle. Who knows? After talking with me she wouldn't have been at her best on the expressway. I'll never know how much of her death was my fault. I'll have to find a way to live with that."

"I guess I will too. But at least we're in it together now." Lucius paused. "What do you think of this? I'll make you a copy of your mother's diary. And I'll buy you a journal so you can make some notes while you're reading. And some pens. You want black ink or blue?"

"I haven't done much writing here," Benny replied. "How about I try them both. See which one feels like me."

"What do you know," Mary Kaye said. "You're starting to sound like Sister Michaeline, or I should say, you're starting to sound like your mom."

Acknowledgments

I owe the fact that I have been able to write this fiction to many people over many years. *Blackbird Blues* fulfills a life-long dream that seemed forbiddingly self-indulgent to a person who from an early age took care of children, spent the 1970s as a newspaper reporter (City Hall) and editorial writer at *The Milwaukee Journal*, before re-tooling and seeing patients in psychoanalytic psychology for three decades. All obviously worthwhile tasks, in contrast to what initially felt like frivolously playing with imaginary people.

I have been blessed with an unusually talented cohort of real people who found ways to convey to me that my writing is worthwhile. And to steer me in directions that have made it more so. It gives me great joy to express my gratitude to a number of them.

I am grateful to Sig Gissler, then editorial page editor at *The Milwaukee Journal,* a master of construction and clarity, who more than anyone taught me to write clearly.

After my time at a Magazine Publisher's Association internship in New York and the years at the newspaper, Stuart Dybek read a number of my early stories and gave me the invaluable gift of identifying me as a writer whose "strength is clear, observant, solid prose" and urging me "to write what came naturally" and "free myself from the weight of trying to be literary." His advice was golden.

Additional thanks to Stuart for sending me to the inimitable Sandi Wisenberg, whose close reading of my short stories was enormously helpful, particularly by helping me break the habit of newspaper concision and learn to write more expansively.

I took several of those stories to the Sewanee Writers' Conference and to the Bread Loaf Writers' Conference. I wish to express my gratitude to them both for including me. While there, teachers Randall Kenan, Robert Cohen, and Frances de Pontes Peebles independently suggested that, given the complexity of my stories, I ought to be writing novels. Many thanks to these three for pointing me down the path that has given me such joy.

Returning from Bread Loaf, having started this novel, I checked into courses at the Writer's Studio at the Graham School at the University of Chicago, where I had earlier taken an excellent class with Gary Wilson, and eagerly enrolled in Kyle Beachy's series of courses on writing the novel. Kyle's mastery of the mechanics of the genre, paired with an unusual gift for teaching and a highly refined sensibility, helped me with style and voice, diction and tone. Many thanks to him for struggling with me through the first draft of this novel—laying down its bones.

To Joey McGarvey, my imaginative and meticulous editor, who shepherded the manuscript through a number of revisions, I am most grateful. Likewise, I'm particularly thankful to Kenneth Warren, a professor at the University of Chicago whose scholarship focuses on African American literature, for his expert advice regarding the behavior, language, and style of the two generations of African American characters depicted in the novel.

Heartfelt thanks to a good number of friends and colleagues who read and re-read the manuscript in various stages, making excellent observations and suggestions, especially Ellen Meeropol, Nina Bernstein, Zachary Schiffman, Rita Sussman, Neal Rubin, and Arielle Eckstut.

Warmest gratitude to Paul Berliner and Stefania Tutino for their astute reading and gracious encouragement.

Special thanks to the folks at Bedazzled Ink Publishing, particularly C.A. Casey for her expert editing and Elizabeth Gibson for her timely and thoughtful engagement. To Angelle Barbazon of JKS Communications I extend my admiration and boundless appreciation for her expertise and ever-present attentiveness. I thank Randy Petilos for his precise and efficient proofreading.

I could not have written this novel without the support and encouragement of my son, Joseph Carney Krupnick, who urged me to start writing fiction after his father, my late husband, Mark Krupnick, died in 2003. Joseph believed in *Blackbird Blues* from the start.

It would be hard to overstate my gratitude to my husband Constantin Fasolt for his nearly daily contribution to numerous aspects of the evolution of *Blackbird Blues*. Coming from a family steeped in literature, he cured me of the worry about playing with make-believe people. The more we talked about the people in the book, the more real they became.

Blackbird Blues is Jean K. Carney's debut novel. Before turning to writing fiction, she spent eight years as an award-winning reporter and editorial writer at *The Milwaukee Journal*, covering Children's Court, City Hall, and Roe v. Wade. She earned a PhD in Human Development at the University of Chicago and trained at a large Chicago inner-city psychiatric hospital. In full-time private practice as a psychologist for twenty-three years in the Chicago Loop, she saw patients from all walks of life and ethnic backgrounds in psychoanalytic psychotherapy. After her husband died of ALS, she edited his last book, *Jewish Writing and the Deep Places of the Imagination*, stopped publishing in professional psychoanalytic venues, and turned to fiction. She has since remarried and is the mother of a son and a son and daughter by marriage.

CPSIA information can be obtained
at www.ICGtesting.com
Printed in the USA
FFHW022308171219
57085832-62668FF